ForBIDden Sky

ForBIDden Sky

The End of the Beginning

Book One of the Dark Wing Series

Stacy Renée Keywell

© 2013 Stacy Renee Keywell
All Rights Reserved.

No part of this publication may be reproduced, stored in a retrieval system, or transmitted, in any form or by any means, electronic, mechanical, photocopying, recording, or otherwise, without the written permission of the author.

First published by Dog Ear Publishing
4010 W. 86th Street, Ste H
Indianapolis, IN 46268
www.dogearpublishing.net

dog ear
PUBLISHING

ISBN: 978-1-4575-1890-4

This book is printed on acid-free paper.

This book is a work of fiction. Places, events, and situations in this book are purely fictional and any resemblance to actual persons, living or dead, is coincidental.

Printed in the United States of America

Part 1

Bidding Day, April 1

Skyler-18

Bidding Day always lands on Birthday. Today is Birthday. They have us all sitting quietly in a room. The boys are on one side and the girls on another. We can see each other, but the room is divided by a glass wall. Naturally, there are more females than males. It always works out that way.

We are not supposed to talk, but no one is monitoring us at the moment. I can tell there are no cameras. None of us here knows what to expect. The bidding process is shrouded in secrecy. Like all taboo topics, we are not allowed to talk about it. We only get to witness the actual bidding once when we represent our own child in the marriage process. Rats, <u>that's</u> not totally true. Only fathers get to witness the bidding process. Being born female, mothers must stay home and wait for the results. Because of this, we have no idea how long the bidding will take. We may sit here for minutes or for hours. We are not allowed to speculate. We cannot take bets on who will marry whom or who will end up a maid.

I sit here super excited. I can feel my heart beating rapidly. I breathe loudly and rather obnoxiously in sweet anticipation that this will almost be over. It sounds like I am wheezing from a sudden asthma attack, and I don't even have asthma. In a little bit, I can finally be happy.

I must be smiling because Antin is glaring at me. His brows are angled, and his lips are turning upward with a nasty grin.

"What are you smiling about, Sky?"

"Nothing."

I do not want to start a conversation with him. He cannot ruin my Wedding Day with his stupid games. Typical Antin, he sits there feeling pretty darn good about himself.

"You think you know who you are going to get, but you don't."

"Shhh. We are supposed to be quiet."

I say this fully comprehending it is either going to make him even madder or yearn to rub in my face the fact that he is going to win the only prize I have claimed for myself.

"Whatever, Sky, but you won't be with the girl you love."

He is so wrong. I am going to be with the woman I love—the woman I have always loved for as long as I can truly remember. I can finally be free to express my feelings. We can live together, hold hands, touch. I can kiss her and not fear punishment.

"Are you scared?"

Paine is nervous. He was not ready to leave his parents' house this morning, be with a girl, grow up, be a man.

"No."

I was ready. I am so close now that I can taste it—her lips, I mean, because her breath is always so sweet. Stop. I refuse to work myself up again. I have already embarrassed myself enough recently. I reassure myself I can wait. Just a few more hours until absolute freedom.

I can barely sit still. I did not sleep well last night. I sat up frozen all night, ready for Birthday. This will be the greatest gift I can give myself, my new wife. All of my patience and sacrifice will finally pay off when the bidding ends and our new brides are announced.

Happiness is not the goal. I am not even sure if happiness is allowed. Here at the compound, we are a community of equality. Everyone works for the common purpose. The purpose is

3

balance. Since I have been born, the community has experienced a great period of balance. The seasons have been consistent. The rain has been plentiful; the crops have provided an abundance of food. Nobody my age has lived through starvation or fear of the elements. Therefore, it has been a period of balance rather than happiness.

Happiness is not encouraged. Smiling, laughing, and enjoying one's feelings are also not encouraged, although I see people doing it. I try not to because I do not want to be punished. I want to follow the rules. If I follow the rules, perhaps I will eventually get my reward.

The compound has just about everything you can think of. It has factories, farms, orchards, a dairy, stores, a common kitchen and dining room where we all eat most of our meals, a school, a museum, a theater, a zoo, a swimming pool, a lake, a beehive for honey, a track and soccer field, and a mountain. Well, actually, the mountain is off limits. We live in the valley shadowed by the mountain, but we are not allowed to roam past the orchards that lead up to the bottom rocks. That is forbidden. To ensure that we follow the rules, the valley is wired with some sort of cameras watching our every move. (Although I have never seen the Watchers or where they store the monitors, I do sort of get called out a bit from going too close to the mountain.) I know we do not have cameras in our slabs were we live, but they seem to be everywhere else. Again, I should know firsthand because they catch me a lot and call for my return home.

I am never caught for anything serious. It does not take much to keep the community in line. People simply follow the rules. The compound lives crime-free. No one has to worry about their children. No locks need to be installed on the doors (well, a small few exist here). We live with very few possessions (especially me), and theft is unheard of here. Well, okay, I am wrong. We must have some problems because we have a court that claims to be all-knowing and unbiased, just in case. If a crime is committed, evidence is produced, and an on-the-spot court is called. Once that happens, they assign a punishment. Usually punishments come in two forms: caning or death. These threats have left most of us too fearful to question the laws of the courts or the community. I am usually just paddled at school for stupid stuff that I didn't really even do.

The community has three kinds of people: Makers, Planners, and Workers. And even though we are all equal, I am a Worker. I was from a Worker, I was born a Worker, I will be a Worker, and I will die a Worker. There is absolutely no way I could ever climb a ladder to become a Planner. Only women can one day become Planners if they are married to Planners, which also means Planner girls can lose their status and become Workers one day. Plus, the marriage process is done through a series of complicated biddings in which we have little choice in the matter. So I am not sure how a woman can try to be a Planner or stay a Planner. We are not allowed to date, and conspiracy to fix a marriage is a punishable offense. Whatever. Since I'll never be a woman, I don't need to figure out how to secure a marriage to a Planner (which is forbidden too, by the way).

Honestly, I have never seen a Maker. I am not sure they even exist. But the other kids in my year insist they do, and Antin even claims he has seen a Messenger. Rumor has it a Messenger does the business of the Makers, but I have never seen one of those either, and they are not part of our hierarch. Who cares? I don't! As well, I never believe Antin, and I don't bother listening too hard into his mind to even see if it is true. He is a worthless, bragging liar.

Antin is the son of a Planner, and he is in my year. He is decent looking and not completely stupid, except he—for some outrageous reason—has always felt a raging resentment and jealously toward me. This condition is based on fear. He is afraid I am better looking. He is afraid I am more intelligent. He is afraid that people like me more. Mostly, he is afraid that even though I am an *S*, I am happier and my life is better. He believes I have the answers to all of the unexplained questions, like I have cracked the code of life, and it drives him mad.

Stupid really, because Antin is not only an *A*, he is number one. Born a Planner's son, he does not live in a slab like my

5

parents and I. He lives in a building surrounded by grass and a garden. He has the most possessions of anyone in our year. He gets everything first, except at school. We sit in alphabetical order at school, and the Planner family who got the number-two son had the nerve to name their kid Aaron, so he got chair number one. So Antin has the second chair in the class at school. But he may eat first. He gets first choice in everything else, including bidding, and he takes advantage of his privileges. He really has nothing to worry about as far as I go. Thus there is no reason for his jealousy. I am an S. I was born an S. I will die an S. I know my place in the community, and it is way below Antin's.

Merry-16

I love watching Sky. Who doesn't?! It is sick, really. Everything he does is beautiful. I can sit and watch him eat all day. The way his jaw moves. The way he breathes. The way he puts food into his mouth and chews. I am fascinated by it. I sit here facing him, lingering in his awesome presence, taking in every detail for the billionth time, relishing the moment, hoping for it to last forever. I yearn to reach out and touch his cheeks. Trace them with my finger. Feed him myself and memorize every movement his face makes. Eventually, he notices me watching him, and he sighs. He gives me an irksome look and grimaces, like he knows what I am thinking. He licks something off his lips and shakes his head. There is not one thing that he does that isn't attractive.

Everyone else agrees. I have asked almost everyone in our year, and they agree that Sky is the most gorgeous, most intelligent boy not just in our year but in our community. I can say with certainty that every girl goes home at night and wishes she will make his bid list—absolutely every girl, I am sure of it. Even the ones that will become maids like Marabelle—not that I would even give her the time of day to ask her. As if she were even worthy of talking to. It is bad enough that we have to sit next to each other. Why does everything have to be alphabetical? Whatever!

Every girl dreams of Sky as her husband, including me. That is what makes our love so tragic.

"Merry?"

I love it when he says my name. His voice is deep and smooth like the factory horns that sound off in the morning.

"It is hard to eat with you looking, Merry," he says.

"I am sorry, Sky. I just can't eat. Bidding is getting closer, and I'm nervous. Our time together is going to end. Sky, I ..."

I am in tears. To capture his attention for so long has been magical. Besides his beauty, Sky is kind and caring. He makes me gifts and writes me love notes. He slips in secret surprises when he can. He is the most amazing person. My fear is that he will not be able to win me with his bid.

"You know how it works, Merry. We can never be together. Merry, I am number forty-three. Forty-three! As in forty-three out of fifty! Forty-two boys are in line ahead of me. They get their lists read before I am even considered. Do you realize what that means? I don't really even have a chance at bidding on you at all! It will never happen. We can never be together, ever."

"I know. I just love you so much."

I weep and push my tray forward.

"I love you, Sky," I say again.

"I know."

"There must be something we can do, some way to stop this. We can change it somehow."

I sound desperate.

"How, Merry? How?"

"I don't know, Sky. Please. Please. Please say you have an answer. You always have a plan, some brilliant idea. Think ... think ... think of one."

"Eat your lunch."

He pushes my tray back and gives me a warm smile. He has this way of always making me feel better. He loves me more than any other boy could love a girl. He must have some plan to keep us together on Bidding Day.

Sky and I walk through the meadow alone. Holding hands unsupervised or during a "non-hand holding" activity is forbidden, but Sky does not care.

"I only follow the good rules," he says and winks.

I love when he winks at me. I shiver as a chill runs through my body. Then he grabs my hand as we walk toward the strawberry patch. Maybe he can sense that I am in a bad mood. Sky always knows how to bring me out of my darkest places.

Most Worker children have to work more than Planner children, so we lose out on playtime. As a Worker child, I was assigned a job this morning, which means no free time until after lunch. I had to wake up early and get into my ugly blue work shorts and worn-out brown work boots, something Sasha has never done and probably never will. The girl just doesn't understand the pain of sleep deprivation or the embarrassment of shabby belongings. She's so lucky to be born a Planner.

"Let's look for butterflies on the way."

Sky always makes work into a game.

"I bet I can spot more than you. Whoever wins gets a prize," he adds.

"I don't want to, Sky. I hate work. I have to get up earlier than any of my friends. They don't have to get dirty or sweaty or pick fruit this early in the morning. It's a weekend for goodness' sake!" I pout.

But Sky always knows how to cheer me up. He sticks his face in front of mine and says, "Fine, I win. And now for my prize."

"No fair," I say.

I can feel my lips spread into a smile. I hate that he always wins me over.

"We can also gather flowers with the berries. I will braid them into a floral crown for the top of your head, Princess Merry."

"Stop it, Sky," I protest. "Let's just get this over with and get back."

But I look forward to his flower tiara as he ignores my protests and laces together the blossoms anyway, humming a happy song.

Then Sky quickly and precisely picks the berries. His eyes always fall to the ripe, red ones, avoiding the green ones and the rotten ones.

"Wanna bite?" he asks me, holding out a perfectly round strawberry close to my lips.

I take it in my mouth, tasting his two fingers in the process. They feel nice. I wanted them to linger in there, but he pulls them out and continues to work.

"Almost done," he chirps.

I cannot concentrate on the berries. I sit and pick at the grass as Sky fills my basket for me. I cannot get the sensation or taste of his fingers out of my mind. I want him to touch me again.

"Ready?" he asks as he stands up.

We wander to the edge of the orchard and gaze at the colorful tree with the mesmerizing fruit.

"Don't you wonder what they taste like?" he asks.

"They are forbidden," I reply.

"I'm aware of that. Doesn't it make you want them even more? I bet they are so sweet. Even sweeter than those berries."

"Probably, but forbidden fruit is not worth the punishment."

"Really? Are you sure?"

I am not sure. Sky is very convincing. He could probably convince me to break the rules in a dash. He could probably convince most people to break the rules. He never fears the rules. They were somehow not written for him, and yet he follows them. He follows them better than anyone in our year.

Sky holds out his palm, and a bird lands on his hand. He hands it a berry, and the bird flies away.

"Ready?" he asks again.

We head back to the dining hall to deliver the fruit and have some lunch.

Skyler-8

I love to draw little animals, especially the bunny with the bell around her neck. She hop-hop-hops around the page. The birds I designed flow from tree to tree, looking for fruit and worms. The cows wander aimlessly around the grassy fields. The giraffe sticks his long neck into the trees, bothering the birds, provoking them to hop on his horns. The hippos laugh lazily in the mud. I stare off into the distance, hoping she will enjoy my latest creation. Writing animal stories is my specialty.

"Skyler-8," Teacher says as she slams her hand down on my masterpiece. "Skyler-8, what are you doing?"

"Drawing," I reply.

Was she serious? Could she not see what I was doing? I wasn't trying to hide my work.

"We are taking a test," she roars, quietly emitting her hot, stinky breath onto my neck the way only a teacher who eats too much white cheese for breakfast can do.

"I know," I reply. Duh!

"Why aren't you taking the test?" she asks.

"Because I already know all of the answers," I respond.

"If you already know all of the answers, then why don't you write them down on this sheet of paper?"

"Because you already know that I already know all of the answers. So why waste my time repeating them? I need this sheet for something new, my latest animal story."

Teacher yanks away my paper and crushes it into a little wad.

"No!" I yell as I see my creatures crinkle sadly into a tiny ball, ripped to shreds by her crooked claws for hands.

Tip-29

"Your son says he already knows the answers, which is why he does not feel it necessary to take his examination!" spits Teacher.

"Does he?" I ask.

"Does he what?" Teacher asks, looking down at me sternly.

"Does he know the answers to the test?"

"That is beside the point, Tip-29. Skyler-8 is required to display his knowledge of the community standards on his examination so we can measure annual progress and scholastic growth. His unwillingness to follow these simple directions goes against the basic principles of the community and is punishable via the paddle. Is this what you want for your son—corporal punishment—or shall you encourage him to follow community protocol?" Teacher demands.

"This, ma'am, with all due respect, does not address my questions. Does Sky know all of the answers to the test?"

"Yes, he does."

I take Sky by the hand. His eyes are red and swollen with tears. I have felt the pain of the paddle in my early days too. Unfortunately, Sky does not take to its effectiveness. The punishment loses meaning with him. He emits his usual aura of injustice. He does not fully comprehend why he deserved the paddle in the first place.

"Why, Sky, why can't you simply follow the rules? If you know all of the answers, just write them down. How hard is that? You are a very smart boy. You possess a great talent. Show it to the rest of the community," I say.

He stares at me blankly, his eyes as blue as the summer sky, like he purely tolerates my presence. He does not understand how much I love him. He means the world to me; he is part of me. He frowns and lowers his eyes to the floor.

"Why does it matter whether or not I know the answers? Seriously, Dad! You know, Dad. You know it does not matter. Why bother showing up to school? I am a Worker; I cannot become anything else. There is absolutely no chance of ever changing my destiny."

Such a small, perceptive boy trapped in my reality. I was born a *T*. Luck afforded my son an *S*, but he understands that still keeps him firmly planted at the bottom of the community. I have no answers for him. He is right. There is no reason for him to do well. He wastes away, brimming with endless talent.

His future is washing dishes, scrubbing horse stalls, mowing lawns of Planners, and working long hours in the orchards.

"It matters, Sky. It matters because I love you. I love you and want you to have as much knowledge as you can get. Learn as much as you are able to. You never know when you might need a skill or a lesson you are being taught."

He looks into my eyes and digests my words. He analyzes them for a moment and nods.

"You are right, Father. I am sorry. I have disgraced you again." He genuinely looks miserable as if he has hurt me.

"It's okay, Son."

"It's just ... not fair, Dad. I can never really do what I want to do and be what I want to be. I can't even be with whom I want to be."

"Sky, you know that's not true. The community is fair and equal."

But sadly, he is right, and it is forbidden for me to say so.

Tip-26

They warned us about the possibilities of this happening on Conception Day, but no couple cares to listen or believe it. The mortality of a child scares most people. Regardless, discussing this topic walks a fine line between acceptable and forbidden. Chatting about the death of a child rarely happens due to its forbidden nature. We are encouraged to converse about more pleasant topics. So I count my blessings with my own child and keep my mouth shut.

The August heat reached a record high tonight on the compound—enough to blow a fuse and keep most of the citizens in the sickly, hot darkness. My own son, Sky, squirms in agitation. He can't seem to get comfortable. Despite my greatest attempts to help, Sky writhes in his cot. My efforts have proven futile at best.

Here's the gist. When my year hit Bidding Day, there was an unusual imbalance in gender. Times back then did not experience the current comfort of a natural balance, and the ratio of men to women fell heavily on the male side. On Birthday, more females had originally taken their first breaths, but by the time Bidding Day arrived, sickness took away a frightfully high amount of girls. The uproar in the community did not sit well with the Planners, and a major population of maids was prepared for a second round of bids. Being a *T*, I worried I would be strapped with a maid. I filled my bid list with as many names as I could tolerate. Few men want to consummate with a secondhand woman. The girl that fit my union did not even appear on my card, but I felt satisfied that she did not come from the pool of maids reserved for the second round.

My wife had a mild attractiveness—not too tragic—although she obviously made it to very few bid lists, if any. We got along okay. Honestly, consummation did not happen right away, but it eventually took place. Then we tried a couple more times before we got to Conception Day.

Conception Day always occurs on July 1. When the community feels there is a need for more population, the latest marriage year gets the date card on the doorstep. Other citizens occasionally qualify for a conception card as well. On rare circumstances, couples that have lost a child may receive a second chance. Men who have lost their first wives and did not create a child may receive a second chance to rebid and have a baby. If their bids result in a union with a maid that is still able to conceive, that couple may also obtain a conception card. I was two years into my union when we got the card. The marriage offered some quaint companionship, but the idea of a baby would make us a family and perhaps bring happiness into an otherwise mundane existence.

Couples can only have one child, thus, the community members have no siblings. No matter what a couple conceives, only one child is born. Couples may only try for a child with community assistance and strictly regulated permission on July 1, and not all citizens are able to have children. Some may experience infertility. Other pregnancies may result in miscarriages. Other families may lose a child after it is born. That child may die right after birth or even before its eighteenth year. Sadly, if that does happen and a couple lose their child during or after pregnancy or cannot even conceive in the first place, another conception card may never reappear. Some of us are given one chance to ever reproduce. This is made perfectly clear during the first informational meeting to help assist with the big day. Couples are also encouraged to consummate the marriage if that has not already happened yet, to make sure things go smoothly (although it is not necessary). Occasionally, marriages field difficulties, and couples do not consummate for a very long time. That is why the community gives each married couple around two years to acclimate. Over the years, the Planners have found that giving couples a longer period of time to get to know each other before Conception Day equals more babies. That is precisely why the Planners tend to be the wisest ones on the compound.

During my year to conceive, an abundance of children were born, fifty boys and sixty-three girls—soon to be sixty-two girls, I suspect! The couple in the slab nearby has a sick child. The father is a *W*, which ties him to the bottom list of Workers. He was one of the unlucky ones who had to marry a secondhand maid. His small daughter, Marabelle, is racked with a high fever and struggles to survive the night in this heat. Her small moans can be heard in the surrounding slabs. Because all of the doors and windows are open to air out the heat, we are all witnesses to the end of her short life.

"Calm down, Sky," my wife says. She tries to put my boy to sleep.

Since he was born, things have been pleasant between us. We finally have something to talk about.

"No," he whines and tosses in his cot.

"Calm down, Sky," my wife says again and tries to push him down, but in his agitated state, he overpowers her grip.

"People must be working on the fuses by now," she squeaks as she simultaneously fans her face and squeezes Sky's hand.

"Ouch!" He wiggles around and escapes her tight grip, even though my wife is practically sitting on him.

"Everyone else here feels the heat too, Sky. We are all hot. Now go to bed!"

"No." Sky's blue eyes glow in the dark like two big fireflies. He huffs and puffs like a crazed animal.

"Do you hear that?" My wife peeks her head out the window.

"It sounds like the animals at the zoo. Something out there is howling."

The animals at the farm start to react to something outside as well. It passes like a wave over the zoo, and then the birds and other creatures around the area shriek as well. Mad screeching permeates the community. The insects create a deafening, nonstop buzz. Something outside scares them too. My ears ache as I am overcome with exhaustion.

"What is happening?" a citizen cries in the darkness. We enter full-on confusion by the heated howls.

"Get those darn animals under control," complains another.

Then a slight breeze tingles my skin. My body drinks up the cool relief. A field of goose bumps sprouts all over my arms and legs.

"Did you feel that?" I ask my wife.

"It's Sky!" my wife cries. "I think his temperature is elevating. Oh no, I don't want him to get sick too. He was with her today at school, you know." Tears roll down her face.

"Wait. It smells like rain. Can you smell that? I think the weather is about to change."

The wind picks up and rushes into the window, blasting our faces with an icy chill.

"What is this?" I can hear confusion outside the slab.

"It is starting to snow."

Citizens rush outside to see the weather inexplicably change at a rapid pace. Flakes gently drop through the open window onto Sky's pillow.

"How can this be?" My wife looks at me, confused.

"It is mid-August."

The white fleet of flakes cools down the air.

"Her fever has broken," a sob-filled father down the way cries thankfully. "My baby will survive the night."

Sky lets out a deep breath, and his eyes flutter and close sleepily. My wife exhales her breath too with heavy relief. We can sleep now that the heat wave has ended, and our child drifts off to his own slumber.

Skyler-16

I can't say I like school. It is what it is. For me, school just prolongs the inevitable, a life of hard labor. When we are born, our mothers get about six weeks' rest with us. Then, especially if you are a Worker, both parents must return to work, and the children go to child care. We stay there until we reach the age of five. At five years of age, we start primary school. We remain with our year until we reach eighteen, and then we must marry and go to work ourselves. While in school, we are organized alphabetically, which keeps me at the back of the room. Planner sons get the spots closest to the teacher. This allows them more access to help if they are lost. Girls are scattered around us. Their parents may name them what they like as long as the name is not duplicated during the same birth year. Naturally, Planner families are given first pick from the pool of female names. Girls are allowed to mix and mingle among the boys, but the rules state to look but don't touch. And when I mean look, I mean we may commingle in the safe confines of the classroom and address each other in a proper yet prudent manner.

Happiness is not the goal, instead it is balance. Balance has no room for hand holding, kissing, touching, or consummating before marriage. We remain pure until union. I follow those rules because the punishment for consummation without marriage is death (unless you are a Planner bachelor who has lost his wife and longs for love needs). Teenage children face the same consequence as two adults who commit adultery. That sort of unsavory behavior is so offensive in this community that the only option is to end those detestable lives.

True, I get several discreet offers from members in the community. In reality, I do not break that rule because I am in love. Sitting in the back of the classroom offers me not only an optimal spot but time to gaze at my true love's hair. I can see her face whenever she turns in her seat or takes a stretch. And I watch her listen to our tedious daily lectures or attempt her class work, although she often appears lost or uninterested in paying too much attention to the world around her. She seems to have tons on her mind. She's a dreamer like me. This way, I can daydream about her and write her notes. I can sit and plan what gifts to send her and glance out the window at the birds who anxiously await my latest command. These things do not fit the rules, but I will not face too much trouble if I am caught. Facing the paddle does not scare me. Plus, who would believe that I command anything around here? After all, I am a mere *S*.

There are precautions that I must take to shield my sweet from being revealed. That would ruin all chances of us ending up together in marriage. Unfortunately, some hurtful consequences result in shadowing the truth, but I believe the end result will reward the both of us. All I may share is that her name starts with an *M*. I take the utmost care in perfecting my transcription of the letter. I can draw it fancy or plain, add colors or hearts. Luckily, *M* proved a very popular letter for girls' names in my year. There are exactly five girls whose names start with an *M*.

Running. They have us running quite often. We require at least an hour of daily physical activity, and running is the easiest for Teacher. I can handle the task with ease. I usually outpace most of my year mates leading the line out front. We must follow the same course each time, starting at the field outside school, looping around the small hills found near the water, and then back to school. If you finish early, you are often granted time to relax on the grass or pursue other leisurely activities.

As boring as running is, I guess it is my strong point. I could complete the course in a matter of minutes, which would leave me with more time to relax, but heading back to school only gives Teacher an excuse to order me around and assign further physical activities for being such a show-off. So I've learned to pace myself around the other students.

Antin loves to feel superior and imagines he runs the fastest. He usually runs near me, very winded, eager to throw insults my way. He figures he can slow me down that way and cut in front of me. His plan never works.

"You're such a virgin, Sky."

"Yeah, we all are."

"Speak for yourself." Antin is laughing at me while trying to catch his breath. Definition, he is barely able to keep up with me, I'm too quick for him.

I don't bother searching to see if he is telling the truth. It is not worth the trouble, and I have better things to think about.

"We are all supposed to be virgins, Antin. That is the rule."

"Good thing you follow the rules."

"I follow the rules because I am in love." Okay, the sick truth is I like to prod Antin in believing my story the way I have concocted it for my year mates.

"Right. Oh, I'm sorry, Sky, are you in love? Is your lover a virgin too?"

"Yes, we both are. We are saving ourselves for marriage."

"Are you sure?"

"Yes."

"So you are sure you know who you get to marry? We'll see, but I think you might be quite disappointed." Antin laughs and gives me a sly grin.

I run past him and lose him. That is enough insults for the moment. Knowing Antin, he will regroup his thoughts and find me later to test my patience.

Just as I get some peace, Paine moves next to me. He overheard my conversation with Antin, and now his head swarms with annoying questions.

"Hi, Sky." He tries to smile as he chokes for air. "We are best friends, right?" he asks as he looks up for confirmation. If he only knew that I detest his insecurities even more than his nosy thoughts. Geesh!

Okay, let's get this straight. I have no friends, especially best ones. I don't want any friends. The community has no room for friends. The structure does not allow for close confidants. I want one thing—my true love for marriage—and that will not happen for a couple of years. Sacrifice has no friends. So I don't get why so many year mates feel we are besties. I tolerate most of them at best. Plus, most take little notice of my obvious manipulation.

"Yeah. Yes, Paine, we are best friends."

He smiles with relief, confirming we are absolute besties.

"Are you a virgin?"

"Yes, Paine, I am."

"I am too."

"I know."

"Do you think Antin really isn't?"

"I don't know."

"Have you ever kissed a girl?"

I get the sense that Paine may have actually locked lips with someone, but laziness stops me from pursuing the truth.

"No."

"Not even Merry?"

"Merry and I are not even allowed to do that. No matter how much I want to touch her, I don't want to face the paddle. I just have to wait like the rest."

"I wonder how far Merry got on the course?"

"She probably reached the water by now. Not at all like Dumb-belle-yucky-smell. She is probably still trying to get up the first hill." I give Paine my toothiest grin.

"Right. I love it when you are mean."

Of course he likes it. Everyone loves when I am cruel. They think I am too good, so when I am mean, I appear more human. It also gives the rest of my year mates license to be cruel, especially to Marabelle. Somehow, if I start it, the rest of the kids feel free to join in on the rotten name-calling.

"I bet you do. The best maid-bounds finish last." I wink and try to run ahead.

"Sky." He still wants to talk. "Are you going to wait for Merry?"

"Of course. She knows where to find me."

I am not like other people, obviously. I'm not sure if there are others like me out there in the community or elsewhere on the planet. I have looked for a very long time. Yet I am still unable to locate my kind. One reason why this search proves difficult is because I must shroud my identity with secrecy. The community might condemn a person like me to death, and that would defeat my purpose of trying to survive my childhood here. It's just that I have these little talents, these enigmatic oddities that others do not seem to possess. First, I can get a sense of what others think. Sometimes I get a feeling of their emotions; other times, I hear entire thoughts. Second, I communicate with animals, especially with the birds around the compound. They keep me company and do my devious chores.

One such chore is to seek out other human life past the natural barriers that contain us. We live in a small community surrounded by a vast lake and a mountain. We have never seen or heard from another human being outside these grounds. How can it be possible that we are the only ones here? So I occasionally send a bird on a mission to find others. In all of the years I have been searching, nothing has materialized. No humans roam the land around the compound. Only wildlife can be found by my search party of birds. Each time I send a scout, I plead for it to fly farther and farther, always with the same disappointing results. The singular spot of human activity resides on the compound. The birds remain devoted and provide company to my solitude. They are the only creatures to whom I can entrust my secret desire. They also help deliver clandestine packages, notes, and gifts to my truest love.

    I sit on the hill next to a friendly crow. It caws, eagerly awaiting an assignment. He can hear my thoughts when I wish it and can answer back. The conversations take place in my mind. No citizen will accidentally hear me talking crazy. I ponder what I should write in my note and how I shall deliver it. I aim for the most effective manner. I have two choices: give it to her in public so others may witness it or have a bird drop it off in private so she may relish it alone. This also changes what type of handwriting I must use. My public display requires a note distinctly written and recognized with my personal script. The private note must look completely different and not associated with me. It needs to look like it came from an unknown source.

Merry-16

I look forward to Sky's little notes. I never know when to expect these surprises. He often composes these little love notes at school and occasionally brings me presents when we are alone. But when his delish letters are delivered during the day, all eyes end up on me, and jealousy lingers in the air. I adore it!

    In the distance, I see Sky take Marabelle by the face, his fingers squeezing her round cheeks. He narrows his eyes and speaks to her quietly. Their eyes lock, they glance at each other, and he pulls his hand down her jaw. She opens the note and rolls her eyes. Sky smiles and laughs. He looks my way and gives me the goofiest grin and walks away.

    "Here." Marabelle hands me the note. Since we are placed alphabetically, Marabelle always sits next to me. She has become the carrier pigeon of Sky's notes.

    "What did he say?" I ask. I can never hear his words to her, but his lips move when he passes the notes to me, so he must have said something to her.

    "Nothing," she replies.

"Then why do you always read my notes?" That really bothers me because the notes are private. "Jealous?" I ask her.

I bet she is because everyone knows Marabelle will end up a maid after Bidding Day is over. You can ask all of my year mates. No one wants to bid on someone so gross and undesirable.

I collect myself and smooth out my work blouse. I like to take my time opening my notes like a nice bar of chocolate. I do it slowly anticipating what it might say this time.

> M,
>
> *Time is running out for us. We were meant to be together, but it is forbidden. Our union was written in the stars, and as I gaze deeply into your eyes, you will know my love is true. I only hope you can love me back one day.*
>
> S

"That is sooooo romantic," Charm gushes over my shoulder.

"Hey, how did you get back here?" She startled me.

"Why can't I get a letter like that? You have been the luckiest girl in our year. You must have sooooo many admirers." Charm wrinkles her freckled nose.

"I suppose, but there is only one boy who truly has my heart, and I realize he is right. Our love is forbidden. He is an S. We will never be together the way we want. He tells me he will find a way, but it's hopeless."

"I bet you are on every guy's bid list."

"And every girl wants to be on *his* list too."

Charm's ruddy cheeks turn even redder.

"I need to talk to him," I say, "but when can I meet him? How can we ever plan our future without being watched?"

The scenario seems impossible. The situation depresses me.

"Ooooh, a new note." Sasha joins us. "I bet Marabelle peeked at it again." She rolls her big purple eyes.

I grab her face. "You are so beautiful. You will be bid on before the rest of us."

Sasha scans the Planner boys and smirks.

"Probably so, but I have my eye on some other interesting specimens too!"

She dares not look at Sky. She knows how I feel about him. It's not fair. She was born a Planner daughter. And even though we are besties, she sees that she is beautiful, and guys love to look at her. I will be really miserable if she shows up to Sky's house on the bidding visitations.

"Calm down, Merry." She must have read my body language. "I get it. Your man is hands off. I wouldn't even think of looking his way. We are sisters, remember? Besides, Sky is an S. Although he is the finest specimen around the compound, he will not be able to provide a large enough stipend to keep me satisfied."

Then she takes her finger and pushes my nose.

"You should seriously consider cozying on up to a Planner boy instead. That way we can continue to hang out and make the community a better place."

She is such a snob. I would rather live my life as a Worker in Sky's arms than a precocious Planner entitled to unspoken privileges.

After school, I return home with my note tucked into my socks. I don't show my parents. I can't. They don't approve. My father will only agree to let me see Sky during the bidding visitations if I sign up for all of the Planner sons. He does not want me to sign up for any other Workers. This breaks my heart, which already aches for Sky's attention. But crying about it does not help. It only upsets my mother and angers my father.

I retreat to my room and pull a slim wooden box out from underneath my cot. When I open it, I reveal all of Sky's love notes. Over the years, I have collected several dozen. I finger through them, displaying tiny pictures of hearts, flowers, animals, and adorable bugs. I hide a separate box that contains dried flowers and other trinkets that Sky gave me. That box lies in the back of my cubby. I try to cover it with feminine products and underwear so that my parents' temptation will be less and so they won't riffle through my things.

Supper time approaches, and I must finish some schoolwork as well. That leaves me with little time to seek out Sky and thank him for the note. He conveniently gave it to me after lunchtime. I will not have access to him during our meal tonight. Instead of placing the note in my box, I put it under my pillow so it evokes sweet dreams of our married life together.

Skyler-16

The snow blankets the hills and the lake. The water froze over the lake about a month ago. Now we have perfect weather for skating and sledding. Obviously, I am the top skater of the compound. I showcase my speed and grace on the ice for all to see. Merry smiles and claps. Antin gives me the finger. Paine and Cecile hover near me, anxious to capture some of my glory.

"Let's race," Paine suggests.

"No," Cecile responds.

Cecile is a Planner son, which gave him a *C* name. His good looks attract a lot of girls until they figure out how dumb he really is. Still, his fine face and good situation often worry me. I keep him close. I cannot let him get in my way and sabotage my future. The moron constantly forgets my views. He requires quick and constant reminders. I have to school that dummy in etiquette and vocabulary.

"Oh, Cecile, then what do you want to do?" Paine loses his patience very easily.

"Let's skate by some of the girls," he suggests.

"Okay," I say. "Who do you fancy?"

"Sasha, for starters," he begins.

"Of course," I agree. "Sasha is very nice. Who else shall we corral?"

"Merry, but she is for you," Cecile says carefully and looks at me for approval.

"Veronica, Clairica, Jewel, Rosette." I list a few names for them. "How about Charm?" I ask.

"Umm, well ..." Paine gives me a torn look. He is not too keen on Charm, but Merry is one of her besties.

"Hey, boys!" Merry greets us before we can agree on what action to take. Charm and Sasha follow behind.

"Too late," I announce.

"For what?" Sasha asks me as she skates quite close, almost hitting me, which prompts Charm to push her into me.

"Oops," says Charm.

I catch Sasha.

"I got you." She happily falls into my arms, prompting Merry to grab her hand and shove her away from me.

"Too late for what, Sky?" Merry asks as she plays with the fringe on my scarf and brushes the snowflakes from my gloves.

"Too late to find you first, ladies," I say and then skate a quick circle around them. They giggle like children.

"Maybe later they will let us make some of those tasty samosas," Cecile says.

"You mean s'mores," I correct him.

"Oh yeah, I always get those mixed up," he admits.

The girls laugh again and exchange glances.

"Look at that." Sasha points her head to the edge of the ice rink. The girls all look.

"Shhh," she hushes them. "Be discreet. We don't want to draw attention to ourselves. I wouldn't want her to think this is an invitation to join us."

"What? Who? Where?" I pretend like I don't know what goes through her mind.

"Marabelle over there," Sasha says and points, turns, and giggles, "is about to face an epic fail."

I can see Marabelle's laces are about to lock together. She takes a clumsy step, voila, her laces lock, and she falls down on the ice.

Everyone laughs. The girls cackle and pinkie-five each other.

Cecile witnesses her fall and starts to skate to help her. I grab his shoulder.

"No," I say forcefully. "She will get the wrong impression! Do you want her showing up to your bidding visitations? Dumbbelle staring at you for eternity once you are forced to marry her? Is that what you want? Huh? I will tell the girls. They will definitely laugh at you." I scare him.

"No, I guess not," he responds quietly. He does not want me to embarrass him in front of the community. He wipes the idea of helping out Marabelle from his mind.

So to save face in front of me, he chuckles and says, "She does look pretty stupid trying to get back up by herself."

A couple small children rush over to Marabelle and come to her aid. They grab her hands and pull her up. One kid comes from behind and hugs her, wrapping his little hands around her waist, smiling like a baby. She adjusts her crooked glasses and thanks them. Marabelle attracts small children more than anyone on this compound. She rotates into child care from time to time. A little girl laces her small hand into Marabelle's palm and leads her slowly onto the ice.

When we were five, Marabelle almost died. Since then, her body healed, but her eyes remained affected. She must wear very thick lenses in order to see. She squints and smirks as snow falls onto her face and melts onto her glasses. She tries her best with the tiny child but can't see well enough to navigate the ice and teeters back and forth.

"Sky." Merry calls me back from my thoughts. She smiles.

"Come skate with me," I tell her.

Merry finds comfort in my company. I guarantee we will spend the rest of the time on the ice together this afternoon.

Tip-37

I could hear my son all night locked in some kind of dream. He flipped around restlessly. I could make out a few words. He was talking in his sleep and moaning loudly. Part of me wanted to shut out the noise, but life in a slab does not grant much privacy. When you have a child, you move from a studio to a two-bedroom domicile and then back to a studio after your child turns eighteen. So I can hear anything that occurs in Sky's small bedroom.

It was a happy dream. He moaned in pleasure, not pain, but when he woke up with soiled sheets, I realized laundry day was not for another week, and I didn't have an extra set.

I open his door and expose his secret.

"Oh, Sky, how could you?" Probably the wrong thing to say to him. Sky turns bright red.

"I'm sorry, Dad," he whispers. "I couldn't help it."

I slam his door and leave him in his humiliation. Why did I embarrass him? I love my son. I wish we could talk about things like this. It is forbidden to communicate about certain topics, so it would be impossible to talk man to man. So instead, I leave him confused.

Sky emerges from his room, dressed, several minutes later. I decide to try to make things right between us.

"No, Sky, I should be the one to apologize. It is normal to dream about girls."

"Dad!" Sky whines, trying to move past me.

"It was about a girl, right? Your dream?"

"Dad, just forget it."

"Was is about Merry? I know how you feel about her."

"Dad, never mind. I'm late for school."

Sky tries to sidestep me again, but I block his way.

"I just don't want to see you get so attached to her. You know how this could end. Feeling strongly about a girl is nice, but you might end up disappointed. I would hate to see you go through that kind of pain."

"Okay. Please move now."

Sky frowns at me and rushes to the door. He slams it as he runs off to eat before classes begin.

"What was that all about?" my wife asks quizzically.

"Nothing," I tell her. "Just teenage boy stuff."

I yearn to tell Sky what I experienced as a boy. Too bad these talks are forbidden.

Merry-17

In most birth years, the female births outnumber the male births. Once we reach bidding age, a handful of girls enter adulthood as maids. Once a woman becomes a maid, her duties range from child care provider, to teacher, to nurse, to a cleaning woman for a Planner family. A maid's life consists of menial labor and absolute servitude. If a married woman's husband dies, she also becomes a maid. Some maids get second chances to rebid during a second round of bidding. They may marry widowers, or like during the dark years before we were born, the unlucky men who were not able to get new wives got a crack at the second lot of maids. By the way, talking about which girls may end up becoming maids is forbidden, so we must discuss the topic quietly and away from prying adult ears.

"I hear some maids are forced to consummate with Planner men in order to take care of their love needs," Sasha informs us.

"Yuck," I say. "How horrible." I am shocked.

"I'm just saying. I have never seen it, of course. That is just what I hear."

"Wow," says Charm, all wide-eyed. She falls for everything Sasha tells her.

We sit in Sasha's room. She is a Planner daughter, so her room is beautiful. Her décor consists of light pink and purple with splashes of hot pink mixed in with black lace accents. Occasionally, I am allowed to visit her when I do not get assigned to any chores. Sasha lives in a real house, not a concrete slab like Charm and me.

"Some maid-bounds in our year will try to visit the good catches, dontcha think? I imagine Sky's card will fill to capacity," Sasha says this to me like it's a fact.

I give her my dirtiest look, but I feel hurt on the inside.

"What, Merry? I'm only stating the truth."

"Yeah," reiterates Charm, "it's not like we have a choice anyway. Our parents fill out the cards for us."

"You do have a choice," I say. "You can tell your parents who you want to see."

"Listen," Sasha replies, "each guy has fifty spots. There are sixty-three of us. Most parents want Planners so that their daughters get more stipends. Those spots fill up fast, but *all* girls want to visit Sky, and he is a Worker."

"Not *all*!" I insist.

"Whatever, but you really need to consider a Planner boy, Merry. Do you want to live the rest of your life as a Worker? You are so smart and beautiful. Wouldn't you rather reap the rewards of a privileged life? Look at my room, my house. I even have better sheets than you. Come on, be honest. You would flourish as a Planner wife, and you know it. Plus, I happen to know most Planner boys consider putting you at the top of their bid lists."

I simply listen to Sasha, devastated on the inside. Maybe Sasha speaks a grain of truth.

"I can't give up ... on Sky," I insist.

"I want to become a Planner," Charm says.

"Sorry, Charm." Sasha looks down at her. "That just won't happen."

Skyler-17

I have to look at the list to see where I work today. With my finger, I scroll down the sheet of paper posted in the main dining hall. Rat's ass! Laundry duty again. I despise laundry duty.

I am young and strong, so I am stuck with pickup today. We all get mesh bags with our slab numbers listed on the exterior, which we fill and hang on a hook outside our doors on designated days. I drive the cart around the compound and deposit mesh bags into a larger white burlap bag. I deliver it to the laundry room once it fills. Then I heave the enormous load over my shoulder and dump it into a machine big enough to wash several hundred mesh bags at once.

"You get clothes clean, Sky." The laundry maid tries to make small talk with me.

"Yes, ma'am. I'll be back in about ten with the next load."

"You good boy. I give you cookie."

I take the treat but then toss it to the birds as I walk back to the cart.

"Thank you, Sky," they chirp.

I head back over to the Planner row of houses. Their mesh bags are larger and get washed more often. They also have more formal wear like suits and gowns. We dry-clean, iron, and press them. The regular laundry maids do most of this skilled labor. I rotate in to pick up, deliver, and fold.

As I walk down the row of rose gardens, a large door opens. Antin appears and tosses a sleek hanging bag at my face. I catch it by the wire hanger just as the sharp end misses my nose.

"Nice catch, boy. Go on like a good lad, and maybe I'll put in a good word to keep you at the laundry instead of your rotation cleaning horse shite. Don't forget to tell the girls downstairs extra starch."

Then Antin tosses a small coin my way. His door slams in my face.

I struggle with my next move. Am I too proud to reach for the coin, or do I retrieve it for my family? I know Antin waits by the door and studies me from the peephole. Swallowing pride wins as I bend down in the dirt. Antin cackles from behind his closed door and walks away. I slip the coin into my pocket for later.

"Where you be, Sky? I wait too long for you." The angry laundry maid points to the clock, spitting and cursing at my slow pace under her breath.

My body starts to ache. I suffered through an entire day of school before work. Plus, I still have studies assigned for homework today. I rarely do my homework, so they seem to fill my evening with extra chores, but when my parents find out I still have schoolwork to do, they will force me to stay up even later to finish it.

On my way back to the slab, I stop at the small store. I touch the coin in my pocket. Each member is allotted a small stipend for extra goods like snacks or fancy clothing. The amount differs depending on jobs. My parents' stipend covers very little for me. They do feed us at the dining hall, but I rarely get enough food. I leave meals with my stomach feeling tight and empty. A boy my size needs to consume more calories, and I have that burning sensation of hunger in my belly most of the day. My parents struggle with guilt because they cannot feed me more often. I seldom complain. I hate seeing their sadness. I make do, but my skinny physique constantly reminds them I need to eat more than my allotted portion.

I walk around the store, slowly assessing what I can afford with my small coin. Colorful yogurts line the dairy case, and crunchy crisps form a bright bouquet on a metal display case. My stomach growls to the point of embarrassment. How is my hunger fair or equal? I dare not ask this question out loud and face the paddle instead of a full belly. I quickly grab a red package of peanut puffs and hand the store keeper my coin.

I rip open the bag and stuff a handful of puffs into my mouth. An immediate buzz of food hitting my tongue gives me a light-headed satisfaction. I was hungrier that I thought. So I decide to grab a couple loaves of bread from the common kitchen on my way home. I can keep one in my room and give the other to my parents. Being thoughtful earns a couple extra bonus points with them anyway.

Merry-17

I see Sky lean against the brick wall of the little market. He rips open a bag of peanut puffs, devours them in about three handfuls, and then licks his fingers. I stand frozen, mesmerized by his presence. He has no idea the power he possesses over me.

I don't want to break the spell by approaching him yet. So I hover in a corner of the building for a moment, out of his sight.

Sky hikes over to the main dining hall. I follow him.

"Hey, Sky." I run a little to catch him.

"Oh, hi," he answers. He looks tired and acts a little out of it.

"Do you have a second?"

"Sure. Just getting some bread to take home."

"Um ..." I try to think of something charming to say. I can tell he is not too interested in talking to me. My heart plummets inside my chest as my disappointment spreads. He seems to sense this as well. He is so intuitive.

"Sorry, Merry. I worked a lot today. I can't seem to concentrate on anything. I apologize."

He smiles at me weakly. Even when he is exhausted, he looks amazing.

"It's okay. I'll hang with you a bit. What did you do today?"

"Laundry. I had to pick up all of the bags. Really a horrid experience. I had tons and tons of lifting, and there was all that driving around the compound. It lasted almost like forever and ever."

"Oh."

I am at a loss for words. I hate it when I can't think of something clever to say to attract his attention. We connect on an amazing level, but I fear what the pool of competition the girls in our year may bring. Many of the Planner girls possess great beauty, talent, and prestige. With their fathers' influences, they may gain some advantage over my lone friendship with Sky. I constantly feel the need to remind myself how he truly cares about me, by reading and rereading his notes and handling the trinkets he sent me. This cloud of hopelessness weighs down on me as Bidding Day grows nearer.

"Okay, Merry, I said I was sorry."

Now he sounds annoyed. My good intentions backfired. The nausea engulfs my stomach. I want him to comfort me before I throw up.

"Merry," he starts again. "What's wrong?"

The tears well up in my eyes, I feel a trickle down my cheek.

"We start dance class soon," I finally say.

"I thought you were looking forward to that."

"I am, but it terrifies me at the same time," I confess.

"Why? You and all of your friends will finally be allowed to discuss boys. That should make you happy."

"It does. I'm ecstatic."

Now the tears start pouring down my cheeks. I probably look horrible.

"But once the lessons are done, we have our big ball, which will lead to the visits, and then, of course, the big day. Our time as children together will end. I'm not ready for this. I'm afraid of whom I may end up with after Bidding Day," I blubber to him.

"I'm sure you will end up happy," Sky tells me.

"Will I? How do you figure?" I ask.

"You can't choose who you fall in love with. I heard that once a long time ago. You can't choose who you will love; it just happens. And when it does, you can't control which person your heart wants the most."

"You are right. I can't even control who I get to marry. At least you get a chance to bid," I add.

"Do I? I'm not sure I really have control over the situation either. As far as I understand about the process is that all I get is a list. One list. My father does the bidding for me, and because he was in the same position as I am now, he doesn't have a clue what to expect either. That's no help to me. You and I are as stuck, as are the rest of our year mates, in a situation beyond our control. So, Merry, please listen to me carefully."

Sky takes my face in his hands. It feels so nice. I love when he touches me. The few times it's happened have made me so happy. I stare into his deep blue eyes.

He continues, "Please do not be disappointed. Dreaming about our happy ending goes against the reality we live in on the compound. You are the most beautiful girl here."

"Shut up," I say. Now I am really crying.

"I mean it. You are the most beautiful girl on the compound. I won't be able to get near you in a year. I'm sorry again. Think of me from time to time. Remember our times together at work, but don't plan on seeing me on your Wedding Day."

"No, Sky, please don't say this."

"I promise you'll be happy. There is more out there than what I have to offer you. I'll see ya."

He turns and grabs two loaves of bread, leaving me to walk home alone to my slab, sobbing.

Skyler-17

I walk home slowly, carrying two loaves of bread under my arms. I scan the sky for birds. I spot a raven and break off some crust of bread. I hold out my hand filled with the bits of food and call him over. I can do this in my head so others do not witness my conversation.

"Come here, little raven. Have something to eat."

It flaps toward me happily.

"Hi, Sky. What can I do for you?" it responds.

"I need another favor. This time, you need to go farther. Please. If you can't, then fly to the farthest point you can and commission another bird to go. Try to contact as many species as you can. I need to search a greater amount of distance. I must find out if there are others out there. We can't be the only people on this land. Please, try to go farther this time." I plea my case by pinching off more bread.

"I can try again, Sky," it answers, "but we have looked for years. You here seem to be the only people in existence living on the land."

"Impossible," I counter. "How can this compound be the only place where humans exist? I refuse to believe it."

"Well, okay, we will investigate. But your kind has not been spotted outside these mountains. Other species exist—bears, wolves, deer, large cats. Some of the hotter lands house monkeys, camels, and fowl of all sorts, but no people."

"Don't give up on me," I say, and by command, I release it into the air to start my hunt.

My search continues, hopefully not in vain.

As I reach the door to my slab, the temperature starts to drop. Living in the valley of a mountain brings cold nights. I sleep huddled under blankets, but I can never warm up enough. Even my duvet doesn't provide ample heat. We use long space heaters in our slab to counter the chill. They plug into the wall. They don't seem to do much. They look a little like toasters, so I often slice my bread and pop it on the grate. This infuriates my father.

"Hello," my father calls as I come through the door.

"Hi. I got you some bread."

"Thanks." He smiles at me. We rarely have anything to talk about. I can tell he wants to a better relationship with me, yet we struggle getting through even a simple conversation. It's awkward when my father tries too hard.

"Well, okay, good night." I try to retreat to my bedroom.

"Wait. Sky, your mother and I want to talk to you a moment."

"What?" I try not to sound too annoyed. Perhaps they will just think I am a normal moody teenager.

"How was your day?" he asks weakly.

"Fine. I am very tired. I've had a long day. I need to get some sleep, all right? Good night." I slam the door for effect. I hear them wish me a good night from behind the door.

I need time to process. I want to wrap my head around the possibility that others do not exist in the world. The compound school limits the information taught. Perhaps no one else on the compound knows the answer. Maybe we are truly the only humans on the planet. Maybe we stay here to protect ourselves from the elements. Between the lake and the mountain, the land is fertile, and food is plenty. Is this why we are forced to stay rather than explore the uninhabited and the unknown?

Honestly, I also want time to daydream about my love. I want to fall asleep and dream about her again. As my luck would have it, this dream never comes. I am frustrated that I am stuck in my room, waiting for that stupid bird to reappear with bad news. I chew on a little bread and drift to sleep, eager to have good dreams.

Merry-17

I warm my hands in the sun. Teacher forces us to sit on a hill during learning choice time. Some students participate in recess, but the older years must choose a scholastic activity. I try to read, but after last night's encounter with Sky, I can't concentrate on the meaning of the words in front of me. My eyes read the same words over and over again.

Sasha sits next to me with Charm. They both pretend to study math.

"I'm so excited! It's almost here. Dance class!" Sasha bubbles over with her nonstop energy.

"We get a turn to dance with all of the boys," Charm adds, her ruddy cheeks glowing an even brighter red.

"That's nice," I say.

"What's wrong, Merry?" Sasha turns to me with genuine concern.

"I can't wrap my head around it, but I think Sky and I had a fight. It didn't seem like it at the time, but he seems angry."

"At you?"

"I'm not sure. I can't tell. Maybe he's angry at me, or maybe he's angry at our situation."

"Wow, you are the only person I know who has had a relationship before bidding."

"Yeah," Charm adds. Words are not her best trait.

"I'm not in a relationship. It's complicated, and relationships are forbidden."

"You are right, but I hear rumors about certain year mates hooking up, so to speak," Sasha says, as she seems to be the master of all rumors and gossip.

"Who?" I ask.

"Not sure—people. Oh, they are only silly stories anyway. Your dilemma is real, unlike those rumored ones. Maybe Sky was tired. The community seems to overwork him. He goes before and after school, sometimes during school. Someone must really have it out for him. He's never home."

"You're right. Wait ... how do you know he's never home?"

"Stop obsessing, Merry. Enjoy this time before it's over," Sasha reminds me.

"What, choice time? I can barely think. This book is impossible to read."

"No, silly, this time! The time we have left together before bidding. After we are married, some of us may not have social time together anymore. Our destinies will be decided, and we will be separated by marriage."

"Hey, guys. Look," Charm interrupts us and points. "Look at Marabelle, coloring like a baby."

"She's not coloring, she's painting, stupid." Sasha hits Charm's head.

"Ouch."

"Sorry, Char. Get this. Dumb-belle has to sit with a little kid because she has no friends. What an old maid. She's getting ready for her duties."

Marabelle lies in the sun next to a younger boy named One. She mixes different-colored paints. I can't tell what she is making on her paper, but she takes a break and leans back, relaxing on the green grass.

At the same moment Marabelle starts to ease her body down onto the lawn, a rock flies through the air and crashes onto her paint palette, splattering a rainbow of colors all over her face. It splashes all over One as he rolls over onto his back, startled.

I turn my head to see it was Sky who threw the rock.

"Ha, ha!" The other boys around him start to laugh.

"Good one!" Sasha shouts.

"Dumb-belle," someone else calls.

"Maramaid," says another year mate.

Tears roll down Marabelle's cheeks as One tries to wipe the paint off her. Sky launches another rock at them, nearly missing One by a fraction of an inch.

"That's it! Head inside." Teacher breaks up the commotion and gathers the hooting students.

Sasha turns to me as we walk inside. "I understand it's forbidden to say, but I hate that girl."

"Me too," adds Charm.

We return to our seats for lecture time.

Again, I have a rough time concentrating on my schoolwork. How do they expect us to learn if we can't sort out our social problems? I can hear paper rustling and a wave of whispering behind me. It approaches my ears like a large whitecap during high tide, reaching closer and closer. Suddenly, I feel somebody tap my arm.

"What?" I whisper harshly.

It's Marabelle. She tries to shove an open note into my hand.

"Here." She pushes it toward me.

I grab it quickly so Teacher doesn't notice.

"Take a shower," I snap at her.

"I did," she responds weakly.

"Why did you open it? Why do you always have to read my notes? They are private," I gripe and purposely turn away from her.

My heart beats rapidly in my chest. I nervously scroll down the note with my eyes. It says...

> *M,*
>
> *I am so sorry! Please forgive me for what I have done to you. I didn't mean it. I get so jealous sometimes. I just can't stand the thought of you being with anyone else. It hurts me to see you so sad. I hate to admit it, but when you cry, I cry too. I know it is hard, but please don't tell anyone how I feel about you. Remember my promise to you.*
>
> *I love you.*

I fold the note and conceal it in my pocket. I want to rush home and put my note away for safekeeping in my box. A rush of relief washes over my entire body. This will make the day much easier to get past. I am happy and light-headed. A large smile spreads over my lips. He still cares about me, and that is all that matters to me.

I walk home slowly, clutching my note to me chest.

"Whatcha got there?"

Startled, I turn.

"Antin, you surprised me."

"Sorry. I didn't mean to. What's that you have in your hand?"

"Oh, nothing." I fold my note up and put it back in my pocket.

"Did you hear the news? We start dance soon. I'm really looking forward to getting a chance to dance with you. Maybe even chat a bit." Antin smiles widely at me.

He is really nice looking—not as handsome as Sky, but not bad at all. He hails from a line of top Planners. As far as I can tell, all of his ancestors received *A* names. His future wife will live with abundance and a hefty stipend. His own child will most likely take an *A* name as well.

"Yes, Antin, sure, I will dance with you." I am flattered temporarily. I need to remember how much Antin hates Sky. It's crazy how deep his distaste for Sky runs. Antin has a passion for detesting Sky and getting Sky into trouble. A bird once pooped on Antin, and Sky was blamed and paddled for it, which is ridiculous. Why would Sky get blamed for random bird poo?

"Merry, I am heading to the market. Would you like to come and get something sweet?"

"Sure, Antin." My stomach grumbles. Dinner won't be for hours. I follow him.

"You look lovely today."

"Thanks, though I haven't done anything different."

"You always look out of the ordinary. Did you see what happened to Marabelle today? It was pretty hilarious."

It was pretty rare for Antin to make a Sky reference, but perhaps he wanted to keep the conversation going.

"I know, right? She's pretty out of it. She just doesn't get it, does she? What an old maid!"

"Really!" he agrees as he opens the door for me.

"Look around," he suggests. "I'm going to get a frozen chocolate. What would you like?"

Antin must really have a lot of coins to be able to afford random snacks. I eye a large chocolate strawberry decorated like an enormously cute ladybug, sitting in the freezer. He sees me and moves closer. He leans over and places his lips next to my ear.

"Is that what you would like? I'll buy it for you."

"Thank you so much, Antin. You are being so sweet. I mean, thanks, Antin. I really appreciate it."

"I don't need thanks, Merry. It's my pleasure. We're friends. That's what friends do. They give each other things. Let me walk you home."

Antin walks me to my door and says, "See you tomorrow, Merry."

"Bye," I say and slide into my slab.

I rush to my room and take out my treat. I sink my teeth into the sweet berry. The chocolate melts around my tongue. I take my time to enjoy my treat. I bet having a large stipend is nice. Then my pocket crunches. I almost forgot about my note. Guilt washes over me again. Did I betray Sky by going with Antin to get a snack? I remove the note and smooth out the crinkles. My eyes tear up again.

"I'm sorry, Sky," I say softly and take out my box from under the bed. I reread his note and flip through the old ones as well.

"Merry, it's time for dinner." My parents start banging on the door.

"I'm not hungry," I say. I crush the candy wrapper and put it in the box. They would get mad if they knew I spoiled my dinner by eating candy that a boy bought me—especially the boy thing. Except if I told them it was Antin, perhaps they would get excited. They are very aware that bidding draws nearer, so attention from a Planner might put them in good moods.

"Okay," they say. Instead of arguing, they leave.

"Great," I say out loud. My stomach grumbles. I suppose I really am pretty hungry, but after taking a gift from Antin, facing Sky at the dining hall scares me. I would rather starve for one evening than see his face. I will tell him I fell asleep doing my homework at school tomorrow.

Skyler-17

As dance lessons start today, the exhaustion creeps over my body. My sore arms ache, and the muscles in my legs burn. My bad behavior fatigues me, plus school, plus work, plus the needy people surrounding me at all times. I hate it! I do not look forward to this mating ritual. We follow the rules with little explanation. Year after year, dance class offers time to spend a moment with each year mate. It gives the illusion of socializing with peers. One last chance at childhood before our adult lives are set, our marriages decided, the date for creating children chosen.

Most of my year mates giggle with excitement. We wait, standing around the perimeter of the gym, separated on either side by gender. We all anticipate who might teach us these magical moves.

A tall, graceful older woman enters the room. Her life as a maid came from the death of her husband. Her attractive face and slim body won her a Planner for a husband, but his poor health shortened her time in her beautiful home. Since she never had a child, she was unable to keep her residence. Women who lose their husbands may stay in their positions and homes until their child reaches eighteen, but she had no child and was forced to live as a maid prematurely.

"Good morning, Teacher," we all say in unison.

"Good morning," she addresses us. "Your dance lessons will start today. They will continue once a week and alternate between your morning and afternoon schedules. First, you will learn the steps alone. No boys or girls will be allowed to touch. Later, you will select alternating dance partners. You will select your dance partners for the second phase by drawing numbers. Since the girls outnumber the boys, they will draw two numbers first, and then the boys will draw one number each for the third pairing. As we rotate, girls who do not have partners will sit off to the side until one of their selections is available. Afterward, you will each practice with every person of the opposite sex. Finally, you will be allowed one grand ball in which you may dress up, be administered one glass of vin, and ask each other to dance. Do I make myself quite clear?"

"Yes, Teacher," we all answer in unison.

This does not sound good to me. It sounds like a waste of time. I am not keen on dancing with every single female year mate. I dread having to smile or make small talk with every single girl here. I definitely feel an illness coming on that may put me in the clinic for a few days over the next several weeks.

I hack a couple fake coughs.

"I'm feeling sick. I'm not sure I can start today."

"Skyler-17, that's enough. I've been warned about you. Straighten up." Teacher shoots me a dirty look. Several of my year mates snicker.

"All right, ladies and gentlemen. Let's get started," she continues.

"Sky is not a gentleman," Antin says under his breath. A couple of students around him laugh. I smile at Merry, and she blushes.

"Enough, children." Teacher cannot see we are verging on adulthood. "Stand up, and form two lines across the room, males facing females, but stand several feet apart."

Merry rushes to stand across from me. Several other girls follow. Some want to be close to Merry; the rest want a chance to stare at me. Most of the less desirable boys and maid-bound girls wind up at the ends of the two lines. I am forced into the middle. Cecile ends up next to me.

He leans over and starts up with me.

"Sky, we're best friends right?" he asks.

I turn away and roll my eyes, dreading another conversation with Captain Insecurity.

"Sure," I answer.

The teacher has us stepping forward and stepping backward.

"What's if I mess up the dance steps? What if the girls laugh? Do you think we'll have a test on this at the end?"

"This isn't a good time to worry about these things, Cecile. We just started. We won't dance with the girls for several weeks, months even."

"Thanks. You always know what to say. I'm sticking here next to you."

"Great. What luck!"

Merry smiles and waves. She has the body of a dancer, thin and tall. Her long blonde hair and blue eyes shine in the light of the gym. She has a small nose and big teeth. Most girls envy her. They compare their own looks to hers to see how they measure up. She sets the standard for beauty on the compound. She gloats about this in her mind. She believes the same about me. Thus we would be the ultimate match. We would create the most amazing child.

I must remind her again soon that the likelihood of our union is slim to none. I hate bursting her perfect little bubble in her brain, but others have their eyes on her. She has to understand a girl as gorgeous as she can't go unnoticed. She is not invisible to the rest. She absolutely attracts the most attention and adoration from our year mates.

"Okay, stop," commands the teacher. "Good, very good, ladies and gentlemen. I think we have had a very good first session. I see a lot of progress being made. You may practice on your own, but practicing with a partner outside class is strictly forbidden. Do I make myself understood?"

"Yes, Teacher," we all say.

"Clearly?"

"Yes, Teacher."

"Good. See you next week."

Oddly, all of that stupid dancing made me hungry. I rush to the dining hall for lunch. Perhaps they will serve something good today like meat and veggie roll-ups with fries. I can eat a heap of them. Why bother getting my hopes up? I see salad, white cheese, bread, and hard-boiled eggs out of the corner of my eye. Oh well, at least I'll get fed.

"Hey, Sky, wait up." Cecile runs to catch up to me. "I just wanted to talk to you for a moment."

"Okay."

"I just wanted to say I hope we remain friends after bidding is over. I understand what Antin says about Planners and Workers not associating together and all, but I don't see the difference. It is all fair and equal, after all. So I don't care what Antin says. I don't want to lose you. I don't want our friendship to end. Promise me, Sky, that we will continue to be best friends. Please. I can't imagine a life stuck with Antin and his buddies."

"Neither can I." I laugh.

"You are so down to earth, Sky. And you always come through for me."

"Cecile, only you can choose to continue our relationship."

"I didn't know we had a choice."

"Then there you go. Do you see Workers and Planners hanging out together?"

"No. But I don't think it is forbidden."

"It might not be forbidden, but it's not exactly encouraged either. I'll be the one trimming your bushes and mowing your lawn. Free time is rarely an option for a Worker."

"Maybe after dinner."

"I think I'll want to spend some time with my wife." I am actually giving him my honest answer, but in his mind, he still imagines us as kids who can play after school.

"I get it. Don't ya want to remain friends?"

"I do, Cecile. My point is that it will be up to you. I won't get a chance to have a say when I work long shifts."

Here's some honesty. I don't want friends. I don't need them. What I need is lunch, and Cecile is wasting my time. This is the reason I stay so thin: not enough time and not enough food. If I run into another person for another useless conversation, I think I'll starve.

"Excuse me," I say, gently shoving him so I can get some food.

As I fill my plate, my father spots me. He aches to talk to me. I am not interested. I try to take three slices of bread, and the server takes off the top slice.

"Only two slices per person, Skyler-17," she says.

"I'm super hungry," I insist.

"Two per person," she repeats.

I give her a big smile, and she rolls her eyes. She slips the bread in my hand from under the tray so no one else can see the extra slice.

"Thanks," I whisper.

Tip-38

I spot Sky sit down in the cafeteria. I notice he scored an extra piece of bread. Guilt overwhelms me. I look at his body. Sky is all muscle and bones. No fat appears anywhere on his physique. He resembles a strong, thin tree. I am unable to provide him with enough food, and the community pushes him to go to school and work long hours. He burns calories but doesn't take in enough nourishment. Vitamins keep him healthy and alive, but Sky can't spare a pound. I badly want to give him some of my portion, but I fear he won't take any food from me. I watch him starve daily. The community assures me they won't deny him proper nutrition. Yet I wonder. In the past, I've taken a risk and asked the leaders. They insist letting an able-bodied young man die is forbidden. Sky will live a long, prosperous life, they say. But do they see what I see? His rib cage? His pelvic bone? His jaw jutting from his face, all skin and no fat? His skeletal body? I often worry about him. My fears greatly annoy Sky. I'd see a doctor about this again, but asking any Planner for the answers I have already received is forbidden. Plus, we are not granted any extra help for our children.

Sky will not be allowed any more sustenance than his allotted amount. I regret to add I lack enough stipend to provide him with more treats or any other types of food beyond the extra dining hall bread found in the cupboard at night.

"Sky." I wave to him. "Can I join you?"

"Sure," Sky says as he stares out into space, his eyes glazed with fatigue.

"Would you like some of my salad?" I offer.

"No, you eat it."

"How about some more bread? I'll split it with you."

"No, thanks. You need it too. You have a long day ahead of you as well."

"I hear you started dance lessons today. How did it go?"

"Fine."

"Do you like your teacher?"

"Sure, she's all right, I guess."

"Any girls you want to partner up with yet?"

"Dad!"

I have annoyed him again.

"Sorry. Perhaps it is forbidden to ask. I remember my first day at dance class. We didn't know what to expect. It was quite nerve-racking. I couldn't imagine who would draw my number, but the whole experience was better than I expected. So just enjoy this time."

"I will, Dad," Sky answers flatly.

I love him so much that it pains me the way we do not connect on a higher level. Sky mirrors my good intentions by showing me a bit of his emotions and affectionately pats my shoulder. Then he smiles. He has amazing intuition and makes me feel better.

"Thanks, Dad," he tells me.

I always wonder how he guesses the right moment to smile or laugh or make me feel all right about our relationship.

"I love you, Sky," I reply.

Skyler-17

Although a perfectly functional pool exists in the community, many swimming lessons take place in the lake. Multiple classes use it at the same time. We swim or canoe or row for sport during school hours. Today is no exception. A few classes of years were ordered to the lake for physical fitness. Teachers sectioned off areas for students to swim laps. Shallow areas are reserved for weaker swimmers. Deeper water is off limits to those who cannot swim well; they are restricted from entering the roped-off area. Instead, this section is reserved for those students who have greater endurance. Teachers frequently test our abilities and divide us into color-coded lanes. Here, younger and older students mix together, depending on the outcomes of the swim tests.

Today, I practice my laps in the red lane reserved for the best swimmers among us. As always, I fail to learn that showcasing my talents means doing the most work. Only five other students achieved red today. The rest of the kids crowd the other lanes.

People walk in and out of the lake. Some splash around and get reprimanded by a teacher and are forced to sit on the beach. As I steady my pace, I feel the wind start to pick up, creating soft ripples in the water. As I push on, the waves slowly build. The water becomes choppy. One teacher blows a loud whistle signifying break time. Most of the kids sit in the sand and relax, but a few remain in the water for a little horseplay.

Suddenly, I hear a whisper.

"Sky," it says, slowly and quietly. I stop my lap and look around to see if anyone is near me. I lightly tread water and listen again.

"Sssskyyyyyyyy ..." it continues.

"Hello?" I say out loud, until I realize I am alone. Nobody else can hear it.

"Sssskyyyyyyyy."

The whisper gets louder. The waves around me get faster and increase.

"Skyler-17!" yells a teacher. "Return to the shore, please."

I swim back listening for the voice.

"Hello," I say. Perhaps it is a fish. It doesn't sound like a fish.

I return to the beach and sit near Merry and some other year mates in the sand.

Out of the blue, we hear a loud scream.

"Aaaahhhhh! Something just grabbed my ankle!"

Merry jumps into my arms, frightened by the scream. We turn and look and see Marabelle. Her face turns pale. Her eyes pop out, and her mouth gapes open. She had been playing in the water with a younger kid named One. He quickly pulls her to the shore. Strangely, this time I can sense her fear and confusion. Normally, she is hard to read.

"Girl!" the voice screeches. Bubbles appearing where Marabelle was playing. "Nooooooooooooooo!" it adds as Marabelle leaves the water.

I look at Marabelle's face. She's in shock. I can't tell if she can hear it too. Tears roll down her cheeks. She pants and barely catches her breath. I hear her heart pounding. I notice One looking at me. Oddly, his mind is completely blank. Did he hear it?

"Something's in there!" Marabelle cries.

Other students respond to this by screaming.

"Calm down at once," orders one of the teachers.

"It grabbed me!" Marabelle insists.

"That's impossible, dear. Nothing is in there. Perhaps it was one of your friends."

"She doesn't have any," somebody offers.

Some students laugh at this.

"Please," she pleads. "I am telling the truth. I swear something grabbed me. It touched my foot."

I run into the water and dive under.

"Yay!" The students stand up and applaud as I search for this monster.

"Sky, you're my hero," someone else yells as I resurface.

"I can't see anything," I report. "Nothing is in there."

More clapping erupts from the crowd on the beach.

"See?" the teacher asks Marabelle.

"Okay, swim time is over! Report back to class!" another teacher yells as we all return back toward the school.

I'm still not convinced. There is something in that lake. I could hear it. I need to find out what called my name. I think some others could hear it too. They won't admit it. I plan on finding out what I heard.

After school lets out, I return to the beach. I recruit a couple of seagulls.

"Something is in the lake," I tell them.

"We know, Sky—fish."

"No, it's not fish."

"Turtles perhaps, maybe some eels."

"No, I heard it this morning. A voice called my name."

"Was it a bird?"

"It couldn't have been a bird. It called my name, and then it spoke to a girl in my class."

"Impossible, Sky. What did it say, Sky?"

"I only heard three things. It said my name, then it said 'girl' and 'no.' It also grabbed someone by the leg too. Please look. Please look for me. Dive under and try to see if you can come up with something."

The birds dive under in search for this magical creature for me. They reappear.

"Nothing, Sky," they say.

"No, I know it there was something—like a person or something."

"No, Sky, there are no people under the water. People only live on land. There are no other people around besides you and those who populate this place."

"I don't believe that. Look again!" I command.

The birds try again in vain. I decide to get into the lake myself. I don't even bother removing my clothes. The water saturates my shirt and pants, and the clothes weigh me down.

The cold water numbs my body. At this point, I don't care. I put my hand in the lake and smack the water with rapid frustration. I was not dreaming. I really heard my name. It wasn't the wind. Something under the waves surrounded me and grabbed Marabelle.

As much as I want to find her and talk to her about it, I restrain myself. I forbid myself from having a conversation with her. What would the other year mates think if they caught us talking? That kid One had witnessed something too because he pulled Marabelle out of the water, but after the rock incident, I'm sure he doesn't want a visit from me. Plus, he kept his mind blank when he noticed me, so I guess he has nothing to say to me right now.

Dripping wet, I sit on the water's edge and watch the sunset. Disappointed again, my life seems to be full of these moments. My stomach grumbles loudly. I bet I am missing dinner. Great, now I am hungry, disappointed, wet, and confused.

Why do I continue this futile search for others? Am I so desperate to find human life that I imagined this lake episode?

No, it's not possible that I imagined this event, because Marabelle reacted to something in the water. Besides, few people around here are squeamish about the fish. We have been swimming in this lake our whole lives. And, and, and fish cannot grab on to people's feet! But why hear a voice now? Why after all of these years? Why haven't I heard this call in the past? Did Marabelle provoke something hidden below the sea?

It's getting late. The moon rises in the night sky. I feel at home with the moon shining down on the sand, reflecting its large ball in the dark water. I just want to stay here and fall asleep. Its glow blankets me with an odd sensation of warmth, like I belong here with it. It soothes my anger a bit.

My parents will probably begin to worry soon. I don't want to cause them more trouble than I already have. So I walk home to greet an angry dad and a teary-eyed mom. Once I cross the threshold, my mom grabs me and cries.

"Where were you? Do you know what time it is? We were worried something happened to you," she sobs.

"I'm fine, Mom, really. Besides, in less than a year, I will be out of the house. Then you won't have to keep track of me."

My father shoots me a dirty look.

"Sorry, Mom. I didn't mean to worry you. I'll let you know where I am going next time, I promise you."

I head to my room, hoping sleep will clear up some of my confusion. As I walk away, I can hear my father complain about me.

"I told you so. He has become so distant. I don't know what to do. Anytime I try to reach out to him, he rejects me."

"He's just ready to leave and start a home of his own."

"He's still so young. He thinks he has all of the answers, but there is so much he needs to learn."

"All in due time. Your son will be married soon and then start his own family. He will have his own worries, and maybe then he will understand what it is like to be a parent. Then he will know what it is like to have a child to care for and love. He will get that chance to love something more than he loves himself."

"Do you really think Sky is capable of loving someone else more than he loves himself?"

If my father even knew! I already do love someone so much that her existence means more to me than life itself. If he even understood how much I love her—that I can't stand looking at her without the ability to grab her and hold her. It kills me to be in the same room as her and not to be able to touch her. If he even knew the time I have spent thinking about her, hoping to dream about her at night, and waking up unsuccessful and disappointed. As I get out of my dripping clothes, I think that this is my life: wet, cold, dreamless, and distraught. I do love someone more than I love myself. I just wish I could get the chance to ask her if she feels the same way.

Merry-17

"That thing in the water really freaked me out the other day. I am not going back in the lake again," I insist to those around me.

We wait to start our next dance lesson.

"I don't blame you. Did you get a look at Marabelle's face? She turned white," Charm whispers back to me.

"There was nothing in there," Sky interjects. "I went in myself. I couldn't find anything. Maybe a piece of seaweed touched her ankle. Most girls are squeamish about seaweed."

"I don't know. She was pretty convincing. The way she screamed scared me away for a while."

"Maybe it was a fish?" he suggests.

"Perhaps. But, Sky, you were brave." I look Sky straight in the eyes. "The way you ran in to protect us all. You are quite the hero."

"Not really. I think people were just trying to make fun of me."

"Not at all. Kids really do look up to you. No one else stepped forward and went into the lake. You are a hero around here."

"Not to Antin?"

"Probably not to Antin, but to the rest of us. You do the stuff other people avoid or run away from."

"I guess."

Teacher walks in briskly, so Sky and I separate to either side. I yearn to talk to Marabelle and ask her what happened in the water, but being seen speaking to her stops me from doing it. I would rather not embarrass myself in front of Sky or have the other year mates poke fun at me for acting too friendly toward her.

The dance session is the same as the last one. We follow Teacher's steps and repeat her dance moves, facing the boys without touching them. I am not able to get close to Sky. Instead, I face Paine, who blushes every time I lock eyes with him. It's completely annoying, and I hate staring at his stupid face. It's ridiculous that Sky can be best friends with almost every boy in our year. They all clamor around him, admiring him. They all want to sit near him at lunch or beg to work during his shift. I rarely get a similar job as he, but I see other girls in our year work next to him. They flirt desperately with him to try to get his attention. It's such a sickening thing to watch, actually.

"Merry!" Teacher shouts in my ear.

"Huh." I drifted off during the lesson, thinking about Sky and the whole water incident.

"Merry," she continues, "you are doing such an extraordinary job that I feel you would be able to demonstrate these moves with a young man."

"Not Paine, not Paine, not Paine," I repeat in my head.

"Sky," she announces.

"Yes, Teacher," he responds.

"Please move forward and join hands with Merry as I have instructed you."

Sky takes my hand in his and puts the other around my waist. My whole body tingles at his touch.

"Now proceed to demonstrate how the dance flows together."

Sky guides me across the floor with ease. I float and spin. I try not to laugh. I can't remember anyone ever holding me this tight, not even my parents. The girls all gasp and giggle. I twirl around like a fairy-tale princess.

"Enough. Separate, please," Teacher demands.

As quickly as our dance started, it ends. We immediately release our embrace.

"Next week, you will draw numbers for partners. Remember, all students will get a chance to practice with each other. Talking, uninstructed touching, and other funny business is strictly forbidden. Do I make myself clear?"

"Yes, Teacher," we answer in unison.

As we leave, Charm runs up to me.

"Wow. I wish you could have seen yourself. You danced so eloquently. I can barely wait for my turn, er, to dance with someone, anyone. What was it like to hold a boy? You held Sky. I mean, wow!" Charm gushes.

"Okay, Charm, I get it. Calm down. I have a lot on my mind right now. I barely noticed Sky holding me."

"Is it the water thingy?"

"No. Now I'm worried about who I will partner up with next week. We don't pick the names we want, we draw numbers."

53

"Well, I can't wait."

"Grumpy, are we?" Sasha slides up to me. "Worried you won't dance with your man next week?"

"You have too much time on your hands, Sasha," I say, smoothing out my hair. "All you do is sit around painting your nails while the rest of us work."

"Just born lucky, I guess, but you can join me. Visitations start soon. Change your mind about signing up for Planner houses? Your nails would look simply delicious if you painted them red, purple, perhaps even flower-petal pink. Think about it, Merry."

The trouble is, I am thinking about it. Being a Worker is exhausting. I can see the toll it takes on my mother. The dark bags under her eyes tell a story of hardship and exhaustion. The calluses on my father's hands bleed from small cracks that form when the weather dries them out. Their bones crack, and their bodies ache. I don't picture myself in their position.

Perhaps it is time to think about practicalities instead of love, partnership instead of friendship. Seven boys hold the title of Planner in my year. It may be time to get to know them better.

Skyler-17

I sense her feelings for me change. Lately, she has put some distance between us. I sense her apprehension to be near me. She has changed her mind about me. I guess it was inevitable. I will eventually tell her that it's normal for her to want to marry someone else. I constantly try to prepare her for the day we won't see each other much anymore, but Merry clings to the ridiculous notion that I alone will be able to concoct a brilliant plan to change the way society works.

From across the room, I see Merry dance with Wills. She frowns. Bad luck landed her with all Worker boys. Wills, being a *W*, is obviously at the bottom, even below me. She also drew Paine's number. I think Teacher felt bad. She favors

Merry. Perhaps Teacher sees she has Planner potential. But because we danced so well for that demonstration, Teacher wanted us to be the "example." So Merry also ended up being my partner (Teacher's choice, a bold yet rare move). Honestly, this also disappointed her. I can't help feeling a little hurt. I am human, after all.

I got Clairica and Veronica for my two other dance partners. I think the numbering and matching of dance partners is fixed. I bet Teacher rigged it, because the less popular maid-bound girls only ended up with two boys each and gather in a pathetic group on the side while the rest of the girls dance with their third partners.

With every lesson, we switch three times, practicing with each partner. The order rotates each time. Now I see the partner-less girls chatting in a corner together, with the exception of Marabelle, who awkwardly stares into space on a bench.

The whistle blows, and we switch. Veronica looks at me, hoping I will say something, so I smile and say thanks. She giggles and finds the next boy as Merry swings into my arms.

"Pathetic. See those girls? I would hate to be them. It's like they already know these lessons are futile. They will be teaching dance rather than using these moves with a husband."

"How is old Wills, anyway?"

"Awful! Do I have the worst luck or what? And I know you are friends with Paine, but how can you stand him? He has the world's worst breath and a big nose. Plus he has no clue how to dance."

"Watch what you say. You may end up marrying him," I tease her.

"Shut up! Bite your tongue. That would be a fate worse than death. I am *not* ending up Paine's wife."

"He does seem to fancy you, and *P* comes before *S*. I barely have a chance with you."

Merry's face turns red. Her guilt spreads over her body as she stiffens. She doesn't want a Worker boy anymore. She wants to relax in the pool with Sasha, pretty painted nails in all. Then when she looks at my face, she remembers that she still loves me, and it confuses her.

"Sky, I—"

"You don't have to say anything, Merry. I'm teasing you. Paine won't marry you. He does have really bad breath, but so do I. I ate onions for breakfast," I say and blow in her face.

"Stop!" She laughs, pretending to be annoyed. "You haven't written me any notes in a while."

"Haven't I? I guess I have been pretty busy. I am scheduled to work a lot. You can stop by and say hi tonight. I'll be washing dishes."

"Sure, if I have time. We have a lot of homework. Gosh, you never do yours, but I'm not as smart as you, so I need to do mine. Plus, my parents don't let me get away with avoiding it like yours."

Here it is. Merry is already making excuses to avoid me.

"My parents don't let me get away with anything. I simply refuse to do it. It makes them very angry when I act this way. The atmosphere is pretty unpleasant at my slab right now."

"Maybe you should try to get along better with them. They are your parents. They love you."

"Perhaps."

The whistle blows again.

"Sorry. Bye. See you later," Merry says and walks away. She has no intention of seeing me later and plans on sitting as far away from me as possible to avoid further confrontation at dinner.

I sit in the main dining hall, nursing a cup of coffee. It's delicious. Only a few of us remain. I contemplate taking a walk to the orchard, but I hesitate. If I go too far toward the mountain, the alarm will sound, and from a loudspeaker, someone will call me back to return home.

The anxiety inside me builds. My seventeenth year is going by so quickly. I must concentrate on my plan. My main goal right now it to get through bidding. I push my cup away as I start to get nauseous. A lump forms in my throat, and I can't swallow. I look around the room to see if anyone notices me. I can either slip out and seek out some birds or head back home and go to bed. My eye lids get heavy, so I choose sleep. Next week, we start our dance rotation where I must practice with all sixty-three girls. The thought exhausts me already. How many of these girls will sign up for a visitation with me? Will interacting with all sixty-three make it worse? Having physical contact with every girl in my year is just asking for trouble. Why can't I declare now that I have already decided who I want to marry? Can we all end this charade now? Why do I have to go through the motions of dancing with sixty-three people? This stupid ritual sucks, and I am forbidden the chance to discuss my feelings with anyone.

As I start walking, I change my mind and head to the gardens instead. Some nocturnal birds flutter around me and greet me.

"Good evening, Sky," they say.

"Hi. I am looking for some flowers."

"We know what you are looking for. We can hear you."

"Okay." I laugh inside.

I sit in the garden and gather some thin branches. I braid them together into a halo and weave in some flowers. I forget their names, but they smell nice. I mostly gather pink, purple, and white buds, creating a floral crown. I attach long blades of grass which give it a ribbon effect. I stare at the mountain, which appears as a dark shadow in the night. Will I ever be able to escape? What is on the other side? Are there any people living there? The birds say no, but why aren't there other people? I refuse to accept no as an answer. I bet they are wrong. My search continues.

Merry-17

I feel bad. I mistreated Sky. Then I didn't visit him after dinner. I know his shift has long ended, so I wait for him to pass my slab. I watch out my window. It's getting really late, and my parents will be angry if I don't get to bed soon. I can't imagine where he's gone. It didn't look like a lot of people ate dinner tonight, so he couldn't have had that many dishes to wash.

My life is becoming one big ball of confusion. I want Sky so badly, but Sasha's words remain stuck in my mind. Why must Sky always stay a Worker? He is smarter than most people. Almost everyone likes him, and he can charm even the sourest people in the community. If life is fair and equal, then why doesn't it seem so?

I hear footsteps approach my window. I carefully sneak out of the slab and make sure it is Sky. I quietly greet him.

"Hi," I whisper.

"Hey," he says.

"Sorry I didn't get a chance to see you at dinner."

"It's all right."

"Where were you just now?"

"Working."

"Really? What took you so long?"

"Huh? What do you mean? I didn't know we were supposed to meet. Did we plan this?"

"No, no. I figured I would find you tonight, you know, to apologize for not saying hi."

"Okay …" he says slowly, sounding either confused or annoyed.

"What's that you have in your hands?"

"Um, nothing."

"Come on, let me see."

"Wait."

I grab his hand. He reveals a crown made out of beautiful little flowers. I blush. Now I discover why he took so long to get back from work. I feel ashamed and even worse than before. I have been plotting a way to marry a Planner, and Sky made me another present. Then it dawns on me. I asked him to do this earlier today. I pushed him to write me a note, and instead, he made me a gift.

"Wow, for me? Sky, I am so sorry! I have been so horrid to you lately. I don't deserve your gifts."

"Here," he says flatly and hands it over. He must be mad. I would be too, so I don't blame him at all.

"Thanks." I put the tiara on my head, and it fits perfectly. "How did you get it to fit so perfectly?"

"Not sure."

"Merry!" I hear my dad call.

"Shoot. Gotta go. See you tomorrow."

"Okay, fine," Sky says sadly and walks away into the darkness until I can no longer see his silhouette.

I run into my room before my parents can see my flowers. If they discover the crown, I'll tell them I made it for myself. They will have no reason to question me. They believe everything I say.

I don't question how they organize the order in dance class. Like my other year mates, I simply do as I am told. Sky doesn't mind getting the paddle, but I do. If opening my mouth is forbidden, then I keep it shut.

We girls stay in alphabetical order, but they sort of cut us in the middle. So the *M*s will start, and the *A*s will follow the *Z*s. The boys stay put, *A* to *Z*, in true alphabetical order. This means I will not practice with Sky again until I reach the end of their line. So it may take a while before I rest in his arms again. Despite my guilt, I don't mind. This will give me a chance to interact with the Planner boys first. Perhaps I can sort out my feelings for a bit. I can contemplate my true destiny. Whatever happens shall truly be equal and fair.

With Marabelle heading up the line with Aaron, I start with Antin first. For some reason, he looks so handsome today. He styled his blond hair neatly, and his blue eyes match his school shirt, which is pressed and starched. He is not as tall or muscular as Sky, but his body is thin and fit. I consider, for a moment, what my child might look like with him. We both

59

have similar hair and eye color. Our child would also have golden hair. Perhaps this child would also be beautiful and happy. It would have enough food to eat, extra possessions to play with, and even a garden to run through. I wake from my daydream as Antin greets me.

"Hi, Merry."

"Hi, Antin."

"Quiet!" Teacher wants us to concentrate on our moves.

"You look beautiful as always," he whispers.

"Thanks. You do too." I blush as I say this.

"I'm not looking forward to dancing with Marabelle," he says and then sticks out his tongue in disgust. I look as she moves the wrong way and then trips on her partner's feet. I hear her apologize quietly. Her partner rolls his eyes, eager to finish this round.

"I hope you will honor me with a dance at the ball, Merry, although you probably decided that Sky will get the most time with you that night."

"Not necessarily, Antin. I haven't given it much consideration yet."

Antin smiles at my comment.

"Perhaps you will allow me to get your cup of vin. We only get one, and you will absolutely love it. My father has his own supply at our home, you know. I've drank plenty in the past."

Then he leans in closer.

"You won't tell, will you?" he asks.

"Oh no, never, Antin. Your secret is safe with me. Antin, you can confide in me whenever you like."

"I trust you, Merry," he says as the whistle blows and our song together ends. "It has been a delight dancing with you, Merry. Remember me when you select your visitations. I've ordered hand-dipped strawberries from the kitchen. The biggest one is for you. I'll put it aside and guard it until I see you."

I am so happy that I can hardly remember to move to the next spot. I want to spend more time talking with Antin. I didn't realize how handsome and sweet he is. Why didn't I notice him before? Did Sky always outshine him until now? Did the distance between Sky and me open my eyes to new possibilities? Sadly, I walk to the next boy.

During the next several songs, I pay little attention to my dance partners. Deep in thought, I just go through the motions to practice for the ball. Each song ends in a blur. I smile at each boy politely and try to make eye contact with Antin with each shift. As I move farther away from him, I find myself hoping he is thinking about me too. When he finally looks my way, my eyes dart away from him. I feel butterflies in my tummy when a voice interrupts my thought process.

"Well, Merry, I guess I'm next." I look up at Cecile, who snorts and turns red.

"Hi, Cecile. How's it going?"

"Um, I'm not sure. I can't seem to get these moves right."

"That's all right."

"Do you think there will be a test at the end? Because if there is, I don't think I'll pass."

"No, I don't think so. You'll be fine." I look back at him, but he's distracted and no longer listening. Instead, he steps on my foot.

"Ouch," I say, trying to redirect his attention.

"So sorry, Merry. See what I mean? I am a dancing disaster."

"Okay, well, Cecile, you need to pay attention."

"Huh? What?"

I glance at Cecile and realize the problem. His eye is on something else. Actually, it is someone else. He is watching Marabelle. His lips sort of move like he is saying something, but no words come out. He must be thinking about a conversation, and his thoughts are forming words on his lips.

"Cecile!" I call.

"What? Oh, sorry, Merry."

"What are you doing?"

"Counting."

"Counting what?"

"The steps. I'm counting the steps so I remember where to move my feet."

"Then why are you looking elsewhere?"

"Oh, sorry, I'm trying to visualize the moves in my mind so I get them right."

"Well, you are not doing a good job of it. You stepped on me. I may need to sit out the next dance because of you."

"Really? Wow. Can I help you to the side?"

He stops, escorts me to the bench, and sits me down. He removes my shoe and

says, "Let me see."

I look down. My toe is red but not bleeding.

"Ouch," I say again, even though it doesn't hurt. I'm annoyed with him.

Cecile gently rubs my toes.

"You'll be all right and dancing again in no time."

He pats my leg and walks away.

Did I imagine him staring at Marabelle? No Planner boy would dare bid on a girl so low in the alphabet and bound for "maid-dom." I look up and see Teacher frowning at me.

"Please rotate to your next partner," she says.

"Sorry. My foot hurt. Cecile smashed it during the last dance. I needed to rest it. I'm fine now. I'll continue."

I get up and greet the next boy. Curious, I look over at Cecile. He appears nervous and tongue-tied.

"I can sit this one out if you like," I hear Marabelle say to him.

"No, Marabelle, stay here," Cecile says as his voice cracks.

"You can dance with her instead." She points to a group of girls waiting to join the rotation.

"But I don't understand. I want to dance with you. I'm not bothering you, am I?"

"No, you're fine," Marabelle answers.

"Did I ever tell you my parents are gone a lot? I get kind of lonely. Perhaps you can stop by …"

As I eavesdrop on Cecile and Marabelle, a loud scream erupts from down the line.

"Ahhhhhh! Help! Help! My back!"

I freeze in my spot. I recognize the voice. It's coming from Sky, and he's in pain.

"Sky!" I shout in a panic and drop my partner's hand.

The music stops abruptly as Teacher rushes to his aid. I run over to him as well and see he has fallen to his knees. Tears gather at the corners of his eyes. He takes deep breaths, and his voice warbles.

"My back. I think I strained it." He crumbles to the ground as the crowd around him gasps with shock.

"Hurry," Teacher commands. "Contact the clinic, and tell them to bring a stretcher."

Sky rolls onto his stomach in pain and scans the crowd for me. Our eyes lock, and he smiles weakly. I crouch down to comfort him.

"You'll be all right," I say, and then suddenly, guilt permeates my brain once more for enjoying my time with Antin. I smooth back the dark locks away from his brow.

"I promise I'll visit you this time."

"Okay," he says. Two porters carefully lift him to the stretcher and take him to the clinic for assessment and observation.

"Class dismissed for the day," Teacher announces as we all disperse.

"Wow. I didn't expect that to happen," Cecile says as he walks out behind me. "Sky is one of the strongest among us. I'd better really pay attention to my technique too next time."

"Yes, it does seem odd for Sky to injure himself dancing," I say out loud, but I guess it can happen to anyone. My mom always says when you turn the wrong way or sneeze funny, you can put your back out. For once, she's right.

I enter the clinic to visit Sky. I picked him some flowers. Not my best idea because I bet he's hungry. Sky eats all of the time, and the clinic won't provide enough food. I reassess. Should I turn around and run to the market to pick up a snack? Well, I suppose it's too late. I'm already here.

"Okay, you may enter," a nurse says to me.

I walk in the room. Sky rests on a small cot, wrapped in a heating blanket. His eyes light up when he sees me.

"I'm so glad you came to visit." He touches my hand lightly.

"I brought you some flowers."

"Thanks. That was sweet of you."

"Did they figure out what's wrong?"

"Not really. They say I must have pulled a muscle while I was dancing. Excellent news—I won't be in the rotation for at least a week."

"I bet Clairica and Veronica won't be happy."

"Why would that matter? We are past that."

"Never mind." I'm not sure what I was thinking other than the fact that quite a few girls will be disappointed that they will miss their turns to dance with the irresistible Sky. But as always, I say the wrong thing and embarrass myself in front of him. Okay, Merry, remove comment, insert foot!

"Hey, Merry, don't worry. That won't affect us. I'll be better soon, and we will still get our dance." He smiles a bit.

"Good. I'm glad to hear that." I don't want to sound unhappy, but I'm still so torn about my relationship with Sky.

"Merry, what's wrong?"

"Nothing, Sky. I need to leave soon. I'm on the list to do some chores. I hate being late," I say abruptly.

"Sure. I understand. I'm glad you came to visit me."

"Feel good, Sky." I leave in a hurry. I don't want Sky to see me cry. It would lead to more questions that I am not ready to answer because I am not sure of my responses yet. I rush to work at the market.

They have me slicing meat and cheese for sandwiches for lunches tomorrow. This will keep me busy, because I need to concentrate so I don't cut my fingers on the blade. I drift a little, and some of the slices come out uneven. The shopkeeper gives me a dirty look.

"Okay, sorry!" I shout. As the evening goes on, my tension rises. I hate being a Worker. I am sick of all work and no play. I need an exit strategy out of this dull existence, and I need one soon.

My slicing technique does not improve, so I guess people will eat ugly sandwiches tomorrow. I don't care. Salad sounds better anyway since the smell of meat starts to nauseate me.

"Hi, Merry." I hear a friendly voice and turn around. It's Antin.

"I just stopped by the market to pick up some items for my parents. They have a little dinner party planned."

"That sounds so lovely," I gush. I hope I don't sound too desperate to him.

"Why don't you stop by later?"

"Am I allowed, err ... I can't. I have things to do, and I doubt my parents will allow it anyway."

"Don't tell. Come by on your way home from work."

"Then they'll for sure catch me. They practically time my comings and goings. They've memorized my entire schedule and go over it with me on a daily basis."

"Too bad. You would enjoy it, and I would love your company. Cecile will be there, and he will bore me to death with his stupid questions."

"Just like at school."

"Yep, just like it." We both laugh.

The door swings opens, and a younger kid enters. It's One. He carries something in his hand, but he conceals it under his work shirt. He approaches us with a sneaky grin.

"While I was gardening by the orchard, I found this!" He pulls out a green garter snake from beneath his shirt and dangles it in my face.

Shocked, I scream.

"What's wrong? Scared? He won't hurt you. He's your friend."

Antin knocks the serpent out of One's hand and pushes him.

"Hey," One says. "Whatcha do that for? Are you scared too? Geez, it's just a little fella. You should see some of the other ones I've found."

"Scram, little kid," Antin tells him and gives him another push.

"Break it up." The shopkeeper walks over to us, looking perturbed.

"Merry, I thought I told you to get back to work. Tell you little friends good-bye. I'm not running social hour here. Serious work must get done," he tells me again.

"Yeah," I say under my breath. "We might have a real sandwich crisis on our hands."

One shrugs and walks away.

"You forgot this." Antin kicks the snake over to him. One picks it up carefully and slams the door.

"He's weird," Antin says and then waves good-bye.

I wave back. I watch him pick up a bag for his parents and leave. As always, I'm stuck alone.

I can tell Sky is back at school because several girls rush to his side as he enters the classroom. I purposely drown out what they say to him, but I'm sure they are trying to flirt with him and gain access to his visitations. Dance class was nice without him. I felt more relaxed dancing with our year mates in his absence. I didn't have to listen to girls gush about his strong arms or piercing eyes.

I've avoided him since our time together at the clinic. I hear he was allowed plenty of rest and time off from doing chores. Out of the corner of my eye, I look over at him. He seems relaxed and well rested. He smiles and greets Paine warmly.

"Did you see Sky is back?" Charm asks me.

"Yep. There he is," I answer flatly to not appear too anxious or excited. I will face him soon enough as our dance approaches. I dread looking him in the eyes. I can't stand the thought of hurting him. We have been best friends for so long, practically most of our lives. I used to tell him everything. Now I don't know what's the matter with me. A wave of chatter wakes me from my thoughts. I feel a tug on my shoulder. I turn and face Marabelle.

"What?" I say under my breath.

She hands me another opened note. I snatch it from her hand and read it.

> *M,*
>
> *As I walked into class today, all I could think about was your beautiful face. Why didn't you look back at me? Are you ignoring me? Did you visit me at the clinic? Didn't we talk? Don't torture me like this. The only thing keeping me going is our dance together. I look forward to holding you in my arms forever!*
>
> *Love always,*
>
> *S*

I crinkle up the note, more confused than ever.

Movies always take my mind off of, well, life in general. I'm not sure how the community acquired so many. We rarely have time to film or write plays like the past generation of residents on the compound. So much work is required around here. Free time is a scarce commodity. Most leisure time is spent roaming the zoo or hanging out at the pool. A few artists exist here and there to contribute work to the museum, but acting is rare. Yet we are occasionally treated to an old film a few nights a month. Most of the compound attends. Nurses wheel in elderly folks. Husbands and wives sit close and secretly hold hands in the dark.

We young people are not to be trusted on our own. We must attend movies with our year mates and sit in rows with our classes. Because of strict rules, boys sit together apart from the girls, who also must sit together. I guess the leaders of our community fear the dark and what possibilities it might bring.

Today they let us pick our seats in the year-seventeen female section. Charm, Sasha, and I huddle close and munch snacks. We brought pretzels with sesame seeds and peanut puffs. Today's film is a comedy. As it starts, I look for Sky. His blue eyes light up in the dark theater as he concentrates on the screen and laughs. I love his laugh. He sits in awe of the moving pictures and forgets the world around him as well. This leads me to wonder what's honestly important to me. These simple pleasures go hand in hand with a life filled with love and belonging as opposed to a life of leisure and loneliness.

The crowd laughs together at a dog chasing a man around the street. He climbs a building with his bare hands. It must be some kind of trick. He jumps into a room and lands in a bed. A sleeping woman shakes her fist at him, and we all crack up. Sky looks my way, and our eyes meet. I quickly refocus my attention back to the screen. As the movie finishes, the crowd breaks out into a wild applause. People cheer and whistle. Moments like this are special, especially to Workers. Our workload lessens our free time. Planners must hold different work hours, because Antin told me about the dinner parties. Worker dinner parties are unheard of in my household. I bet Workers probably cook those meals for the Planners and their ever-entertaining lifestyles.

"Wow. Best movie ever!" Charm gushes.

"I've seen it." Sasha tries to act cool and show off.

"I saw some guys checking you out, Merry," Charm says and nudges me.

"Really?" I wonder if it is anyone good.

"Sky, for one."

"Obviously!"

"Wills."

Ick!

"Paine."

Whatever!

"Asher."

He's younger; no chance of bidding.

"Cecile."

I don't think he was looking at me.

"And, um, Antin."

"Wait," Sasha interrupts. "Did you say Asher? He's a little kid."

"Only by a few years."

"True, but we can only marry year mates. Marrying younger or older only works if you are a maid. And that can only be done in second-round biddings, thus almost impossible. Asher wouldn't even think about Merry."

"Maybe he was looking at someone else. Marabelle occasionally takes care of the

younger kids."

"Let's change the subject." I am hyperannoyed by their topic of conversation and need to focus on something else.

"Okay," Sasha bites back. She sounds bothered too.

"It's just that I am sick of talking about boys and dancing and bidding and marrying."

"What else is there?"

"I don't know—something, anything!"

"Work? Homework? School? What else do we have in our lives?"

"Nothing," I say. I am tired and defeated.

"We can gossip," adds Charm. She's always a good companion who can breathe life into our conversations. "I hear Marabelle still sleeps with a doll."

Sasha laughs at this.

"So, Charm, are you snooping around her window or sending others to do your dirty work?" Sasha asks.

Charm turns bright red, which usually makes her resemble a pomegranate.

"Don't lie and tell me you never check out slab windows," Charm says.

It's true. We learn so little from teachers and parents. Peeking at others is the only way to educate ourselves about personal issues. That is how we find out about relationships behind closed doors.

It's obvious we girls are tired, and it's getting late.

Sasha responds, "Touchy! We'll talk later."

As I head home alone, I realize tomorrow is my dance with Sky. I get nervous. What will I do? My friends are annoyed with me. I have no one to confide in because Sky would normally be that person. But now my future seems unclear, and I would rather stay home sick than face Sky. I bite my lip to keep from crying.

The wind blows my hair gently. Birds gather around Sky's window. I bet he's been feeding them bread again. It drives his father nuts because he hates the noise when he's trying to sleep. Plus, he's constantly getting on Sky to clean the poop.

I finally reach my slab and run into my room. I consider flipping through my notes, but I'd rather sleep. My eyes close, too heavy to leave open. I drift slowly, deeper, deeper, deeper, deeper into my pillow. Out.

"Nice to finally see you again, Merry," Sky says awkwardly as he slips his hand into mine. I must look confused. "You know, as a dance partner. It's been a while since we've danced last," he adds.

"You took a break from dance altogether. Remember?" I tell him.

"Serious injuries," he responds and smiles. "I'm still healing. I might lounge in the pool a bit, perhaps even in the hot tub. Just in case you're free, you may want to join me. I might even sneak in a nice fruity drink to sip while I relax."

"That's so enticing, really. I might have to work. They need people to pick up the slack at the dairy. For some reason, they are short staffed. I strain the liquid out of the cheese."

"Fun."

"Messy and wet."

"At least you don't have to clean the stalls at the farm. I get to shovel manure all day next week. But don't worry; I'll shower really, really well for the ball."

"I almost forgot it was coming up."

"Promise to save me a dance?" he requests.

"Sure."

He winks at this. My heart skips a beat when he does this to me.

"I bet you're excited to dance with Marabelle next," I say.

"What?" His body stiffens at this comment. His hands jolt and tense up for a second.

"Huh? No, Sky, it was a joke. Plus, I don't mean next week. I mean right now, right after me. Remember? We have to rotate in about thirty seconds."

"Oh yeah, that. For a second, I got so caught up in the moment with you that I forgot all about everyone else around us. I'm so used to dancing with you. Plus, I've been absent for a while."

The whistle blows, and our song ends.

"Bye. Have fun," I tell Sky.

"Right," he says as we move to our next partners.

My next partner is Terrance. He is slightly adorable but a *T*, so his place is at the bottom. We greet each other, and the music starts.

Next to me, I hear a shaky voice crack, "I can't do this right now."

I turn to look who it came from. It was Sky. He was facing Marabelle and grabbing her hand to dance. As I turn, I see him throw her hand back down and step away quickly.

Barely audibly, he says, "I'm sorry," and runs out of the room. Our year mates murmur around me, speculating what just happened.

"He's gone. Just vanished," I hear someone say.

"He ran outta here. Does anyone know why?" someone else in our group questions.

"That was weird," Terrance says to me.

Marabelle stands alone in her spot, tears streaming down her cheeks. I almost feel bad, but I don't know what to say to her.

"What happened?" another maid-bound girl runs over to her and asks.

Marabelle shrugs. She's as clueless as ever. Moments later, the community loudspeaker goes off.

"Skyler-17, return to the compound. You are in violation. Leaving the compound is strictly forbidden. Skyler-17, return to the compound."

The message repeats itself a few times and stops. I assume he has stopped fleeing and is heading back.

From time to time when rules are broken around here, the compound speaker goes off as a warning. It doesn't happen often, but Sky frequently sets it off when he wanders too close to the mountain.

"I need to check on him," I tell Terrance and leave the class without permission.

Sky is probably the fastest runner of the community. It took him no time to reach the outskirts of the compound. It takes me a while to find him. As I reach the orchard, I see him lying on his back under a pomelo tree, eating some fruit.

I rush over to him. His eyes are red as if he had been crying.

"What's wrong?" I ask.

"Nothing." He takes a peel and throws it into the distance.

"What do you mean 'nothing,' Sky? What happened in there? One second, we are dancing, and the next, you yell at Marabelle and run out. Did she say something to you?"

"No."

"Did she do something to you?"

"No."

"Then what?"

"Just forget it. I'm fine."

"Have you been crying?"

"What? No! Some pomelo squirted into my eye. Can't I be alone here for just a moment, a second, an instant? It's not like I can leave or anything."

"Why do you want to be alone? Why do you want to leave here? Leave me?"

"I don't." He turns, looks at me, and then gets up.

I follow. He should have a friend at a time like this. He walks over to the forbidden tree and points at the iridescent fruit.

"You should take one," he tells me. "Try it and see what happens."

"No, Sky, it's forbidden."

"It won't be when you become a Planner. Nothing is. I've seen them, drinking vin, having parties. You can taste the fruit, and when you do, tell me how it is because I'll never get to, and you know it."

I suddenly change my heart and change my mind. I want Sky. I've always wanted Sky, for my friend and for my husband. What was I thinking when I decided the life of a Planner is better? I'd rather be a Worker in love than a Planner alone. If anyone can solve a problem, it's Sky. He will make our union happen.

As these thoughts run through my head, I see him grin.

"What are you thinking now?" I ask.

"It's just you and me against the world. Come on. Walk me back before they ready the paddle for my behind."

I yearn to grab his hand, but I don't want to make his punishment any worse.

"I guess you'll be shoveling a lot of manure now, Sky."

"I guess so." He chuckles.

It's good to see his humor reappear. His laughter always confirms my feelings for him.

I slowly get ready for the ball. My hair needs to look perfect. Sasha lent me a few items like lipstick and a white bow to wear as a headband. I own one dress. I hope I don't embarrass myself. It's a bit short. I've grown several inches since the last time I wore it. My mother does not have enough time to adjust the length. She tells me a shorter dress won't hurt me this close to bidding. I'm not sure what she means, but my father refuses to explain.

Charm knocks on my door. She is wearing a very brown, very dull gown. She waves and jumps up and down, smiling uncontrollably.

"I'm so excited! I can't wait for tonight. I hope I get to dance. Do you think anyone will ask me?"

"You look beautiful tonight, Charm. I'm sure you'll have a lot of offers."

She spins around to make her dress twirl. It barely moves, but she doesn't notice.

"My first cup of vin. This has to be the best night of my life," she trills.

"Calm down, Charm. We aren't even there yet."

"I know, so hurry up. You are stunning. No more primping. Let's move."

"Hold on. I can't leave until my nails dry. Sasha lent me some of her polish."

My first manicure. I display my rose nails for Charm. It's truly a night of firsts for all of us. Yet I am realistic. They give us one night, and then they take it away. Many of us will marry soon as party-free Workers. Then others will face a lonely life of maid-dom like Marabelle.

Charm finally coaxes me out of the slab, and we walk to the dance. It takes place in the same room as our lessons. Tonight, teachers have transformed a plain gymnasium into a glowing paradise. Candle-lit lanterns hang from the ceiling. Colorful tulle covers little tables which are decorated with tea candles and chocolates. A long table overflows with bowls of treats like peanut butter puffs and mini-veggie burgers. A tiny punch fountain flows with a pink, bubbly beverage. Then one singular table is set up with vin. We are allowed one cup, and a stern teacher with a good memory stands guard. Glasses of attractive, dark aubergine liquid awaits us.

Charm pulls me into the room, and Sasha attacks me with a hug.

"You both look so amazing. Look at this place. Can you believe it is the same stinky gym where we took our lessons? Some of the boys here look hot! Some even smell good tonight. My future husband lurks out there somewhere."

Sure, Sasha is excited. She believes she will stay a Planner. She is probably right. Her father holds a high position. He has probably already made some backdoor deal she doesn't even know about yet. Rumors of prearranged bidding often surface around the community. But let it be known, such actions are forbidden.

"I am going to ask every boy I can to dance," Sasha adds. She rushes off to start her quest.

"Well, it's just you and me," Charm says as we walk farther into the room.

I would love to eat some of that scrumptious-looking food. I have been so nervous about tonight that I skipped breakfast and barely choked down lunch. Now I'm starving, but I don't want to ruin my dress or smudge my makeup. The boys don't seem to care as they grab food and stuff their faces. Paine couldn't care less. He has crumbs all over his face, and his dress shirt has a punch stain. Then I start to wonder where Sky is and if he is even going to show tonight.

I usher Charm to a table facing the door—so I can spot him first—but far enough away to give me time to appear casual. I don't want Sky to know how anxious I am.

Marabelle enters cautiously. I barely recognize her. Her makeup and pink dress transform her from an awkward mouse into an adorable princess. She shows off her thin waist with a tiny belt, which is funny. I always thought she was a bit chubby under her frumpy, baggy work clothes. She still wears her goofy, thick specs, but I guess she can't help that. Judging her face, her paint-mixing talent paid off; her make up is flawless. She quickly shuttles to an obscure corner of the room and camouflages herself by blending in with a table decorated in pink lace. She rests there alone.

"Was that Marabelle?" Charm asks "Wow, I didn't realize how pretty she is. I mean, you are prettier—like the prettiest girl here, for sure—but she sure made herself look nice tonight."

"If you like that sort of mess," I answer. "One night won't change the fact that she is maid-bound and has no friends her age. Only babies and little kids hang out with her, and like you said, she still plays with dolls."

"Jealous much?"

"What? Are you kidding me? Why would I be jealous? Over a pretty dress or a nice shade of lipstick? Please."

"Okay, whatever you say. Wanna get some snacks from the table?"

"You get us a couple plates of treats. I'll save our table. It's a prime people-watching spot. Someone else might grab it if we both get food."

When Charm gets back, I pretend to pick at the goodies. Sky has yet to show, and it makes me nervous. Charm scoops crisps into her mouth, carelessly getting crumbs on her chest. I sweep chip dust into a pile and push it into a corner. The fifteen minutes we've been here feels like an eternity. The ticking second hand on the clock hanging from the wall puts me in a hypnotic trance.

I am lifted out of the fog by Sky's arrival. He makes an obnoxious grand entrance which sends most of our year-mate boys into a wild applause, shouting loud cheers and clapping him on the back. Who knew how much they really loved him? Antin smirks because of their sudden display of male affection. I pretend I didn't notice him and wave at Veronica, who sets down her punch and walks over to chat.

Before Veronica can reach me, I hear his voice.

"Hi."

"Hi."

"You look beautiful tonight."

"You too. I mean you look handsome, not beautiful, er ..."

"I brought you a rose bouquet. You can pin it on your dress. That's why I was late. I was finishing up, and I didn't realize the time."

He puts a tiny bouquet in my hand. He'd used tea roses and baby's breath and then wrapped them in a bow. I try to put it on my dress, but my hands shake a little.

"Here, let me help you." He calmly pins it on me. I tip a little from light-headedness. Sky steadies me with his hand and places it around my back.

"Will you dance with me?" Sky asks.

"Yes," I say and wave good-bye to Charm as Sky pulls me on to the dance floor. I forget every move we've learned, but Sky's feet flow as if he were floating on air.

We twirl around the room like lovers in a musical. I feel like I am standing high on the mountain and can see our entire world from here. Over in another corner of the room, I spot Cecile. He stands to the side, looking confused and worried. He scratches his head, unsure of his next move. He stares off into space. His feet rock back and forth not to the rhythm of the music but trying to decide where to put them. Why must he always look like a clueless dolt?

As the song ends, Sky leads me in Cecile's direction. Antin lurks nearby, partnerless and friendless. Sasha tries to catch Antin's eye. This sea of busyness distracts me for a moment.

"Merry? Hello?" Sky taps my shoulder. "Can I get you a cup of vin now?"

"Yes." I smile gladly.

At the small, pink table, Marabelle checks the clock and stands up, smoothing out the skirt of her dress. Cecile's feet finally decide to walk away from the dance floor toward my direction. I hope he doesn't ask me to dance in Sky's absence. Antin seems annoyed by the whole evening and also moves over my way. Thankfully, Sky returns with our two cups. A stray, pushed-out chair blocks his path, and before Sky can react, he trips, and the glasses of vin fly through the air and land on Marabelle's petal-pink gown, soaking her long curls and googly glasses as well.

She lets out a cry. She squeezes her eyes shut and pulls off her dark purple-stained glasses. Tears roll down her cheeks, creating watery purple lines. The vin ruined her dress. People around us stop to watch her reaction.

"Excuse me," she says and pushes past us. Her night at the ball ends.

"Sky, how could you be so clumsy?" I ask. "That was my only chance to taste vin. They only give us one glass." I shake my hand at him. "They won't refill if for you. My chance to try it is ruined. I may never taste it ever again!"

This sends Cecile running in the opposite direction.

"Sorry?" Sky offers, but it's too late.

"Here, Merry," Antin sweeps in and offers me his hand. "I'll let you have my glass."

"Really, are you sure? Gee, Antin, you really don't have to do this."

"I don't mind. Some of us are gentlemen and treat a lady with respect."

I accept his hand and leave Sky standing in his puddle of vin. I spend the rest of the night dancing with Antin, ignoring my best friends and Sky. We move together naturally and comfortably. I even allow Antin the chance to walk me home. I want to kiss him good night, but that would be forbidden and a punishable offense.

As I enter my room and start to take off my dress, I remember my flower bouquet. I remove the pin and hold the buds in my hand. My head spins, perhaps from the vin. I mistreated Sky over an innocent accident. How could I have been so mean over a glass of vin? I feel sick to my stomach. I owe Sky a huge apology. The next time I may see him could be during the bidding visits. This was my last chance to win over Sky, and I blew it. Who would want a wife that gets upset over a spill? I cry myself to sleep again.

Bidding Visitations

Antin-17

I already know what's going to happen during bidding. The outcome is inevitable. Being born a Planner brings privileges no ordinary Worker can dream of, first pick being one of them. Since I have already secured my happily ever after, these visits are a waste of my time. Perhaps I can have a little fun with it—flirt, tease, maybe even humiliate.

Each male is entitled to fifty slots. Mine are filled with a wait list of sad hopefuls. Cecile can't even fill half that.

The maids clean the drawing room and fluff pillows on the white couch. They set trays of food and punch on the coffee table. Brightly colored pastries fill a plate, and stacked tea sandwiches rest on a multileveled platter. Crystal jugs of fresh lemonade and iced tea sweat as the large chunks of ice filled with frozen fruit melt within.

Father informs me that young girls enjoy this type of refreshment, and he advises me to use my best behavior, especially with my first guest, Marabelle.

"Antin, please hear me out. A Messenger informed me to make sure Marabelle made the list. They required me to persuade you to strongly consider her as your first choice. This mandate comes directly from the Makers. They assured me of the severity of this proclamation. So please do me the favor. Seriously think about making Marabelle your primary bid to take on as your wife."

I look around.

"Is this some kind of joke? Are you going to break out laughing at any moment 'Ha! Ha! Ha!' and let me know you are kidding? No, really, let me know you are joking! Any time now."

"Antin, please. I need you to stop fooling around and hear what I am saying. The Makers want this union. They decide, and we follow."

"Seriously, Dad, have you even seen a Maker? Do they even exist? Or a Messenger, even? Who sent you this message? Who did you talk to?"

"It was the father of … um … a younger Planner boy. Then he let me speak to the Messenger, and he told me—"

"Oh, okay, I see how this works. Someone just makes this stuff up."

"No, not at all. I believe, Antin, and so should you. Makers and Messengers don't need to appear for us to have faith. Going against a decree like this, acting disobedient, may cause problems. It could tip the balance of harmony on this compound. We don't want to see what happens if we displease the Makers. You never had to live through the bad times. You are lucky, and you don't appreciate the abundance because you never experienced the harsh years."

"So this is all on me? Please. I don't buy it for one second. This is ridiculous. Why do I have to be the one to follow the Maker's orders? Why can't someone else do it? Like someone a lot lesser than I. Like Cecile or Paine. Or Sky perhaps. He does everything he is told to do. Make him do it. And Marabelle? Really? Who is she? A daughter of one of the lowest families in the community? Father, her mother was a *maid*!"

"Marabelle and her family work as faithful servants of this community and the Makers."

"Right, servants. She belongs to the order of maids. It's a known fact."

"The known facts, Antin, are that the Makers are giving her to you as your wife, and now you must deal with it. Greet her graciously, and get along."

Father curtly leaves me alone and calls in Marabelle. I wait for her to arrive. I'm seriously worked up by this sudden decree. Who cares? I hate Marabelle and don't want any part of her presence in my life. How embarrassing! Does my dad hear what they call her? Does he listen to what people think of her? This can't be happening. Why does she have to step foot in my house? I might turn to stone by simply looking at her deformed mug. Oh no, here she is. I look up, and she stands before me wearing her raggedy work clothes.

"Well," I shout at her, "come in and sit down!"

"No ... thank you."

"What do you have to say for yourself?"

"Nothing. My father dropped me off here."

"So you didn't sign up for a session with me?"

"What? No! I didn't sign up for any sessions. I would rather not subject myself to this humiliating process. I'd rather be alone than marry you, Antin! I'd rather not marry anyone. I would rather be free to do what I like whenever I desire rather than have a husband to give me directions."

"Then your wish shall be granted. Therefore, I've changed my mind. I shall keep you in my life as my personal maid taking care of all my desires."

I grab her hand to sit her down.

"No, get away. Don't you dare touch me. I will never submit to you. You are beneath me, Antin."

She struggles to take her hand away, but I squeeze it harder.

"I will never be beneath you, Marabelle. You'll see. Things won't end well for you."

"Ouch, you're hurting me! Let go!"

I release her and shove her back a little.

"Get out!" I scream. "Get out now! Leave! Now!"

I hear my voice echo down the corridor as Marabelle runs away.

"What happened, Antin? What did you do?" My father enters, looking worried.

"Next!" I shout at him.

Merry-17

I wait in the lobby of Antin's immaculate house. I brushed my hair out straight and put on a pink minidress. I'd painted my nails using the rest of Sasha's polish, but I've picked off half of it as I nervously stand here. Other girls in my year join the line behind me. They've all adorned themselves in their best outfits. I imagine certain girls feel they have an edge being daughters of Planners. So I've got some fierce competition.

As we all linger, an angry girl rushes past us so quickly that the gust of wind she leaves behind blows my hair out of place. As I smooth it back in place, I recognize the face of the girl. It's Marabelle looking quite livid. A loud voice echoes through the corridor.

"Get out! Get out now! Leave! Now!"

Marabelle turns back and looks at us. She scowls and shakes her fist in defiance at the voice. We make eye contact. I start to feel bad for her situation and give her a sympathetic grin. She shakes her head. Her eyes sadly droop. Marabelle whips open the door and leaves.

Antin's father walks toward us, smiling warmly.

"Merry, please," he calls me and leads me to a lovely room filled with fresh flowers and delicious foods.

I turn and say, "Thank you." I shyly sit down, trying to remember I am not wearing work pants, so I need to keep my legs crossed together.

"Hi, Merry. It's sooo nice to see you," Antin says warmly.

"Hi, Antin. Was that Marabelle who just left?"

"Yeah, it was."

"Things didn't seem to go well."

"No, they didn't. First of all, she was somehow invited. She didn't even make the first cut on my list. Someone forced her to be here. Then she wasn't very pleasant to me."

"Wow. Sorry to hear that. Maybe she was in a bad mood. It seems like she's been through a lot lately. Like getting abandoned on the dance floor in class and getting vin dumped on her dress at the ball."

"All thanks to your friend Sky."

"I don't want to talk about him right now."

"Of course. Agreed."

Antin pushes a tray of bright red chocolate ladybugs my way.

"Here. I told you I would have these made for you."

I take one. I don't want to take a bite and ruin my lipstick, but I would also hate to insult Antin. I take a small bite and put it down on a small crystal plate.

"Delicious. Gee, our time is almost up. Well, Antin, is there something you would like to ask me?"

"No, not really. I just like being with you. It feels so natural for us to be together. An interview isn't necessary. We don't even need to speak. I like hanging out with you. We would make the ultimate couple."

"Really?"

"Yes, we would sort of be a power couple in this community. Merry, I am number one here."

"First pick? But I thought there was a boy above you?"

"Nope. My parents liked my name. That other family knew they had the number-two spot. They weren't supposed to use a name before mine, but Aaron's parents snuck in an extra *A* to try to best mine, but the community didn't buy it. He is considered an *AR*, not an *AA*. So my family secured first spot for the bidding. A Messenger told them yesterday."

"A Messenger, really? No one has ever even seen a Messenger. Amazing! Your parents actually talked to one?"

"Yep, my dad."

"That's incredible … I—" I start to say something when Antin's dad knocks on the door politely.

"Antin, I'm sorry. This session has ended. The next young lady awaits her appointment."

"Okay," he says to his dad, and then he turns to me. "See you tomorrow, Merry."

I blush when I realize Bidding Day starts tomorrow.

"Good-bye," I say as I get up and leave.

As I leave Antin's, some of my year mates give me nasty looks. I try to be the better person and smile back. I check my schedule. Sky's house is next. I walk more slowly than I should. As I approach his tiny slab, his line looks longer than Antin's. Perhaps it is because Antin lives in a larger house or maybe because my year mates want one last look at Sky's face before he becomes an ineligible, happily married man. No one knows how this will turn out. I have no clue who Sky will actually marry.

I greet the girls in line around me and wait for a bit. Sky's father calls my name. He doesn't resemble Sky that much. He isn't as tall or as handsome. His build is not nearly as muscular, and his posture is poor. He stands bent over a bit. He's too young to look so old. A Worker's life is a hard life, and it has definitely taken its toll on Sky's dad.

I enter the miniscule slab, and Sky sits in a small chair facing a tiny couch. Chips fill a couple small bowls, and a jug of water rests on the cracked coffee table.

"Hi, Merry." He smiles, not at all embarrassed by the meager offerings. I bet he's never had a glimpse at the amazing spreads Planners have to offer.

"Sky." I start immediately sobbing. "I'm so sorry. I didn't mean to leave you at the ball like that. I love you."

There, I said it. I love him so much. I want to be with Sky so badly and marry him, be his wife, and have his child. I don't want to be a Planner after all. I'd rather be old, bent over, and happy.

"I know, Merry. I'm sorry too. I just ... I just ... you know, I don't want this disappointment to affect our married lives. You are aware of the odds that we won't end up together. Please be strong, for me."

I put on a brave face and wipe away my tears.

"I will." My words crack as they leave my lips. "For you."

"Here." He hands me a box. "I have a present for you. Don't open it until you are married. It is something only you and your husband can share together. Promise me you'll keep it shut."

"I promise," I say.

"Good. Then let's spend the next few seconds taking our minds off this situation."

"Okay. Did Sasha visit you?"

"Yeah." He laughs. I fume.

"Of course. I knew it! She couldn't stay away."

"Now, now, Merry. What does it matter? I won't marry Sasha. She's a Planner girl. She'll be taken long before my name even comes up. Some Planner boy will snatch her away."

"That's true." Inside, I'm relieved.

"Sky." His father pokes his head into the small room.

"Oh, I'm sorry. I guess time is up. Here. Don't forget your present."

He picks up the package and puts it in my hand. I leave, clutching the box. I decide to skip the next couple of appointments and run home for a bit. I carefully close the door to my room in case my parents return from work. I place the box on my bed and stare at it for a while. I decide what he doesn't know won't hurt him.

I slowly unwrap the box and open the lid. I peek inside. A large magenta orb shines from within. I reach to grab the round object and take it out of the box. Here before me, I hold in my hands a piece of fruit plucked from the forbidden tree.

Skyler-17

My Visitation Day finally ends in exhaustion. Fifty slots filled with fifty anxious girls

chatting my head off in hopes of finding their ways onto my bid sheet. I simply listened and responded politely fifty times. I wish I could have told them it was too late. My mind was already set. I've made up my mind, and there is no going back, no changing the course of my decision, the decision that I made many, many years ago. As a small child, I knew what I needed to do to get here, to Bidding Day. So now I can hardly breathe in this ridiculous anticipation. My hands sweat and shake. I wring them together nervously, waiting for my father to appear.

We need to discuss his plan of action tomorrow. I pace the small living room in our slab. Tomorrow, I leave this home and start a new life with the woman who will be my wife.

"Dad?" I call out, anxious to talk.

"Sky, ready for this? I'm not. I love you. You grew up so fast. You are still so young."

"Dad. I'm not going anywhere. I'm just getting a new slab, probably pretty close by. We are in the same section of the alphabet."

"Sure, Son. Fine, let's see." He takes out a sheet of paper to place the names of my female year mates for bidding. "Who would you like to marry?"

"I just have one ... Marabelle, please."

"Marabelle?"

"Yes, Marabelle."

"Are you sure, Son? Because I've never seen ..."

"Please, Dad, do me this one favor. That's all I ask. I want Marabelle. I love her, Dad. Just write one name. I won't have anybody else."

"But what's if she is on someone else's list? Don't you want a backup name, just in case?"

"Trust me. She won't. Write 'Marabelle.' That's all." I point to the top line of the sheet and look up at him.

"Does she feel the same way about you?"

"Yes."

"Are you sure? Does she even know?"

I don't answer; it's irrelevant. I look into his eyes, pleading to be heard. My father sighs in confusion.

"Not Merry?" he asks.

"Marabelle," I enunciate in case he does not understand.

"Fine, Marabelle it is."

I smile, I laugh, I jump up a little and hug my dad.

"Thanks. I love you."

Tip-38

My son leaves me in confusion and hops to bed. In almost eighteen years of his life, I've never heard him mention Marabelle to me, ever. He centered his existence around his year mate Merry, a beautiful blonde who is noticed by the entire community. Now he tells me he has been in love with this girl Marabelle his whole life, a tiny dark-haired girl with goofy glasses, who almost died when she was young. Disease stricken, she was left clumsy and myopic. As far as I can tell, most people merely tolerate her presence, and my son, brilliant and beautiful Sky, wants to marry her. I wonder if she even knows. I hear she is considered maid-bound. Some other disappointed girl will take her place in maid-dom as my son vies for his pale little princess.

Skyler-17

I lie awake in bed. Sleep won't come. I'm too excited. I try to slow my breathing. My heart beats fast and skips around my chest. I mouth her name with my lips. Marabelle, Marabelle, I love you, Marabelle. I unconsciously grind my teeth. My body tenses up, stiff as a board. I want to call the birds and tell them. I want to speed up the night and push the sunlight to day. I look out my window at the full moon. My body sweats, and I can hear my loud, uncontrollable breathing. I'm so happy that tears trickle down my cheeks, burning my eyes.

Marabelle, I want so you badly that I can taste you in my dreams. I try to force myself to dream about her again, but I can't do it. I wipe the big smile off my face, but it reappears. The combination of the stars in the sky and my tears in my eyes blur my vision. One more night and a few hours left without her. I get to finally hold Marabelle in my arms and tell her the truth about how I feel and what really happened between us.

Look! I have been a good boy! I have followed all of their rules! I have worked hard, behaved. I haven't touched a single female soul. I've abstained from consummating with a girl and stayed a virgin for marriage. I haven't even touched a girl with my lips, even though some of my year mates claim they have. And even though I've held my face so close to Marabelle's I could have touched her lips so easily, I dared not to blow my cover. Thus, I've played their game, followed their rules. Now I want to collect my prize.

Part 2

Bidding Day, April 1

Skyler-18

April first represents all things new. All babies born to the compound are born on April 1. Through strictly controlled conception dates and medical science breakthroughs, all people here have the same birthday. Doctors, nurses, and new parents miss the annual Birthday celebration. Instead, they rush around the hospital in the yearly tradition of mass chaos and confusion. More than one hundred ladies crying in pain while nervous men pace the floors. Hospital staff members work like mad to complete all births within a twenty-four-hour period of time.

Elsewhere on the compound, happy citizens receive a slice of cake and an extra stipend as a present. Younger children occasionally get a toy or some sweets. Most attend the Birthday parade or participate in fun games at the pool or school field.

The rest of us practice the tradition of Bidding Day. Fathers meet in a room to witness the secret process of marrying their children, armed with lists of desired suitors. My year mates and I rest in a quiet room—boys on one side divided by a wall of glass with girls on the other side.

Marabelle sits proudly holding her rag doll, clutching it tightly in her hands. I must be smiling because Antin is glaring at me.

"What are you smiling about, Sky?" he whispers.

"Nothing."

Merry glances at me, but I ignore her.

"You think you know who you are going to get, but you don't."

What does that even mean? I ignore his taunting. I think I'm starting to drool. I wipe my mouth. I love her. I want her. Antin is still staring at me.

"Shhh. We are supposed to be quiet," I tell him.

"Whatever, Sky, but you won't be with the girl you love."

How does he know? It's getting warm in here. I have to pee so badly, not because I need to go to the bathroom but because I am so excited. Like a dog, I'm so happy I want to pee all over the place and mark my new territory. I can hear my breathing getting louder. I feel faint. What is taking so long?

The girls are crossing and uncrossing their legs, looking bored and terrified. Some already started to cry. Some twirl their hair. Others bite their lips.

"Are you scared?" Paine asks, poking me.

"No," I say. "Shut up!" I think to myself.

A voice from the loudspeaker makes an announcement. I hold my breath until I am blue and dizzy.

"Bidding is now officially over. All unions are final. Workers will gather their belongings and report to their new slabs with their spouses. All maids will gather their belongings, register their names, and then report to the assigned dormitories. All Planner couples will report to the formal hall for a meet and greet to review the procedures for Wedding Day, May 1. The couples have been paired as follows … Antin-Merry."

The voice starts the long list of names.

"Cecile-Sasha."

Some people look pleased while others burst into tears.

"Paine-Charm."

I can't take in anymore. I explode inside.

"Skyler-Marabelle."

"Woohoo! Yay!" I jump out of my seat. Everybody stares on both side of the glass, even though the girls can't hear me.

"Marabelle! Yeah! All right!" I continue shouting.

I dance on my chair. The guards outside the room approach me nervously, so I jump off my seat and pound on the glass.

"Marabelle!" I shout, waving furiously at her. She stares back, confused.

I pound again, smiling and waving like an idiot. She must think I'm a lunatic.

"Skyler-18, settle down quietly!" They issue a first warning over the loudspeaker. I return to my seat and sit down as they finish the names. I clap my hands together, laughing hard.

Antin's and Merry's mouths both hang gaping open for different reasons, accompanied by shocked looks on their faces.

"Yes," I say to myself as quietly as possible. I don't want to face a beating the first day of my marriage.

Cecile gives me a sad, hurt look.

I turn to him and say, "Piss off!" Now it is his turn to look shocked.

The new maids cry, their sad fates sealed. Veronica blubbers. She didn't think she would end up alone. She was sure she had a shot at finding a mate.

They finally release us in order, handing the males their new keys. I snatch mine and dance all the way to my new slab. I unlock the door. Maids cleaned each slab the night before, so all of the slabs still smell like bleach and ammonia. I don't care. I eagerly await Marabelle's arrival.

She finally appears in front of me with a small bag and her doll in her arms.

"Good," I say. "You brought the doll I made for you."

"What?" she asks.

Before she can react, I pick her up like a baby and carry her over the threshold of our new slab together. I hug her tightly, squeezing so hard she can hardly take a breath.

"Sorry," I say and release her, only to come after her with a hundred kisses all over her face, her cheeks, her forehead, her hair, inhaling the smell deeply as I kiss it.

I catch her off guard and scare her a little. She looks shocked and very confused.

I'm having a hard time reading her mind. It's a bit muddled.

She looks around the room and back at me.

"I'm Marabelle," she finally says.

"I know," I say, grabbing her hand and pumping it up and down in an exaggerated handshake. "I'm Sky. Nice to meet you." Then I pull her hand toward my mouth and start kissing that as well.

She pulls it free.

"Is this some kind of joke?" She still looks around like someone is going to jump out and surprise us and return her to the maids.

"No, we are married."

PS: all Worker unions are final and start immediately without ceremony or celebration. Once our names are declared together, we are married.

"I'm Marabelle, you know, not Merry."

"I know, Marabelle. I only put one name down on my bid sheet—yours," I chirp happily.

"Why?"

"Why? Because I love you. I was hoping you loved me too. We have so much in common, you know. I just love everything you love. We are going to get along so well and have so much fun together. I can't wait! Are you excited too? I mean, what do you want to do first? Let's go for a walk. No, wait. Do you want to look around the slab? Hey, I have an idea let's ..." I talk to her a mile a minute, too excited to get my words straight. Then I look at her face and see she is still so confused and a bit overwhelmed.

"Gee, I'm sorry. Let me start again. I realize I have a lot of apologizing to do. I owe you a big explanation. I was hoping you would listen to my story so I can share all of my secrets. I think after you hear them you'll see me in a different light. Please come sit down with me."

I lead her to our new couch. I take her little, bony hands in mine.

"Do you like me too?" I ask.

"Yes," she says very slowly, almost hesitantly. "But I don't understand."

"You will, though." I start caressing her hands. My head spins. I start to absorb her feelings simply by the touch of her hand, and it blows my mind. Touching her causes my own emotions to run wild, and I start to cry. I look away for a moment. She wipes my eyes with her finger, and I grab her face and kiss her lips gently for the first time, and then I hug her again.

"I love you," I muffle through her dark curls. "Will you dance with me?" I ask.

I stand up and reach for her hand. I try to be gallant, but then I just grab her body and whip it against mine.

"This will be our first wedding dance."

I don't go through the elaborate dance moves we learned in class. I pull her close and simply rock back and forth with her in my arms.

"I don't get it. You didn't even want to dance with me in class."

"But, Marabelle ..." I laugh through my tears. "Didn't you get why?" I think about it. "Of course you didn't. Why would you? I'll explain. I promise."

"And at the ball, you threw punch all over my dress."

"Yeah, sorry. Don't you understand why?" I ask as if my motivation has been nothing but obvious.

"Not really."

"I couldn't let anyone else be with you. I had to do it to protect us. We couldn't be together if someone else wanted you. I must have made you seriously miserable at times, but I tried to make it up to you. I sent you notes to explain. Remember? And I made you all of those presents— like your doll—to keep you happy."

"You made this doll?"

"Yes, for you."

"Weren't those notes for Merry?"

"Merry? No! They were for you. Why would I ask you to read them if they

weren't for you? I had to give them to Merry so I didn't get caught, so we didn't get caught."

"But, huh?"

"Marabelle, bear with me. I'll explain it all."

We sit back down, and I kiss her nose. I pull her close in my arms and lean back.

"Get comfortable. I want to tell you our story."

Skyler-8

For a very long time, I followed Marabelle. When I was little, I used discretion, but I could tell others noticed. Noticing means danger. Danger means losing forever. I had to outsmart them.

They all felt Marabelle was delayed. She walked later than others. I used to try carrying her around the nursery. Her speech was delayed. I used to try answering for her. They wanted to keep her with crybaby Cecile and his runny noise. I used to try telling them she wasn't stupid like Cecile was. That got me in trouble and made Cecile cry harder. Deep concern from the elders surfaced about my odd behavior, and suspicion arose. I learned to back away. I watched at a distance. I feigned distain. I threw them off my scent. I vowed to make up for my rotten behavior by sending gifts and secretly encoding my adoration in devious notes and pictures.

I recruited help from those around me, involving them involuntarily in aiding my plan. Their unconscious roles were key to my success. The unfortunate cost involved Marabelle's sadness. I expect her to fall into my arms once I reveal my plan, which will take about a decade. We will both be rewarded with happiness and togetherness.

For now, I stitch a rag doll together for her. I add yellow strands of yarn for hair and paint blue eyes on its face. I dress it in blue work clothes. I disguise its intentions behind a doll that looks like Merry. In case I get caught, I'll hand it to Merry and say I made it for her instead. The more desirable I make Merry, the less desirable Marabelle becomes. The less desirable Marabelle becomes, the better the chance we leave the compound together like we planned. I stuff the doll with old T-shirts and pillow fluff. I draw a beautiful pink mouth that reminds me of Marabelle's full lips.

I wish I could sleep with the doll for a few nights, but I risk my father confiscating it. He would frown at this notion of playing with rag dolls. I had a teddy once, but he got rid of it. He told me only babies hold on to stuffed animals. I cried, and he told me little boys shouldn't play with dolls. I don't want to play with the doll. I just want to feel close to Marabelle for one night.

I decide against keeping the doll any longer than I need to. I solicit a raven. I call to it, and it flaps to my window.

"Fly with this doll. Drop it into Marabelle's window, and place it on her pillow."

It caws back at me and picks up the doll. As soon as my parents fall asleep, I sneak out of the slab. I peer into Marabelle's room. I spot her curled into a little ball in her bed, a tiny fairy face resting for the night. The doll is tucked under her arm. She rests her belly on its little body. This confirms that she found her gift. I have the urge to climb through the window and fall asleep on the floor next to her. I would be able to do it if I could guarantee that I wouldn't fall asleep for the rest of the night. I could hear the screams of terror in my head if I got caught. I could imagine the elaborate punishment that would go along with my crime. Therefore, I decide against it and return home.

I settle back into my bed with a bittersweet feeling. Planning your future is forbidden, and it sure is hard work. Choosing your love is not an option, but I disregard that advice as well. I was warned about feeling too attached to any one person due to the bidding process, but how do they expect us to like our friends? I call to the birds to sing me to sleep; my mom won't do that for me anymore either. They gladly assist. I resist the drowsiness at first but then drift deeper into the darkness to the tune of a hooting owl.

Marabelle dances in a grassy field with tall weeds. Butterflies flutter around her. She laughs and sings to herself. A few butterflies take off into the air. Marabelle follows, carelessly swinging her arms in joy. I trail behind her, quietly giggling at this stealth game. I enjoy my time with her, even though we stay apart, and she has no clue I'm around. I send some birds to hop around her feet. She claps in delight at the finches who dance around her toes. I twirl around in a circle on a hill at a distance, falling over dizzily. We play together separately. I lie on my back and watch the clouds blow past, looking for shapes of animals.

Then, as always, it hits. When it hits me, it hits me hard. Marabelle doesn't get to rest beside me and play my game. She thinks I hate her. She plays alone a lot. The little ones like her, but our year mates do not. I've poisoned their minds with lies, and they mostly believe the stories I tell. It's disgusting how little time it takes to seduce people into believing you.

I want to call out to her. I want to run to her and grab her hand, reassure her it will be all right. "I love you, Marabelle!" I cry to the birds. They call back.

"Look at all of these birds sitting in that tree."

Merry has found me. She points and then she rips a paper I've kept hidden in my hand away from me.

"Hey, another animal story. For me?" she asks. Merry tosses her blonde hair

behind her neck and bats her eyelashes at me.

"Sure it is. I know how much you love them." Another present for Marabelle stolen.

"What are you doing out here? Can I join you?"

"Why would I say no to my best friend? Would you like to look for shapes in the clouds with me?"

"Yes. Um ... I see an elephant, a cake with frosting, a large heart. I'm bored. Let's do something else," Merry says.

Marabelle is gone. I've lost track of her, and she is out of my range of vision. My heart sinks. I'm stuck with Merry.

"Sure. Let's go." I reluctantly follow Merry back to the compound to do what she want to do. Boring!

Skyler-16

I'm a bit discouraged. I thrash my hands against the concrete before I enter work to rid myself of these images swimming in my brain. I want something that I can't get. I detest yearning for the forbidden deeds. Why do they have to be forbidden? My body works against me here. At some point, a switch was flipped, practically overnight, and now these little urges pollute my brain in which I have very little control over. Who can I turn to in order to explain this development? Why must I suffer alone? One day, I am drawing animals, and the next, I want to grab Marabelle and do things I can't explain. As always, discussions about this topic are forbidden. We learn about love needs by sneaking peeks into married couple's windows. We know where babies come from—pregnant women roam the community—but that's not what I want to ask. I want to ask if others have the same hunger as I do. I wonder if I am normal. If I am sick. If I am in need of help. Or perhaps nothing at all is wrong.

I wash dishes as Marabelle washes and slices fruits and vegetables. She has a small waist which I am drooling over right now. She normally wears baggy clothes, but today, her work shirt is tied in a knot at the bottom to stay out of the way of her chores. Her chest looks like two perfect scoops of ice cream or a couple of cupcakes. Her bottom is round like a pillow. I scrub the dishes, roughly cracking the skin on my fingers till they bleed. I have trouble concentrating. I breathe hard and heavily. I grind my teeth, trying to control my thoughts and focus on my own chores.

Marabelle peels beets. Juice splashes all over her arms and legs. Flies swarm to drink the sweetness off her body. I want to be a fly. When she is done, she takes a knife and slices lettuce so fine that it melts in your mouth when you eat it. I've seen her other talents too. She can core and peel an apple in one unbroken movement. The long peel spirals to the floor, revealing white flesh as pale as her skin. I want to peel her clothes off like an apple. I can't stop myself from these dumb daydreams. I'm probably not normal.

After food prep, Marabelle cleans the dining room, picking up used plates and sponging up spills. She sings and dances to herself, wiggling her hips as she brings me the trays of dishes and silverware to wash. I bite my lip until it bleeds. My entire body double-crosses me and goes crazy. I'm dizzy and can't make eye contact. I don't dare talk to her. I might reveal my feelings to the lunch crowd.

I sense a traitor among us. Marabelle's cute ways attract another set of eyes in the room. Cecile finishes his meal slowly. His mind contemplates talking to her as well. He and I share a similar confusion. (Maybe this is normal after all.) Yet we can't even turn to each other for comfort. We go about growing up in confusion and solitude.

Still, I'm glad Cecile and I cannot share our thoughts. I might strangle the notion of Marabelle's body out of his lungs until he takes his last breath and passes on to the unknown.

I make eye contact with him. He cheeks grow red with shame. His thoughts were not overly pure. So I summon Cecile to rip him away from my prize.

"Hey, Cecile, what's up?"

"Ya workin', Sky?"

"Yep, you're so lucky. You'll never wash a dish in your life."

"Sure, I guess."

"Can you believe who I got stuck with today?"

I motion to Marabelle, roll my eyes, and laugh. He chuckles, embarrassed from getting caught looking at her.

"Uh ..."

"I mean, what luck! Now she really needs a shower. Disgusting!" I whisper in his ear so she won't overhear the conversation. Then I wink.

I look over at poor Marabelle. She's covered in fruit juice, but I smell like dirty dishes. Surprisingly, Marabelle always smells very sweet, kind of like honey and cinnamon, or vanilla and lavender, or oranges and apple blossoms. I can't imagine how she does it, but I assume that she must mix some sort of oils and perfumes together. Whatever it is, I want to lick it off her. Now

I'm the one, again, who is embarrassed by these deeply forbidden thoughts. I frown.

"Did you finish your homework?"

"Nope. I didn't get it," Cecile says.

"Great. I guess I can't copy yours, then," I say back.

"What do you mean? I usually need to copy your work, Sky. You always get it. Not me. I'm sort of stuck on the first page."

I reluctantly suggest tutoring him. This makes Cecile very happy. He slaps me on my sweaty back and leaves.

We are running, and Antin is bothering me about being a virgin again.

"You're such a virgin, Sky."

"Yeah, we all are."

"Speak for yourself."

Do I really need to listen to his tiresome cackle? I would love to be with someone, obviously, but approaching Marabelle at the wrong moment is not worth the risk of punishment. I'm ready to be close to her, but she does not suspect my feelings. If we were allowed a bit of freedom, would she even be ready to return my offers of affection? I'm so pent up with frustration I could punch Antin in the face, break his nose, smash his teeth, and bloody him to a pulp. He should really back off!

"We are all supposed to be virgins, Antin. That is the rule."

"Good thing you follow the rules."

"I follow the rules because I am in love."

Oops!

I search his thoughts, going as deep as I possibly can.

Merry.

That's who I see.

Relief.

My plan is foolproof.

"Right. Oh, I'm sorry, Sky, are you in love? Is your love a virgin too?" he asks in a sarcastic puppy-love voice.

What a moron! He could probably turn me in for talking about love. He would rather torment me.

"Yes, we both are. We are saving ourselves for marriage."

And death does not seem too appealing right now either, so I guess celibacy.

He goes on and on and on with his idiotic rants. He is the best pawn at perfecting my cover.

I speed up, and once I get rid of Antin, Paine moves in. So insecure!

He pumps me for information about Merry. You marry Merry if you like her so much, you daft baby.

I ponder running and hiding a bit. Would I get into trouble? Would they find me and give me the paddle? They have our lives so tightly scheduled that they would notice my absence right away. Plus, all of my besties would start to worry and report me missing. My plan has been foiled before I can even carry it out. Marabelle is probably still about a mile behind me. I could double back, grab her, and try to run to freedom. But that wouldn't work either. That would double foil my evil plot and put us both in jeopardy of never seeing each other again. Then where would I be? So I'm stuck here between Antin and Paine, biding my time before bidding.

The full moon makes me antsy. I punch a tree trunk to take away the pain I feel for Marabelle. It helps erase this persistent longing for her. I can't get rid of it, but with each blow, I ease the pressure a bit. It takes the edge off. Tears streak my face as I shred my hands. How do the other mates deal with their feelings? Do they even have feelings?

If my father finds out that I've left home, he'll kill me. If my mom saw my hands, she would sob and get me in trouble with my dad. When I get home, I'll just pour a bottle of antiseptic on my wounds. My cuts seem to heal pretty quickly anyway. I smash the tree for the last time. I don't want to kill it.

The moon hangs so low that I reach out and try to grab it. "Free me," I say. The nocturnal birds screech in delight. I shiver and contemplate going back home. I insulted Marabelle again. When we were running, she was too far back to hear me, but I still did it anyway. Then I lied to Paine. He enjoyed my cruelty. People seem to enjoy rotten behavior better than kindness. I dig my nails into my dirt until my fingers ache and bleed. I am not really trying to punish myself to make amends; I just grasp at adequate release for my pent-up frustration.

I chant, "Please, Marabelle, please forgive me!" I braid tiny white flowers into a bracelet. I plan on tossing it through Marabelle's window on my way home. Then I'll shower away the evidence of my midnight escape. This was the only time I could go and hide from the world unnoticed. The darkness cloaks my flight from the community. But I realize it is a temporary fix for my longing to leave. I head back to my prison. But as I reach her window, I stop. Then I trace a heart in the dewy condensation with my finger. I hope it lasts till morning.

"Hello, little fairy. I see you flitting around in your own kingdom inside your mind. Please notice me!"

During class I sit and stare at Marabelle as she daydreams.

"No? Fine. I'll write you a little note. Maybe you'll take notice now."

She can't hear me, but a little bird smashes into the window, which startles a few people and causes them to jump. I ignore it. Can't draw too much attention here, now can I?

I get out a piece of paper and think about how I can phrase my words to delicately encode them. Will she comprehend my code? Will she remember what I promised? Probably not, but I owe her a little reassurance. Okay! Maybe the reassurance is for me. Whatever! I'll write her anyway.

M,

Time is running out for us. We were meant to be together, but it is forbidden. Our union was written in the stars, and as I gaze deeply into your eyes, you will know my love is true. I only hope you can love me back one day.

S

I get up the courage to deliver the note myself. I walk over to Marabelle and kneel down on my knees. I love her lips. They are uncontrollably full and pink, and I have the urge to press mine against them, but I can't. It would be so wrong on so many levels. I catch her eyes and stare into a garden of green like a lush forest. I gaze, so maybe she will get the picture. I forget myself and reach to touch her face. I can't stop myself as I stroke her skin. It is soft and a bit bumpy. I pull it so close to mine I can smell her sweet breath. It smells like mint leaves. I linger longer than I should in this moment. Marabelle is unsure what to do and freezes. I can't read her because I am too busy feeling her skin, stroking her face.

"Read it," I command her.

Marabelle hesitates. She eyes me, perhaps a bit skeptical and unsure of what to do.

"Read the note. Then give it to Merry."

I release her and grieve. Our time together ends. It's so hard to let go. Why do I have to leave? Can't I just stay next to her for a little while longer? The pain increases each time we have physical contact that must end. All eyes are on me. Whoever said I wanted to be a role model in this dumb community anyway?

Any interaction with Marabelle, no matter how small, means I must do something to save face. So I smile at Merry and laugh to indicate I'm just playing, that note was really meant for her. She's confused by the fact that Marabelle must always read these notes. She simply figures Marabelle is just jealous. I love Merry's insecurities. They go a long way in my own plans. Girls surround her and squeal in delight. Pathetic. They are easy targets.

From a distance, I spot some little kids. They walk by us in a line led by an old, strict teacher, bitter from years of lonely maid-dom. Most of the younger children wear frowns of frustration. They do not enjoy their dry lessons from this angry woman. One kid recognizes Marabelle and gives her a thumbs-down. Marabelle responds with the same signal. A kid at the end of the line sees her too, gives her a thumbs-up, and then spots me looking. He immediately pulls away his hand and stuffs it in his pocket to continue his not-so-cheery march.

Very odd!

Cecile begins to annoy me more and more every day. He sits ahead of Marabelle so she can stare at the back of his head. She can watch him drift away from the lesson into an idiotic stupor. She can also see him turn toward her to catch her attention and flirt. He is too handsome for me to ignore. He'll drone on, "Girls like me at first, but it never lasts, blah, blah, blah." But Marabelle is too nice to be cruel to Cecile. She might attempt to steer him away, but his persistence to get near her may break down her resistance. Especially since he is so good looking ... until he opens his dumb mouth.

I cozy up to him to pester and pry. I continuously persuade him to look elsewhere. I don't want to use brute force yet. Cunning skills and social pressure should be enough for him to cave.

"Who do you fancy?" I pry.

"Sasha, for starters," he says.

Good boy. Now keep it that way. We hang out on the icy lake. I skate in circles, rambling names of year-mate girls he should want to like, all the while wondering if I can find Marabelle in the crowd. Someday she and I will come out at night and skate alone, arm in arm. I'll bring her favorite coffee and cake for a midnight picnic on the ice. Then my mind goes to other things I want to do, so I blush from my forbidden distraction.

"Hey, boys." Merry joins us with her besties in tow.

"Too late," I answer.

"For what?" Sasha gets dangerously close, checking me out for her own selfish desires. Charm pushes her into me, and Sasha relishes in my touch.

"I got you," I say, keeping up with my festive end of the charade.

"Too late for what, Sky?" Merry asks. She reeks of jealousy as she plays with my scarf.

"Too late to find you first, ladies." I am so convincing I almost vomit at my performance.

"Maybe later they will let us make some of those tasty samosas," Cecile says.

Probably not, dummy!

"You mean s'mores."

Please let Marabelle hear how stupid you really are!

"Oh yeah, I always get those mixed up!"

"Look at that." Sasha indicates to the rest of us that she means Marabelle.

I get an odd sense that she is jealous of Marabelle. I can't figure out why. In her mind, Sasha feels she is the most attractive girl here, thus she should connect more with me. She and her friends despise Marabelle, so why would she suddenly feel threatened? Maybe she sees Cecile admiring her, but I am not picking up Cecile. That's because it's my image floating in her head.

"What? Who? Where?" I play dumb.

"Marabelle over there is about to face an epic fail."

Marabelle falls. Everyone laughs.

I keep the urge to run and save her to myself. Sasha keeps her eye on me for a reaction. I am stone cold, and her apprehensions about me dissolve until Cecile makes a start to come to her aid.

"No." I grab him, ready to humiliate his efforts and keep Marabelle out of Cecile's mind.

"She will get the wrong impression! Do you want her showing up to your bidding visitations? Dumb-belle staring at you for eternity once you are forced to marry her? Is that what you want? Huh? I will tell the girls. They will definitely laugh at you."

Cecile sadly agrees. He wonders why I am so mean, but I don't care.

"Sky, come skate with me."

Duty calls. I have a big show to put on in front of my year mates. I get the strength to put on my BFF face.

The bright moon lights my way down a pebbly pathway. The little rocks shine like sparkling jewels. Marabelle looks my way and laughs as she runs into a small garden. I chase her, laughing too. She wears a white, sheer dress. I can make out her naked body underneath. I think she has wings, black ones so translucent I can barely make them out, or maybe it's smoke swirling around her in the darkness of the night.

Marabelle stops and turns. She takes her finger and motions for me to follow. I gladly obey and run after her. I trick her and take a shortcut around a tree. As she arrives, I jump out at her and yell, "Aha!" She yelps in surprise and jumps into my arms.

We fall to the ground, and I roll on top of her. She doesn't stop me. She lets me kiss her, and then I don't know what's happening. I breathe hard. I can't speak. I try to say her name, but it gets caught in my throat. The only sound I get out is an "ahhhhhh!" My heart beats so fast it feels like it's being ripped from my chest, flip-flopping and taking flight into the air like a bird. I grab her hand and squeeze tight. Marabelle squeezes back. I feel a happy release. Then someone or something starts to pull Marabelle away from me.

"No!" I yell, tears dripping down my face. Who is taking her from me? It took so long for us to be together. I call her name.

"Mmmmare ..."

I sit up in my bed in a panic. Sweat pours down my back. I'm wet all over. I still feel my heart pounding, and I feel around my bed for her. It was a dream. I have the urge to call for Marabelle, but she's not here. She never was. I want her to come back. I want to go back to sleep and look for her.

I see my doorknob turn, and my father walks in on me. This is very annoying.

"Oh, Sky, how could you?"

Privacy is a real issue in this slab.

"I'm sorry, Dad. I couldn't help it."

How am I going to go back to sleep now?

He leaves and slams my door.

It's time to take flight and leave. If I find Marabelle, maybe she would agree to go. But somehow, I doubt she will. In reality, I need to tough it out a little while longer.

I get cleaned up and dressed. I will tolerate these two people I call parents until I get my own place. They will not be invited to come with me when I escape. I wish they would leave me alone. Especially my dad. Oh, and no more bonding time!

Once again, my father's back for more.

"No, Sky, I am the one who should be sorry. It is normal to dream about girls."

I don't have time for his pep talks.

"Dad." I try to get away from him.

"It was about a girl, right? Your dream?"

"Dad, just forget it."

"Was it about Merry? I know how you feel about her."

Sure, Merry, whatever you want to think. In fact, spread that rumor around the community. Make sure the entire compound knows. Shoot, I must have said something in my sleep.

"Dad, never mind. I'm late for school."

Now I'm really angry and anxious to leave. My dad insists on pushing this issue. He tries desperately to make this sappy father-son connection.

"I just don't want to see you get so attached to her. You know how this could end. Feeling strongly about a girl is nice, but you might end up disappointed. I would hate to have to see you go through that kind of hurt."

Nice lecture. Is that what happened to you? Well, it won't be happening to me, Father!

"Okay, I know, Dad. Please move out of the way now."

My stomach grumbles. It would really suck if this conversation cost me breakfast. I run to the dining hall to get some food.

As I arrive at the dining hall, I spot Marabelle. I feel my cheeks burn. We shared something special last night, and she doesn't even know it. I can't face her right now to even ignore her. I stare at her chest. Oops! Bad idea. I hide behind a beam and watch her get coffee. Marabelle loves coffee. Two sugar cubes, half steamed milk, half hot coffee. I quickly grab some corn flakes and eggs and pour myself some hot coffee. What would happen if I ditched school? Would the cameras spot me? Would I get a paddling or just a stern talking to?

I decide to return to school this morning after all. Getting in trouble would invite more useless conversations with my dad. I'd rather sweep a stable than talk with him.

Skyler-17

My time is so often wasted putting up with Merry and her continuous confusion. She loves me, she loves me not, she loves me, she loves me not, she loves me. And she really does! Wishing, hoping, waiting for me to give her a sign from the Makers that I have a plan and can solve all of her problems so we can finally be together but live in privilege. I try to tell her the truth to cushion the blow of reality, but her head stays steady in the clouds.

I give it to her straight.

"Remember our times together at work, at school, but don't plan on seeing me on your Wedding Day."

How much more straightforward could I get with her? She doesn't buy it.

"No, Sky, please don't say this."

What more do you want, Merry? I have little stipend, and I don't really love you. Deep down inside, she really hopes to marry Antin. She refuses to admit it to herself. I'll deliver her to him. Two shallow people are meant to be together. It's as if she were specially created from a part of him for his own enjoyment. I will grant them both this wish so I can take Marabelle. That way they can live in his beautiful house with an awesome garden together.

"I promise you'll be happy. There is more out there than what I have to offer you. I'll see ya."

The birds go farther. They bring back olive branches which I throw to the ground. I know vegetation exists beyond this compound as does water, mountains, air, and sky. I need proof of life—not of animals, but of humans. I have faith that they can somehow expand their search, go farther than they dare, summon strange creatures to aid this mission. What a lonely world this would be if we were it. Perhaps they don't look like us. Perhaps they speak other words. Perhaps they live freely with fewer rules. Perhaps their customs differ from ours. I don't care. This lonely planet invites human life to take over and populate its hills and valleys, forests and deserts. Why would we be so unique? This community certainly can't be the lone population of humans on this earth!

Walking to school, the wind blows softly on my face. I stretch out my hand to feel the breeze. It rushes around my fingers, and the sensation soothes me. I listen as the air roars around the leaves in the trees. I find birds in formation above, changing direction with the fickle wind. It's nice. I'm at peace alone. I do not look forward to reaching my destination.

Choice time? It's more like waste of time.

I grimace. Teacher shakes her head, warning me to not get on her nerves today. She doesn't have the strength to put up with my ever-shifting moods. She thinks to herself, "Mr. Chameleon, changing shades with every backdrop." I contemplate giving her the finger and getting kicked out of here.

I lean back, squinting at the sun. I should take a nap. I survey the area. Marabelle mixes colors. Her paintings turn out a bit juvenile, but she mixes paints with beauty and

ease. It's like when she peels an apple; it comes naturally. Her skin glows in the light. Her full lips pout as she concentrates. Thinking about her makes me woozy. Suddenly, I pick up a weird vibe from where she sits. I can't read his mind. Odd. It's blocked by a strong will. Who is this kid? I focus my eyes and see some little kid named One. He sits dangerously close to Marabelle. It bugs me. Marabelle cozies up to her young friend. That should be me. I feel more at ease knowing that he can't have her. It is forbidden by the community to marry outside your year. Only year mates may marry each other. But sitting that close is forbidden by me. So really, he can't have her. She is mine, and One must pay. My blood starts to boil. My hands shake in anger.

I pick up a rock and launch a warning shot. It smashes Marabelle's paint palette and splashes her. Those two should know I am an excellent shot. I could have easily hurt them, but I intentionally missed. I shock One as we make eye contact. As furious as he seems, he averts his eyes and looks away.

People high-five around me and taunt Marabelle in response to my jealousy.

I immediately regret my decision. The fire inside urges me to run to her and beg for forgiveness. It shouts, "Tell her the truth! Explain your rash actions!" I can't expose myself like this. I will make it up to her. I owe her a thousand more kisses. I slap my forehead in anger to prevent myself from crying in front of the entire school.

Teacher commends herself on confirming my ability to single-handedly ruin outdoor choice time. She verbalizes an "I told you so" in her head. I raise my eyebrows at her, thinking, "Yep, you were right." And if anyone were to even ask, I would openly say, "I told you not to trust me." I'm weak when it comes to Marabelle and getting what I want.

We return to the classroom. I want to vomit. Help! I can't take it anymore! I want to die right here and now. Marabelle, I am sooo sorry.

I need to apologize right now. I had planned on making her something sweet and hiding it near her pillow, but it might be too late. Perhaps I'll do that as well. But right now, I rip out some paper and write her a note. My hands shake. I'm a bad person. How will she ever love me? I wish I could just get in her head and validate that she feels the same way about me. I know once I get her alone, she will return my love.

> M,
>
> I am so sorry! Please forgive me for what I have done to you. I didn't mean it. I get so jealous sometimes. I just can't stand the thought of you being with anyone else. It hurts me to see you sad. I hate to admit it, but when you cry, I cry too. I know it is hard, but please don't tell anyone how I feel about you. Remember my promise to you.
>
> I love you.

I work hard in the main hall kitchen. I melt white and dark chocolate and pour it into a mold of a dove. I drop bits of cherries and nuts into it and pop it into the fridge. When it solidifies, I will wrap it in red cellophane and toss the treat into Marabelle's bed. I'll hide. She'll look around and wonder who gave it to her. She'll shrug and enjoy, like always. In less than a year, I'll confess. We'll have a good laugh about it all.

"Sssssssssssssssssskkkkkkkkkkkkkkkkkyyyyyyyyyyyy yyyy!"

The voice plays over and over in a continuous loop in my dreams. This eerie voice haunts my sleep.

"Sssssssssssssssssskkkkkkkkkkkkkkkkkyyyyyyyyyyyy yyyy!"

Even now, I search for it. I imagine myself back at the lake at night, splashing my hands furiously on the sandy bottom, trying to grab on to it.

"Sssssssssssssssssssssssssskkkkkkkkkkkkkkkkkyyyyyyyyy yyy!"

"What are you? Who are you? Where are you?"

I yell louder and louder. I can't seem to locate the voice.

"Come out! Show yourself! I'm not afraid of you!"

"Gggggggggggggggggggiiiiiiiiiiiiiiiiiirrrrrrrrrrrrrrrrrrrrllllllllllllll-lllll."

Now it calls for Marabelle, and my body freezes.

I feel movement below. Waves crash against my bare chest.

It starts to look for her. I can sense its urgency to get hold of Marabelle. It knows her. It pictures her face.

"Stop!" I yell.

The water calms around me. It retreats back into the blackness of the lake.

I spring up from my sleep, gulping for air. I can't breathe. I choke up some water, and it splashes onto my duvet on the bed.

"Help," I mutter weakly.

I did not mean to do this. I alarm my parents and arouse them from their deep sleeps.

"Sky? Are you okay?" my mom calls from her room.

"Fine, Mom. Um, just a dream. Sorry for disturbing you. Go back to bed."

"Are you sure?" she asks.

"Yes, sorry."

"Good night, then."

"Good night."

My string of dreamless nights ends with a fierce nightmare. I try to push the wet remnants off my lap. My hand brushes against some thing odd. I pick it up to examine it further. It's a piece of seaweed.

My hand touches Merry's back. She enjoys my touch as she laughs and giggles in my ear. She imagines herself a fairy-tale princess. I preoccupy my mind with Marabelle. I still worry that the day at the beach frightened her. My year mates continue to congratulate me and talk me up as their hero. I yearn to talk to Marabelle and comfort her.

Teacher eagerly pushes my union with Merry. Merry's friends stare green with jealousy as we demonstrate what we have learned. At the same time, most of my male year mates hunger to touch Merry as I do in front of them. She appears to be the most desirable female on the compound. Her blonde hair bounces with grace down her back. She bats her eyelashes for all to see. She screams inside, "Look at me!" The boys daydream about her alone with them on Visitation Day or perhaps even their wedding night.

"Good," I say to myself. "Compete for Merry's attention." She is free for the taking. Come get her, boys. You can have her. All of you. She'll make you really happy, I promise. Look how beautiful she looks in my arms. She can cozy up in yours too. Bid on her name! Bid! Bid! Bid on Merry!

Weak-minded Merry goes back and forth on her feelings for me. I'm sick of hearing her back and forth pros and cons about me in her mind. Now she waits for me in the darkness and snatches another one of Marabelle's gifts. Oh well. It's all right. I was having some seriously forbidden thoughts about it anyway. As Merry grabs the floral halo, I figure it saves me from more humiliation of being caught by my dad. But it cost me the happiness of seeing Marabelle smile for a few minutes.

I walk away from Merry, leaving her hungry for more time together. The darkness creeps around me and sucks me into deep reflection. I think about the day long ago when I tried to truly escape. What would have really happened? I was so young. Perhaps I was too young to even take care of myself, let alone another person. Could a small child live apart from the community in the wilderness and survive?

As I think to myself, firing off random nonsense in my brain, my hands begin to tingle. A small spark flies into the air like a candle and then is instantly extinguished by the wind. I clap my hands together furiously. I bring my palms up to my eyes and inspect my fingers. I focus my eyes to scrutinize what just happened. I must have imagined this.

Great, I'm seeing things.

I'm being driven crazy.

I run home and dive into my bed before my parents even consider conversing with me about the day. I'll shower tomorrow. I've had enough. I need an escape plan or at the very least some quiet rest and time away from my mates.

Dance rotations start. They force us to dance with every female year mate. One hundred twenty-six sweaty palms to look forward to pressed up against mine. I only desire two little hands, and currently, they rest inside Antin's grip. He dances sloppily with Marabelle, repulsed by her mere presence. He eagerly waits for their turn to end. Antin hopes to purge Marabelle from his life, mostly because she confuses him. He's angry because Marabelle sports an orange and ginger fragrance. It's light and refreshing, and her smell makes him uncomfortable because it's so delightful that he would rather die than admit her scent entices him. He avoids embarrassment by acting rude. I sigh in relief. Antin and Merry try to flirt in secret, and Marabelle barely registers them.

On the other hand, Cecile concerns me. His mind moves closer and closer to declaring his hidden feelings for Marabelle. Her perfume practically knocks him off his feet. I hear his heart racing, and my blood starts to boil. As much as I want to grab him and smash him into a wall, I can't. I must concoct a plan to separate those two immediately.

Cecile and Marabelle converse as they dance. Cecile gathers his nerve to invite her over. He imagines being able to talk to her alone to confess his crush. He imagines her face bright and happy upon hearing this good news. He starts to long for other types of attention Marabelle can bestow upon him that may or may not be forbidden to think about. I must stop them. I must end their time together.

I instantly drop to the floor, arching my back and twisting with dramatic pain. I rest helplessly on my knees.

"Ahhhhh! Help! Help! My back!"

I scream as loud as my lungs will let me. My hurt voice echoes through the ears of my year mates. All concerned eyes fall on me as I writhe on the floor. I force teardrops out of my eyes so the year mates can witness my pain as the droplets roll down my cheeks.

"Sky!" Merry panics.

"My back. I think I strained it." I collapse into a fetal position as the crowd goes wild with predictable shock.

"Hurry! Contact the clinic, and tell them to bring a stretcher."

This allows me to really ham up my performance. I roll in pain. I'm afraid someone will laugh and claim I'm a faker. I look around to make sure the crowd buys it. They do.

"I promise I'll visit you this time," Merry calls.

"Okay."

Don't bother.

The porters carry me off to the clinic for assessment and observation.

Time off for good behavior from my wonderfully convincing performance, here I come!

A cold, rough, bony hand sweeps my forehead. It's tiny and reassuring. Startled, I grab it. I open my eyes and try to focus on the face above me.

"Marabelle!"

"Shhhh!"

"Marabelle, what are you doing here? Am I still at the clinic?"

"You're not sick." Her little hand caresses my forehead one more time, and then she pulls it away.

"I know I'm not sick, but why are you here?"

"You're dreaming. Go back to sleep. You don't want to wake the others."

"No, I'm not dreaming."

"Are you sure?"

I look at her. She wears a worn, dingy nightgown. Her pale face glows from the light of the moon outside the window by my cot. I'm still in the clinic. The nurses told me I may be here awhile to determine what happened at dance practice. Now Marabelle stares at me in the dead of the night. I want to take her in my arms and hug her. I yearn to tell her to stay, keep me company, and talk. I want to confess that I'm lonely without her.

"You're not sick," she reiterates. "I've got to get back home."

Marabelle stands up and walks away. Her image dissolves into the darkness of the

clinic.

I sit up.

"Wait!" I call loud enough for her to hear me down the corridor.

"Sky?" My mom's face hovers over mine. "How are you feeling, baby? Did you have a bad dream?"

"What? No. I was talking to someone. Did you see someone leave? She was just here."

"Sky," she speaks calmly and slowly, "no one is here. We are alone. I have been by your side the whole time. You must have been dreaming."

She picks her hand up to feel my forehead, and I block her.

"Wait, Mom, you don't need to do that. I'm not feverish."

"Sure, okay. Whatever you say."

I can tell my mom is disappointed. She stood guard over me, and I let her down by not appreciating her vigil by my side. I can't get over my own upset. My heart sinks when I realize Marabelle was nothing but a moonlit mirage.

My mother starts to rearrange my covers and pillows.

"Let's get you comfortable and back to bed."

She brushes some crumbs off my sheet.

"Little messy, huh?" I say.

Then she lifts a long, curly strand of hair from my hospital gown.

"Some nurse must have shed on you." She scrutinizes it a bit and then tosses it to the floor.

My return to class turns me into a champion. My year mates clamor around me. Paine and Cecile slap me on the shoulders, happy to gain back my company. I talk to Paine a bit. He seems relieved that I'm back. Girls approach me and chatter in my ear, asking how I feel and inquiring what happened. Some wonder if they can assist me, you know, by carrying my books, my lunch tray, perhaps.

As always, Marabelle ignores me. She keeps me at a distance. She's inaccessible. I'm dying to wave to her and call her over. I don't care anymore about what is or is not forbidden. I need to ask her about the night at the clinic. It couldn't have been a dream. I didn't imagine it. That hair proves she came to check on me. My mom probably fell asleep and missed Marabelle's visit.

Merry wanders around the room, miserable and avoiding my glance. She sets the scene so perfectly for me to deliver another note to Marabelle. By now, I find it hard to believe Marabelle thinks these notes are for Merry. They are too personal.

M,

As I walked into class today, all I could think about was your beautiful face. Why didn't you look back at me? Are you ignoring me? Did you visit me at the clinic? Didn't we talk? Don't torture me like this. The only thing keeping me going is our dance together. I look forward to holding you in my arms forever!

Love always,

S

The sealed letter makes its way to Marabelle. She opens it and reads the contents. She reacts indifferently to it and passes it to a moody Merry who screams for joy inside her head.

My stomach somersaults. I can't swallow. My hope diminishes. Marabelle frowns in the distance and walks away. The life force inside of me floats away with her every step, leaving me alone once again. I don't get it. How can she not know the notes are meant for her? She finds herself friendless. I see her empty eyes counting down the minutes to maid-dom. Merry's dumb performance convinces Marabelle. In fact, it fools the whole community into believing that I'm chasing Merry. I don't know if I should laugh or cry. I could laugh all the way to Bidding Day. Or I could cry, give up, and throw myself off the mountain. I definitely keep these forbidden thoughts to myself. I'm not sure anyone here understands what I'm going through.

Movies here are so awesome. I love them. I can sit and relax in the dark and stuff my mouth with junk food. Most of the time, I can never get enough food around here to satisfy me throughout the day. But on these days, they treat us to extra stipend to buy peanut puffs or spicy shrimp chips. I indulge in chocolate orange slices, so sweet and juicy, squirting onto my tongue. I eat half of my stash even before the movie starts. I probably look silly. I bet my face is a chocolaty, powdery mess, but I don't care. I'm famished. I dump the box of cocoa nibs down my throat, barely chewing them. I rip open a bag of sponge cake and stuff three at a time into my mouth.

Paine turns to me. He can't believe how much I just consumed in one minute.

"Hungry, Sky?"

"Yes." I spray him a little with my full mouth. He doesn't seem to notice I got crumbs on his shirt.

"Wan some?" I ask, crunching loudly.

He looks at his slightly rounder body and then at mine.

"No, thanks. I brought my own." He holds up his small bag of pretzels.

I laugh at the movie. I wish we would be allowed to watch them more often. Maybe they think we would get clever ideas from it, and they wouldn't want us to be too clever.

Midlaughter, I make eye contact with Merry. Too late to take that back. She'd been waiting all night to catch my eye. She would have sat and stared until it happened. I go back to ignoring her so I can enjoy the film. I clap and whistle. A movie like this could calm me into a zombielike submission. I'll keep that bit of info to myself. Wouldn't want that tidbit used against me.

Just as I finally relax, the crowd starts to thin out. I see something odd out of the corner of my eye. Asher, a younger kid, smiles at Marabelle and gives her a thumbs-up. She responds by smiling back and giving a thumbs-down. As the rest of the community disperses, this small gesture catches me off guard. I know Marabelle takes care of the little ones, but my hands immediately want to react. They start to tingle again. I massage them to get the urge out of my system. I've seen this before, but it didn't register as much as it does now. My head spins. I get up and leave. My hands still ache, so I press them against the cold wall outside the theater. As we get closer to Bidding Day, things make less sense than ever.

"Sky, Sky, Sky, Sky."

Some birds fly over my head and squawk out a greeting.

"Do you know why my hands hurt?" I call to them.

"No," they answer and fly away.

"Well, me either!" I shout to them.

"Me either," I say out loud in the darkness.

Ever wake up in the morning and feel the sun is shining just for you? Ever look up and think the light seems a bit brighter in the sky? Ever look at the shapes of the clouds and see secret messages like large hearts or the face of a loved one winking down at you?

Well, today is my day. The day is just for me. Marabelle and I will have our first dance together. I will finally get to put my arms around her in public and not worry about judgmental eyes or scorning year mates. My dance will be camouflaged in broad daylight for all to see, and nothing about it will be forbidden.

I am giddy when I greet Merry.

"Nice to finally see you again. You know, as a dance partner. It's been a while since we've danced last."

Merry is easy. It's fun to play with her mind. She really buys every word as do most of my year mates.

"You took a break from dance altogether. Remember?" she responds.

"Serious injuries." I act all casual toward her. "I'm still healing. I might lounge in the pool a bit, perhaps even in the hot tub. Just in case you're free, you may want to join me. I might even sneak in a nice fruity drink to sip while I relax."

I tease her with nonsensical invites. They work me to exhaustion here. Who would ever allow me more free time? I'm a Worker!

"That's so enticing, really. I might have to work. They need people to pick up the slack at the dairy. For some reason, they are short staffed. I strain the liquid out of the cheese."

"Fun."

"Messy and wet."

"At least you don't have to clean the stalls at the farm. I get to shovel manure all day next week. But don't worry. I'll shower really, really well for the ball."

"I almost forgot it was coming up."

"Promise to save me a dance?"

"Sure."

I wink. I need to make a public spectacle of our alleged relationship. Our year mates must really believe I love Merry for my plan to truly work. Antin doesn't worry me too much. He lusts after Merry. It is Cecile. I don't just need to distract him, I need a stronger force to keep Marabelle's name off his list.

"I bet you're excited to dance with Marabelle next."

Merry's comment catches me off guard. I didn't expect it and wonder if she

knows. My brow sweats, and I start to worry.

"What?"

"Huh? No, Sky, I don't mean next week. I mean, now, right after me. Remember? We have to rotate in about thirty seconds."

"Oh yeah, that." Relief spreads over my body. Merry feels she might have upset me for a moment, but I backtrack and patch up my error.

"For a second, I got so caught up in the moment with you I forgot all about everyone else around us. I'm so used to dancing with you. Plus, I've been absent for a while."

121

The whistle blows. I'm so excited I could cry. My nerves return as I process the fact that Marabelle and I will touch moments from now.

"Bye. Have fun," Merry calls to me.

"Right."

I quickly move away from Merry. I might faint from excitement. The crazy anticipation makes my hands shake. The shakes move up my arms, down my legs, through my voice. I can't walk. I force my legs to move toward Marabelle.

"Hi."

"Hi."

We greet each other shyly in unison. I lick my dry lips. My arms grow heavy, my teeth chatter. The music echoes in my ears as it starts a new song. I reach for Marabelle's hand. It feels so nice. My other hand creeps around her waist, and I pull her close to my chest. At this moment, my body starts to betray me. Weird desires from my crazy dream surface, and I can feel my embarrassment rise at an inappropriate time. I risk utter humiliation. Is what I feel is forbidden?

In a moment, how much I love Marabelle will be revealed for all to see. I want to die. Tears well up in the corners of my eyes. The room turns into a blur of hazy faces. I wanted this time together so badly, and now I have ruined it. Will Marabelle ever forgive me for what I have to do? I must abandon her now and leave the premises immediately. I will explain later, for she is innocent and can't really comprehend what is happening to me, even though she is pressed again my body. Seriously, I barely understand why this has to happen to me at this moment.

"I can't do this right now," I scream. Poor choice of words, I know.

I throw her and step away. Poor choice of action, I know.

"I'm sorry," I tell her quietly and say to myself, "I love you."

I run as fast as I can so that my poor, bent-over posture doesn't register with my year mates. I make it to the edge of the compound in no time. I yell with frustration hitting, kicking, and throwing everything that gets in my way. I scream and cry.

"Why???!!! I hate you!!!!!! Release me!!!!!!! Get me out of here!!!!!!"

A scared flock of birds takes off.

"Aaaaaaaaaaahhhhhh!!!!!!!"

I sound off the alarms, and a loudspeaker goes off.

"Skyler-17, return to the compound. You are in violation. Leaving the compound is strictly forbidden. Skyer-17, return to the compound."

I collapse. My face is stained with tears. I grab a pomelo from the tree and accidentally break several braches as I angrily rip off the fruit. As I start to peel the skin, the juice sprays my eyes. It stings horribly, and I curse loudly.

Footsteps approach me. Predictably, Merry has found me and comes to confront me. She reaches out to me as a friend. I understand that she feels genuine concern. I would rather grieve the lost opportunity alone, but Merry craves this reassurance that I love her the most.

"What's wrong?"

"Nothing."

I throw the citrus peel. There's no way to shake her and stew in my misery solo.

"What do you mean 'nothing,' Sky? What happened in there? One second, we are dancing, and the next, you yell at Marabelle and run out. Did she say something to you?"

"No."

"Did she do something to you?"

"No."

"Then what?"

"Just forget it. I'm fine."

Seriously, she can't take a hint. I'm not discussing my private life with her. Who does she think she is, getting into my business? When this is all over, I don't want to talk to Merry ever again. I'm sick of her moody nagging. I need my space.

"Have you been crying?" Merry doesn't quit asking her twenty questions.

"What? No!" I respond in my meanest voice. "Some pomelo squirted into my eye. Can't I be alone here for just a moment, a second, and instant? It's not like I can leave or anything."

123

My message gradually sinks into Merry's pea brain.

"Why do you want to be alone? Why do you want to leave here? Leave me?"

"I don't."

I stand, stretching my legs to release the tension from this rough afternoon. I walk away, but Merry remains at my side like a confused puppy. A devious idea creeps into my head. I grin and move toward the forbidden tree. I slowly turn to Merry and say in my most seductive voice, "You should take one. Try it and see what happens."

"No, Sky, it's forbidden."

I start to scare her.

"It won't be when you become a Planner. Nothing is. I've seem them, drinking vin, having parties. You can taste the fruit, and when you do, tell me how it is because I'll never get to, and you know it."

My voice melts like chocolate into her ears, slow and warm, enticing and devious. I win her back and push her mind into my darkness. I face Merry and smile so she can see the good side of my darkness.

"What are you thinking now?" she asks me.

"It's just you and me against the world. Come on. Walk me back before they ready the paddle for my behind," I hiss in her ear and draw her even closer.

She will return home and reassure her friends our relationship is stronger than ever.

The ball doesn't mean much to me. I set my mind on Bidding Day years ago.

Attending this parade of silly adolescence doesn't interest me at all. I realize I agreed to dance with Merry. She'll be waiting for me to arrive. She'll sit there on edge, surrounded by her admiring friends. That sacred cup of vin will be offered to us peons as our induction into adulthood as we enjoy our final moments before the rest of our miserable lives begin. I would much rather stay in my bed and count the cracks in my ceiling. I do consider showing up to see what Marabelle is wearing. Looking at her from afar cheers me up, sort of, when I am not ruining everything around me. Then it dawns on me. If I don't show, someone else may move in on her. I must go and stand guard of my property.

My mom claps her hands with joy when I exit my room, dressed for the ball.

"Oh, I knew you would change your mind."

She squeezes my shoulder. "You look so handsome. Wait until your father sees you."

They clamor around me and beam with pride.

"It's just a dance, geez. Calm down, you two," I say, severely annoyed.

"I understand, Sky, but you won't be in this house much longer. We enjoy these last few memories we can make together as a family. You'll move on soon to create your own family and eventually your own child."

I grimace and roll my eyes at them. Are most teenage boys ready to have a child? Are they even ready to discuss having one? I rarely hear Merry and her friends discuss babies. Who am I kidding? Merry probably has a name picked out for every letter of the alphabet for a boy and a girl.

I shoo away my parents and hunt down a tea rose bush. I quickly assemble a bouquet and pull a pin out of my shirt. I need to look official when I arrive at the school.

I walk in fashionably late to the cheers of my year mates. It's nice to feel welcome. I must get over that need to fit in or care what others around me think. Marabelle doesn't care.

Speaking of Marabelle, a flash of pink catches my eye, and my little fairy takes my breath away. I've never seen Marabelle look so beautiful. She sparkles brighter than any other girl in the room. Yep, I've learned my lesson, and I vow to contain myself this time. There is no need to react so eagerly in front of the whole school. I exercise self-discipline and put on an ambivalent face.

Merry plays her own angle and pretends to ignore me. I can use her to keep close to Marabelle and dance in close range to her—stand guard, if you will.

I walk up to Merry and start.

"Hi."

"Hi."

"You look beautiful tonight."

"You too. I mean you look handsome, not beautiful, er …"

"I brought you a rose bouquet. You can pin it on your dress. That's why I was late. I was finishing up, and I didn't realize the time."

Merry takes her gift with shaky hands, so I offer to help her pin it. She beams at me. I'm ready to make a move to the dance floor, so I ask Merry to dance. She eagerly pulls me toward Cecile. He stares in Marabelle's direction, which immediately worries me. I gather a plan in my head. But it's no use. I'm too clouded by the emotions in my head.

Cecile's inner yammering distracts me as I dance, until I sense Antin in the midst. He's angry at me and hungers for Merry's attention. He composes his own plan to humiliate me in front of our entire class, which could work in my favor. I offer to get Merry a cup of vin and set in motion this mouse-trap of a game we are all playing.

As the dark purple liquid is poured into my two cups, Marabelle rises and fixes her skirt. Cecile, that daft jerk, finally gets up the nerve to ask Marabelle to dance. His foot slams down in her direction. Antin reacts to my arrival with the cups by pushing a chair in my way. I could have easily avoided this setup because I knew it was coming. Antin grins with his superior ego, not realizing he is my pawn in this game. I purposely trip, losing control of my two cups of vin, unfortunately destroying Marabelle's gown in the process, thus keeping Cecile and his ulterior motives far, far away. Mission accomplished.

I'll make it up to her. I promise. I'll make a hundred new pink dresses. I'll secure her a thousand bottles of vin. I'll dance with her to a million songs. I just needed to get rid of any unnecessary competition.

Poor Marabelle storms out of the room, tearful and alone. I hope to be able to comfort her later. It's only a matter of time before I can.

Merry ignores me the rest of the night. She might as well. I didn't intend on hanging out with her here anyway. I put on my friendliest face and socialize with some other year mates, mainly Paine, who is a nervous wreck over visitations. I assure him for the billionth time that it doesn't matter how many girls sign up to see him; males have the final say in who goes on our bid lists. The girls don't really get to bid. They are the ones being bid on! It seems like it takes an hour to explain the process. Then I explain that I don't really know what I am talking about. I'm just repeating what I've heard.

As the ball winds down, I grow pretty bored. I made sure I ate a lot because it's rare for me to find this much food. I feel bad that Marabelle can't share these treats with me. She isn't the kind of girl who is afraid to eat while others watch. I've seen her go to town in the dining hall. Plus, she eats a lot of the sweets I've sent her. I've seen that too.

I walk home alone in the darkness to await my bidding visitations. With fifty girls, it's going to be a very long day!

Skyler-5

The heat suffocates us as we sit simmering in the nursery. Teacher reads us a boring story. Her bland voice puts us to sleep. It's only morning. Nap time starts after lunch. We barely finished our breakfast. I lick my cracked lips to try to heal the blisters. My eyes roll to the back of my head. The rest of my year mates doze on and off as Teacher neglects us. Merry rolls up in her mat and spins herself toward me. I consider kicking her away, but the skyrocketing temperature prevents me from moving. My legs stick together with sweat and carpet fibers.

A child nearby takes shallow breaths. I turn my cheek to see who it is. It's little Marabelle. Her skin has turned pale green as she struggles and gulps for air. She suffers alone. Teacher either refuses to notice or refuses to care about her littlest student.

I reach my hand out to touch her forehead, and it burns. A tear drips from the corner of her big green eyes. "Let me help you," I try to tell her in my mind, but she can't hear me. Her lips turn blue. I slide over to her mat and pick up her limp body and cradle it in my arms as the story ends. I rock her back and forth a bit, hoping to comfort her. Nobody seems to notice or care. I care.

Teacher releases us to play outside, and I help lift Marabelle to her feet. She doesn't speak a word to me. Poor Marabelle lets out a whimper and stands on her wobbly legs.

"Come on," I finally say and pull her across the grass.

Marabelle stumbles behind me, unable to keep up. My pace is too fast for her. But as Marabelle slows down, I pull her harder and drag her, increasing my speed, covering more ground, getting closer to the edge of the compound. Marabelle's delicate body shivers. She gives off intense heat. I stop briefly so she can catch her breath. Instead, she vomits and shakes with tears. I pick her up in my arms and carry her like a baby in order to reach the orchard. My feet pound against the ground. I see the mountain ahead.

"Marabelle, Marabelle, can you hear me?"

Her limp body jiggles in my arms as I run.

"Marabelle, we are leaving. I promise to take care of you. You'll be safe."

"Help me," she finally offers in a soft voice. "Please take me back."

"No."

"Please, I'm scared."

"I'll take care of you. I promise. What are you afraid of?"

"Dying."

I stop and collapse to the ground with Marabelle in my arms. I cry.

"Don't die, Marabelle."

The speaker goes off. "Skyler-5 and Marabelle-5, please return. Leaving the compound is forbidden. Skyler-5 and Marabelle-5, return now or face severe punishment."

My hands shake, and I have to make a decision: keep running or go back to the compound. Either way, I might lose Marabelle. I gently put Marabelle on the ground and pick up a pomelo. I take off a piece of skin and squeeze a little juice into her mouth. She coughs most of it up, but I want to keep her lips moist. I smooth back her hair. I've made my choice. I put my mouth close to her ear.

"Marabelle, listen. I'm going to get you some help. Just promise me you'll run away with me once you get better. Okay? Just you and me."

Marabelle's eyes flutter. She's trying to see me clearly. Her heart pounds in her chest. For some reason, it sounds very loud to me.

Finally she spits out, "Okay." Her voice is hoarse.

I nervously lean over, almost placing my lips onto hers when the speaker sounds off again.

"Skyler-5 and Marabelle-5, this is your final warning to return to the compound. Failure to do so will result in harsh punishment."

I pick up Marabelle's limp body and rush her to her parents' slab.

I knock on the door, and a very worried woman answers.

"She's very ill," I tell her.

The woman snatches her daughter and slams the door in my face.

Two very disappointed people, my parents, grab my hand and drag me back to my

slab.

The heat grows more intense as night falls. Marabelle's moans can be heard by the surrounding slabs. I grow restless, which frustrates my mother. I refuse to sleep while Marabelle suffers.

"Calm down, Sky," my mom demands.

"No," I respond.

"Calm down, Sky." My mom exerts her force and tried to push me down into my cot.

The sweltering heat has knocked out the power, and the darkness engulfs me. I am being swallowed up into this intense fear of losing Marabelle.

"Help her!" I scream to the birds. "Help her! Help Marabelle! Please hear me! Help!"

"Help! Help! Help!" The birds outside react to my call, agitating the animals nearby. Cows from the barns start to moo and push into each other, kicking at the fences. Dogs howl wildly at the moon. Horses whinny anxiously, setting off animals at the zoo. Tigers and lions pace their cages, growling, scaring the camels, causing more birds to screech.

"Help her!" they shout back.

"How?" I scream.

"Change the weather!"

"How? What do you mean? I can do that?" I'm confused.

"Help her, Sky. Help her, Sky."

I'm screaming so loud on the inside that I miss the sound of the wind. My heart pounds in my chest.

"Do you feel that?" my dad asks.

"It's Sky. I think his temperature is elevating. Oh no. I don't want him to get sick too." My mom knows I was with Marabelle.

"Wait. It smells like rain. Can you smell that? I think the weather is about to change." My dad stares out the door of our slab.

The wind blasts around my face through the window.

I let out a shaky exhale from my lungs.

I must save Marabelle. I think about cold, icy glaciers. I concentrate on easing up my breathing and slowing down my heart, calming down my body. I feel a sudden relief-like sensation. I shut my eyes, visualize Marabelle, and smile.

"What is this?" someone cries nearby.

I hear voices outside.

"It is starting to snow."

I relax even more.

"How can this be?"

I am almost there.

"It is mid-August."

I'm feeling pretty good.

"Her fever has broken."

I'm shutting my eyes.

"My baby will survive the night!"

I'm fast asleep.

She made a promise that we'll be together. I'll hold her to it, and we'll leave

together soon, once she is well. Marabelle's heart belongs to me, and no one else will have her.

Bidding Day, April 1

Skyler-18

All of my deep, dark feelings pour out of my heart. Softly, my desires leak into the room. My secrets reveal themselves. I spin my tale with the precision of a spider perfecting every web of truth winding around every angle of my story back to today. As I speak, I stare directly into Marabelle's green eyes. I check for a reaction, though she gives little back. Although she looks me in the eyes as well, I pick up no sign that she cares. She wears no expression of emotion on her face; it is stone cold. The only sounds she makes are her soft breaths. Her chest goes up and down as she listens quietly. I try to smile as I tell her how I feel.

I stand up and take her hands and lift her off the couch. Then I drop to one knee.

"Marabelle, I love you. I've always loved you. I've spent my whole life trying to hide this from you and the world. Now I would love to spend the rest of my days making it up to you. I want to start again and live life all over from the very beginning, but this time I want it to be with you. Marabelle, will you marry me?"

Marabelle listens carefully to my speech and takes a moment to contemplate what I've taken so long to say. Finally, she smiles and answers.

"Yes, I will."

I stand back up and hug her. Then I take her face and kiss her on the lips.

"Good, because I'm not sure you would have been able to return me if you had said no."

We both laugh at this. I take this as permission to kiss her again. My hands slowly creep around her waist. There is no way I can let go of her tonight. Happily, I pull Marabelle closer. She does not resist. In fact, this time she returns my affection and holds my back with her little arms. At some point, I started crying because tears have rolled down my neck, but I don't care.

Part 3

Skyler-18

Letting go seems more difficult than ever. I held Marabelle tightly all night. I'm not sure that was comfortable for her, but she fell asleep anyway. Poor thing woke up to me kissing her all over her face. I realize she could barely shower as I held on to her, smothering her face with my lips. I figure some soap and shampoo must have rubbed off on me too. Thus I'm clean. Then getting dressed and walking out the door proved very challenging for her this morning. I have a very tight grip and tailed her every move. Affection outside the slab is deemed forbidden, even for married couples, but we walked to the main dining hall together holding hands.

We are scheduled to work the kitchen today. I appreciate my luck since newlywed Workers don't get time off or even any celebratory party favors. They just get to be together a month prior to Planner couples who must prepare for their wedding ceremonies. In this respect, I am grateful to be a Worker.

As Marabelle heads to the vegetable prep station, I quickly kiss her good-bye—also forbidden, by they way.

"Bye. I'll miss you," I tell her.

"Ummm, I'll be right there," Marabelle responds and points her finger a few feet away from my dishwashing station.

"Oh yeah," I say, drunk with love. I blow her a kiss, and she waves at me awkwardly.

My dizzy head spins thinking about her, and us, and last night.

I pay little attention to my task while Marabelle gets to work rolling and slicing the lettuce into those thin strips that melt when I eat them.

"See you at lunch," I shout to her, louder than I need to.

"Okay," she answers in a manner that lets me know that she is no longer paying attention because she is singing something in her head. From time to time, I hear her la la la las.

Marbelle and I have the early shift. The cafeteria starts to fill up with other Workers starting their shifts and Planners looking to eat breakfast. From a distance, Paine spots me. I keep a low profile to avoid him. He wears a miserable expression on his face. Things did not go so well with his new bride. Paine never really fancied Charm. As with most of my year mates, he desired Merry. He even included her on his bid list, hoping I would never find out. Now I gather he realizes I couldn't care less who he put on his list. His bloodshot eyes plead to make eye contact with me. I turn away from him and continue to work, pretending I don't notice.

Paine gives up on trying to signal me in a subtle fashion and walks over to chat. I dread his conversation. I have nothing to say to him.

"Hey, Sky."

"Hi."

"So ..."

"So, Paine? I'm kind of working, so what do you need?"

"Are we still friends?"

"Sure."

"How did you get, um, how was your, um ... What did you ..."

"What do you want, Paine? I'm kind of busy."

That is a lie. It's not too hard to wash a dish and talk to him at the same time.

"Sorry. I confess I'm having a hard time putting what I want to say into words. Things didn't go well for me, as you might have guessed. I hear things turned out, uh, differently for you, like I mean, ya know, things went, um, well, um, for you yesterday ..."

I start to get angry. My face gets hot as I slam down a tray. I glance at Paine. There is no way he can't tell my face is turning red.

"What are you getting at, Paine?"

"I heard you consummated your marriage."

"That's none of your business!" I yell at him loud enough for him to step back. I don't need Marabelle overhearing any of this conversation. It would completely embarrass her. She is very modest. Plus, I don't want her to see me act this way. From now on, I only want to show her the kindest, sweetest side of Sky.

I pick up the full tray of dishes and nudge him out of the way with a sharp corner. This move surprises Paine. He's hurt. He thought we could discuss anything. He believed friends could confide in each other.

As I walk away, he persists in questioning me.

"Wait, Sky. I'm sorry. Please stop. I'm sorry if I offended you."

His demands are ignored. I rush to the serving station with the clean dishes and stack them furiously.

"Sky, please," he urges on in a low voice. "Please tell me. What's it like?"

"That's private, Paine," I say loud enough to cause the bustling cafeteria to pause and watch our conversation.

Paine drops his eyes to the ground.

"I didn't mean to pry. Just that you, Marabelle, well—"

"Don't let another word come out of your mouth," I warn. Words and images swirl in his brain. Paine seeks several explanations from me. He doesn't understand how I suddenly like Marabelle enough to have a perfect match. Paine wonders why rumors of my alleged romantic evening have swept the community so quickly while he slept on the floor in a room with a weeping bride curled in a ball of the cot.

"Back off now. You and I aren't having this conversation, ever! In fact, I seriously doubt our friendship right now. Please leave. Get away from me. You and I are through. Don't ever approach me to talk ever again," I say firmly until Paine backs away from me and sullenly leaves, unable to reply.

In all of this commotion, he forgets to eat and must work light-headed and miserable. He is truly lucky I did not threaten to kill him after what he tried to do to us. Try working while starving with a death threat on your mind!

Anxious to dine with Marabelle during lunch, I brush off

this conversation. Many more unnecessary talks with mindless year mates will follow, no doubt, but I would hate to have bad vibes resonate because nothing else matters to me now that I have Marabelle.

Tip-39

Robotic. Mechanical. That's how Sky appears as I enter the main dining hall. Hollow. Blank. Plate after plate scraped clean and put in the machine. Not existent. Apathetic. He doesn't acknowledge anything around him. Water sprays the caked grit off pots and pans. We people around him float back and forth like ghosts, bothersome yet invisible.

My wife warned me to lay off him and not push him into eating with me. She tried to remind me what it was like being married and spending moments alone with a female for the first time. She implored me to understand that he'll want to be with Marabelle and get to know her better. I countered with the fact that I think Sky already knows Marabelle very well, although deep down inside, I know it's not true. Sky never spent his time with this particular girl. In fact, Marabelle was never mentioned in our home. This whole marriage came as a surprise to the entire community.

My curiosity about his choice of mates eats away at me on the inside. Out of the blue, Sky hits me with a name of a girl known to be maid-bound and expects me to believe she is his true love. This is a girl who almost died when she was young, has no friends her age, walks around the compound like a clumsy daydreamer, and my son, wanted by all female year mates, selects her as a perfect match? Even odder, my son is the one who cultivated relationships with the most beautiful girls in his year. My son is thought to be the most attractive, intelligent, and athletic teen on the compound. My son was supposed to be in love with the gorgeous Merry. So basically, from nowhere, he begs me to bid on this peculiar girl as his one and only choice for marriage.

"Why does it matter?" my wife begged me. "Leave your son alone to his own happiness," she said. But now does he look happy? From where I stand, Sky wears no expression at all. As I approach him, his eyes barely register my presence.

"Sky, how did Bidding Night go?"

"Fine."

"You must be happy. You got what you wanted."

"Yep."

"Want to sit and eat with your old man during your lunch break?"

"No."

"Really? I thought we could talk about, you know, things."

"Sorry. Too busy."

With every word, I lose him. I am having a hard time working out my feelings. A day ago, I had a little boy in school. My house included a son who slept at home. Three people lived together as one family. Nighttimes were for listening to my baby's breath as he slept safe and sound. Now I face eviction from my slab, back to a smaller studio in an older section reserved for empty nesters. My child has entered the workforce. For his hard work and growing pains, he receives an awkward bride and a twelve-hour workday. No cake. No gifts. No congratulations. No celebrations. No accolades. Not even a day of rest. So here he stands, back at work, eyes red from fatigue. I'm doing my best to reach out to him.

"You've got to eat some time, Sky. Come on, please!"

"I'm going to have to decline right now. I'm eating with Marabelle. We would like to be alone. Sorry."

Sky's mannerisms turn formal. He does the best he can to not offend me. I must admit I'm hurt. I'm not ready to give up on him. But I'll give him some space.

I retreat and go eat. From a distance, I spot Sky and his bride. They carry trays to the most secluded spot they can find in a busy cafeteria. As they eat, they smile. Their legs are turned toward each other, and their knees touch under the table. Their quiet talk includes hushed giggles as they mouth what must be intimate secrets into each other's ears. Unlike the majority of the newlywed Workers, they appear happy and rather enamored with each other. The correct reaction would be happiness and pride. I should be proud of my son and ecstatic to see him so in love. My honest reaction is jealousy, because, well, he was never this happy about family, friends, school, or anything in life, until now.

Merry-18

The luxury started as soon as I was bid to Antin. As Workers filed to their new slabs, Planners attended meetings filled with exotic treats. I never understood how different our lives were until I attended the first luncheon following the bidding process.

Yet somehow as I followed the small crowd of newly bid Planner females out of the holding pen, I didn't feel very festive. I'd just witnessed Sky's exaggerated performance during the bidding results where he climbed up on the furniture and danced for the stunned crowd of year mates. At that moment, my heart broke. Somewhere behind me, Sasha cried uncomfortably in disbelief that she and Cecile would soon be married. I'm willing to bet we'll have some hard feelings, because she'd had her hopes up for getting Antin.

As for me, it's not exactly like I am displeased with the results. Sky and I had many heart-to-hearts about the odds of us ending up together. Then, as bidding approached, we sort of grew apart. Plus, Antin treated me kindly whenever we encountered each other. The true origin of my pain stems from the perfect match.

The community gets very few perfect matches during bidding. In fact, perfect matches are so rare that no statistics exist on the matter, although openly discussing them is forbidden. A perfect match results when a boy only bids on one girl and that girl's name does not appear on anyone else's list. It is a perfect match because said boy only wants to be with one girl and risks his entire bid sheet on her, and no other boys requested that girl to be their wife. Thus there is no competition. Said boy wins, and the two end up together. Allegedly, since there is no negotiation, a perfect match can be honored first because it is the easiest. Organizing a perfect match is not only difficult, it is forbidden. No male or female is allowed to negotiate with each other or their fellow year mates to get the chance to wed using a perfect match. Secret setups are illegal. Plus, we are not to have relationships with each other or prearrange them for the future bidding either. But here we are processing the end results of our Bidding Day, and Sky not only got who he wanted, he got her first. He got his perfect match.

The excitement over Bidding Day rumors often lasts a month or longer. We occasionally get to hear about who we think bid on us and who didn't. My name ended up on several lists, I guess. Perhaps I should not be surprised. But I am most bothered by the talk about the perfect match. I think people intentionally say something about it in front of me to get a reaction and gauge how I feel. The truth is, I don't know how I feel. I do know I am hurt by it and don't really understand it. How did it happen? Why? I struggle with the idea of confronting one or both of them about it. When I see them together, it's like a kick to the teeth. I hold back my tears and try to act nonchalant so people don't point or gossip about me. But I would be a fool to think they aren't already talking about the entire fiasco behind my back.

Several Planner girls and I rest in leather cushion seats as maids paint our toes. Wedding preparations include many meetings and tons of pampering. Our official ceremony takes place in a month's time, so every aspect from head to toe must look perfect.

"I still can't believe we had a perfect match," says Greta, another Planner about to marry.

"I don't want to talk about it," I say. I feel tears welling up in my eyes.

"And to Marabelle. I thought she was maid-bound," Greta continues and then looks down at the maid massaging her feet and adds, "Sorry."

"Enough already. Every time someone brings it up, it feels like a slap in the face," I respond.

"What are you so grumpy about?" Sasha adds. She hurts too. Cecile is an idiot. "You are marrying Antin, the most sought-after Planner in our year."

How can I counter this comment? She's right, except Sky would really be the most sought-after boy in our year, period.

"You are going to have to face her ... soon," Sasha continues.

"Who?" I ask.

"Marabelle, duh! She mixes the best colors. No doubt they will schedule her to do makeup. She'll be serving us at the reception as well. Sky too. All year-mate Workers serve as wait-staff at the year-mate Planner wedding reception."

Sasha says this with such confidence. She's such a know-it-all. Maybe I should remind her she's lucky to remain a Planner. A couple of guys down, she would have ended up a Worker. At least I'll get to see Charm that night. I hear she's extremely miserable with her outcome too. It's not that I'm miserable. I like Antin. I'm confused. I can't wrap my mind around Sky's bid. Maybe it was a mistake. Maybe his paper said Merry and his dad read it wrong. Could his dad have been nervous and called out Marabelle instead? With these thoughts, there is hope that this perfect match was a perfect mistake.

Cecile-18

How can I explain how I am feeling? Confused? Betrayed? Is it common to go through this anxiety after bidding ends? Have the past yearlings felt similar? Did my father experience the same? Obviously, it is forbidden to discuss these matters with him. I only know one thing: someone here talked to him before I did. Someone said something to my dad about Marabelle which prevented me from listing her, and I think I know who.

Sky walks around ignoring me as he collects garbage from the bins in the main dining hall. Even though I loathe confrontation, I urge myself to talk to him anyway. I trusted Sky as my best friend. Now he has proven to be a backstabber.

"Sky, wait up," I call. He persists in ignoring me.

"Sky, I want to talk to you," I say again.

Sky stops suddenly and turns around, leaning in too close for comfort. He towers over me, looking down with his piercing blue eyes. He seems to be flexing his chest in order to intimidate me. I never noticed how lean and muscular he has become. I stand up to him. I refuse to be afraid.

"Ssssky, please. I just want to ask you something."

"What?" he asks in a seriously nasty voice.

"Why did you choose her? I'm starting to believe that you knew how I felt, and I'm really kind of hurt. I thought we were best friends."

"Did you ever say a kind word about her to me?"

"Well, no, but neither did you, um ..."

"Did you put Merry on your list?"

"Yes," I admit. "I didn't do it to hurt you. It's kind of fair game."

"Really? Fair game? So you can bid on Merry who you thought I liked, but I can't bid on Marabelle who I thought you hated?"

"No, I didn't hate her. You are twisting my words."

"Am I?"

"You had a perfect match, Sky. You had to have known. You saw me talk to her while we danced, the day you got hurt ... Sky, did you tell my dad? Did you tell him I liked Marabelle? He was very angry, and I didn't tell him. Was it you?"

"No. I've never talked to your dad in my life."

"Are you sure? Who could have done it?" I don't believe him. Sky is a liar.

"Maybe it was a little bird who did it," Sky barks. Then he turns and walks away. But before he gets too far, he turns back around and approaches me. He puts his face close to mine and says slowly and clearly, "Just so we understand each other, you need to stay far away from us! Especially her. Far, far, far away!"

With that, he leaves to resume his garbage collection.

My gut feels empty. If Sky didn't tattle, then who did? I consider Antin, but he hates Marabelle more than anyone in our year. It only makes sense that Sky did it. Now I'm stuck with Sasha, who hates me. During orientation, we were assured that most girls take bidding pretty hard. They need time to mourn their childhoods and make a resolve to start anew with a happy marriage. We were told most girls turn around their attitudes and become loving wives. I've known Sasha all of my life, and I don't think it is in her to love me and play the happy housekeeper. Then there's Marabelle. From a distance, I see her smile and hold hands with her new mate. I even hear rumors about their happy wedding night. At our meeting, we were told consummation does not always occur on the first night, but people love gossiping about Sky and his perfect match and his happy little love slab. I shake with rage. I really, really think he knew how much I cared for Marabelle, but he took her anyway, and I was forbidden to even bid on her name. Perhaps we are not best friends after all.

Merry-18

The dress hangs perfectly on my body. A white satin ribbon accentuates my waist. Tiny crystals and pearls cover the bodice. Pale embroidered roses decorate the full skirt which covers a large hoop slip underneath. I should feel honored to wear such a gorgeous wedding gown. I've seen Planner brides in the past. I never dreamed I would become one of them.

Sasha was right. Bowing down at the hemline sits Marabelle. She pins the bottom of the dress so I can walk down the aisle. When she finishes, she is supposed to do a trial run makeover and then deliver my dress to the head seamstress.

Marabelle does not utter a word. I do not enjoy this uncomfortable silence. I stand in a row with several other Planner brides-to-be. They chat away with their Workers, gossiping about their upcoming nuptials. I wonder how I find myself paired up with

Marabelle. She doesn't appear to be happy with this match either. As she weaves the pins in and out of the fabric, Marabelle pricks her finger.

"Ouch," she says to herself and sticks her finger into her mouth. She has very large lips like pink rose petals.

"Make sure you don't get any of that blood on my dress," I snap. Marabelle refrains from responding. Instead, she searches her kit for a thimble and slips it on her pricked finger.

Immediately after making this snotty remark, I'm mad, only at myself. I can imagine Marabelle running back to Sky after this session. One look at her finger will send him into some sort of kissing frenzy. I can see him trying to make her feel better, all the while making a public spectacle out of it—then perhaps chastise me for insulting his injured bride. These two have only been a couple for like two weeks, and they walk around like they are the only two people who exist on this compound. They run around hugging and kissing and displaying every forbidden act of affection they can think of without worrying about getting caught. They act like two little children on a summer day, completely disregarding anyone around them.

Tears well up in my eyes again. I can't stand not knowing why Sky chose Marabelle and not me.

"Marabelle, Marabelle," I say, but she won't look at me. Instead, she continues to work on my dress.

"Marabelle," I persist. "Marabelle, why? Why you? Why did Sky choose you?"

Finally, Marabelle looks up. Our eyes meet. Her lips part as if she has a response, but she doesn't answer. She goes back to working quietly.

"Please, Marabelle. I'm sorry. I don't mean to be rude. But seriously, you didn't have a prior relationship with him, and you know it. What was the connection? He wasn't even nice to you." I can't help myself. Words start pouring out of my mouth like tears.

Marabelle stands up with her color palette full of makeup.

"Look up," she says, instead of replying to my question.

She darkens my lashes with a sort of black paint specially made for eyes. I think it's called mascara. I feel her bony fingers brush against my face. Her hair smells like a mix of a floral bouquet and coconut milk. Her skin smells like cinnamon and vanilla beans. She wipes my cheeks with a brush covered in soft pink and colors my eyelids bright lavender. She lines my lips with a colorful pencil and shines them with a sparkly gloss.

"What do you think?" she asks when she finishes the job.

I turn and face the mirror. Marabelle does possess a certain talent for applying makeup. I've never looked more radiant than this moment. Antin will be knocked off his feet when he sees me on our special day. But I can't help wonder what Sky will think when he sees me this way as well. Will he regret keeping my name off his bid list?

Marabelle unzips the back of my dress and gently helps me out of it. She carefully places it in a garment bag to take to the seamstress. I listen to her soft breaths as she works. I imagine Sky stays up at night to listen to her sleep, enjoying her little breaths and kissing her funny little face. Fine, I'm still jealous. I can't seem to move on from Bidding Day. Maybe it is because I still have to wait for my own relationship to start. Here I'm thrust into this bizarre limbo while the man I love enjoys the company of this girl who stands in front of me, working as my aide. Perhaps by next month, he will be all but forgotten when I marry Antin.

Quickly, Marabelle packs her supply bag so she can make a fast getaway.

"Marabelle, please," I beg her, although I'm not sure what about. Marabelle probably does not have any answers. How would she know why Sky would pretend to hate her so much, spend so much time antagonizing her, and then sweep her off her feet and lead her into matrimony? Was it a trick—part of his master plan to reunite himself with me?

"Don't leave just yet, Marabelle. Talk to me. I need to know. I'm getting married soon. Why are you the one who got a perfect match?"

With shaky hands, Marabelle finally says, "I'll see you in two weeks on your Wedding Day. Make sure you have a clean face for your makeover."

And with that, she walks away, leaving me in my bustier and slip.

In the evening, Antin and I meet for a candlelit dinner for two. We don't need to eat in the main dining hall for dinner like the Workers. Planners have different options for meals.

He looks very handsome. His blond hair has grown out, and it's brushed a bit. He takes my hand and warmly kisses the top of it.

"You look gorgeous as usual," he greets me. "How do you like your apartment room? I secured the best view facing the lake. Our new house is being renovated. It will be ready in two weeks for our wedding night."

"It's just lovely. I'm not used to living by myself. I've spent my whole life in a slab with my parents."

"It's only temporary. You'll join me in a couple of weeks. I hope you're not too lonely."

"No, not at all. It's kind of nice spending time alone."

"I'll visit you more often, I swear. It's totally my fault that I haven't been around enough. I've been very busy finalizing all of the minute details. You wouldn't believe how much time it takes to create perfection. I'm having a garden designed for you. I'm including a birdbath fountain, a hummingbird house, and a strawberry patch."

"Wow, thank you so much. No one has ever gone out their way to do so much for me. I'm honored."

"Honored? That's nothing. You're my wife—to be, that is. I want your life, our life together, to be absolutely perfect. Merry, you are the most beautiful woman here."

"Antin, we are alone. I'm the only woman here." I giggle.

"Here, on the compound. Everyone agrees you are the most stunning woman alive. Merry, I love you, and I'm so happy we are bid together for life and marriage."

"I didn't realize how romantic you were, Antin." I blush.

"I got us something special." He holds up a small carafe of vin.

"Oh my! How did you get that?"

"We only have enough for two glasses. They say you shouldn't drink too much if you aren't used to it or you'll get sick."

"Who gave it to you?"

"Well, I know the person with the key. It's kept locked up because overindulgence on vin is forbidden. You know him too. It's Sky. He has the key to the cellar door."

I look down at my lap. I pick up my napkin and blot my lips like I am wiping off a crumb from our butter rolls. Does Antin suspect how I feel about Sky? Is he testing my reaction to this torment? Or is the vin a romantic gesture?

"To life," I say as I pick up my glass.

"To life, together," Antin responds and clinks my glass. He smiles and takes a sip. "Mmm, good."

By his reaction, I gather it was not a test. He wanted to make me happy. We enjoyed such a good connection over this last year that Antin has probably disregarded Sky as a passing phase.

"So what are we eating?" I ask.

Antin uncovers the plate and reveals two small birds covered in some kind of sauce.

"Quails in sesame seed sauce reduction, wild rice pilaf with almonds, and pickled radish."

"Yum, I've never even heard of this dish."

"It's quite a delicacy."

"I can't get used to this."

"Merry, you are a Planner now. Our lifestyle is not going away. You can breathe easy. Your working days are over. You're with me now, and you'll never have to worry about being a Worker again."

Antin-18

I've outdone myself again. Merry lapped up every bit of luxury I provided her and has not looked back one bit. Sky is clearly out of her mind. She didn't even flinch when I mentioned his name. I didn't even glimpse a flicker in her eye, especially when I presented her with two cups of vin.

Sky, on the other hand, was not too pleased when I procured the precious liquid from him. Apparently being one of the more trusted men on the compound, for some crazy reason, Sky was presented one of the few keys to the cellar. Planners like me are allowed to ask for vin for special occasions. Obviously, a romantic dinner with my future wife qualifies as special.

Last night, I went to his new slab after dark and peered through the window again. His wife was curled in a ball under a blanket as Sky slept protectively close to her. I pounded on the door and startled them both. Sky came to the door wearing only a pair of shorts.

"What do you want?" he sneered as he opened it a crack.

"I need you to open the cellar. I need some vin."

Sky rolled his eyes and sighed deeply.

"You need to get me some vin now. I need it for tomorrow," I reiterated.

Sky stood and stared at me for a moment.

"Come on now, Sky! Get your work clothes on, and get your key."

"Fine."

Marabelle peeked from under her thin sheet. Two large green eyes squinted at me from their small cot. She kept trying to focus her eyes. Her glasses are very thick. She probably recognized my voice, but I couldn't be sure. I wondered if she was naked or had some clothes on under there.

"Let's go!" Sky roared and slammed his hand hard against the door, knocking it back a bit.

"Watch it," I growled.

I followed him to the main dining hall, toward the back of the kitchen to a small wooden door. It looked like a narrow closet. Sky took a key from around his neck and unlocked the door. We went down a spiral staircase to a damp room filled with large oak barrels. Bottles lined metal shelves every which way, all labeled with different grape or fruit types and different years. Sky walked over to a metal spout and filled a small carafe with some grape vin.

"You can start with this," he said, handing it to me.

Then he held out his hand for me to leave the cellar and walked behind me. He locked the door back up without saying another word.

"She's mine, you know. Merry is mine, and there's nothing you can do about it now. I bet you thought it would turn out differently, but it didn't. In fact, I bet you knew I would get her first. Is that why you didn't even bid on her? You're just a loser, Sky. You always were, and you always will be. That's why you and your loser wife will always serve me. Just remember that on my wedding night when I have Merry all to myself. I'll be back later for more vin."

Then I spat on the floor, almost getting his shoe.

Sky looked at me in the eye, smiled, and walked away, leaving me in the dark kitchen with my carafe of vin.

Paine-18

"Don't you dare yell at me!" Charm shouts in anger.

"Hey, I thought we were friends!" I yell back.

"Yeah, we were. I didn't realize we would have to get married!"

"Be nice to me. I haven't done anything mean to you."

"Oh, really?"

"Excuse me. That's what we are supposed to do!"

"Don't you dare rush me. I'm getting used to having to wake up to your face every morning."

"Whatever. You make me sleep on the floor. Why can't you be more like Marabelle?"

"Don't you dare!" Charm screams even louder. "I can't believe you even went there. Never compare me to Marabelle, ever!"

"Hey, I heard Sky and Marabelle connected on *the very first night!*"

"I get it! Everyone heard that! It was impossible not to. We don't even live that close to them! You need earplugs to live in this part of the compound if you want to sleep at night!"

"You should be doing whatever it is that Marabelle does, and I should be acting like Sky."

"Oh, great, there you go again. I don't care how many times you've crept past their window lately. You can stay on the floor for now."

"I'm telling."

"Who are you going to tell? No one cares. No mandate has been issued for us to consummate our wedding. Some couples don't even try until they're ready to have a baby. So you stay far, far away from me!"

"Nice! Well, Charm, I don't even like you in that way, but I'm stuck here with you anyway. How many other lists do you think you even made it to? I bet you would have become a maid if it weren't for me. Cecile didn't want you! None of my other friends bid on you. Sky certainly didn't bid on you. So you should calm down and show me some gratitude."

This sets off Charm into a crying rage, but it's true. She was at the bottom of my list, and I can't say I know anyone else who wanted her. I was just being nice. I didn't think I would actually have to marry her. How strange is it for Sky to have a perfect match with a girl that in eighteen years he never indicated that he liked even as a friend? Even odder, she is the same girl who seemed to have endured Sky's most devious torments. And now she showers him with constant affection. But here I sit in my new home with a lifelong friend, fighting with her and sleeping on the floor. Why do I suffer while Sky basks in marital bliss?

"I'm sorry, Charm. Please don't cry. We seem to be under a lot of pressure. You are right. We don't have to be like ... them. Can we start again? I'll take it slow. I want us to be friends again, like we were at school."

Charm calms down, sniffles a bit, and wipes a bit of snot from her nose.

"Okkkay." Her voice shakes a bit as she talks. "Maybe I'll let you share the bed tonight."

I smile, and we both crack up.

"Thanks, I'll take it!"

Skyler-18

I'm really starting to notice things about Marabelle that are similar to my own characteristics. Really, I swear! I can't say how seriously exciting this is. These are minute things really, barely noticeable by any person on this compound. In fact, if I didn't pay close attention myself, I would have missed them. But I do pay attention. I pay attention to everything she does. I watch her every move. I hope she doesn't mind. I wonder if she even knows.

Anyway, for one thing, Marabelle appears to possess acute hearing. Her inability to see well may have something to do with it. As we lie in bed at night, it's easy to hear the obvious noises—for example, people walking back and forth on the pathways around the slabs. But the less obvious sounds—like a wild animal in the distant woods or a baby crying from a separate population of housing or a bird soaring high in the trees—are the ones Marabelle registers in her ears at night.

I've seen her react on several different occasions. A baby will cry from far away, and her eyes will flutter open. I see her awaken in the darkness.

"Go back to bed," I'll whisper and stroke her face to calm her back to sleep.

Other times, raccoons will fight and screech late into the night in a distant wood. This causes Marabelle to shiver and hide under her little blanket.

"Don't be afraid. I'm here with you." I lift the covers and reassure her of her safety with me.

"I know," she'll say.

"Are you afraid?"

"No, I just don't like to hear the fighting. It bothers me." Then with a kiss, she'll drift off to sleep once more.

I'll take my hand and smooth out her long hair until her body relaxes and her breathing grows steady.

Crazy enough, once Marabelle rests peacefully, I talk to her. I confess my love to hear and beg for forgiveness. Occasionally, she will actually hear me and respond in her sleep.

"You don't have to apologize. Really, it's okay."

"No, it's not. I vow for the rest of my life to make up for any cruelty I have inflicted on you."

Sometimes she squeezes my hand as her eyes roll to the back of her head. Once, she told me, "No matter what happens, I love you the most."

Planner Wedding Day, May 1

Merry-18

My hands shake from my nerves. Walking around on an empty stomach doesn't help calm me down. In fact, the nausea makes my head spin a bit. The other Planner girls and I get dressed and prepare to walk down the aisle. Sasha struts around in her stunning

gown, flashing rehearsed smiles into a mirror. She chats happily about her plans after marriage while avoiding conversation about who she'll be married to.

Marabelle helps me into my gown. It fits perfectly and just barely hits the floor, the perfect length to sweep the ground without dirtying it while I walk or dance. She covers my shoulders with a plastic sheet and applies my makeup.

As I stand here in my dress, I feel so alone. The two of us barely acknowledge each other. Marabelle keeps her eyes averted and avoids my gaze. I do wonder if she is silent because she is actually concentrating on doing a good job or if she is trying to avoid another confrontation. The other girls insist Marabelle's colors are the best they have ever seen as they chat away with their own assistants.

Out of the corner of my eye, I spot Sky. My heart thumps inside my chest. I blush at the fact that he sees me in my wedding gown. He sports a black suit with a white shirt. He is one of the waiters, but he could pass for one of the grooms. He doesn't appear to notice me. Instead, he peeks his head in the door and makes googly eyes and silly faces at Marabelle. She laughs. I don't remember him being so immature. He continues his antics by making silly sounds and saying weirdo stuff. Marabelle giggles until tears drip down her chin. Finally, a maid walks by and chases him away. When he's gone, all eyes land on me. Greta and Sasha wait for my reaction. I stand paralyzed. He didn't even say hi to me or congratulate me.

"I'm starving! I haven't had a thing to eat. I can't wait until tomorrow when I don't have to wear this tight dress. Then I can stuff my face," I say.

This seems to break the ice, and the other girls laugh. They haven't eaten either.

"I haven't eaten a full meal in a month," Greta confesses. "I didn't want to look fat on my wedding night."

We all agree we haven't taken advantage of the Planner feasts they've offered since Bidding Day.

Marabelle stops applying my makeup and packs her bag. She leaves without saying a word. Like Sky, she wears a waitress outfit, only with a black skirt instead of pants. As she goes, it's obvious her skirt does not fit that well. Because Marabelle has such a small waist and a curvy backside, her shirt untucks at the bottom, and her skirt gapes open at the top.

"Someone needs to lose weight," Sasha says, too loud, as usual.

The others snicker. I do not. I turn to the mirror and check out my own body. My body looks like a rail compared to hers. I'm so lean that my top goes straight down to my flat bottom. Is that what Sky wanted, curves? Did he prefer a brunette instead of a blonde? Did he want someone short and not too tall? Was he attracted to everything I wasn't this whole time?

I lift my eyes to the mirror and stare at my face. I'm amazed. I touch my cheek to make sure it's me I'm looking at. I don't even recognize myself. Marabelle worked some kind of magic. I've never felt this beautiful before.

"Merry, you look gorgeous," Greta gasps.

"Why didn't I get Marabelle?" Sasha snaps.

"Antin won't even recognize me. I'm going to knock him off his feet."

"Calm down, girl. Save that for tonight," Sasha says and then laughs at her own cleverness.

I'm dying to remind her that she will have to face Cecile tonight, and I'm willing to bet she would be very upset if I did it in front of the other girls. A girl fight is not worth the trouble on Wedding Day.

"Ten minutes," a maid says, popping her face in the room before rushing out.

Seven girls dressed in white line up on the white lace runner. Seven white dresses sparkle under the candlelit pathway. Seven veils blow softly as the wind cools the spring air. Fourteen high heels wobble under seven girls who rarely get a chance to wear anything other than school flats. Hundreds of eyes witness the slow yet steady march of seven new brides. I head up the line as the ceremony starts.

The pool area has been transformed into an elegant stage. In the darkness, candles light up hundreds of floral arrangements. Tea candles float inside lily pads in the pool. The community sits in a semicircular pattern as the brides walk to the new grooms. Violin music plays in the background. My parents smile and cry as I pass them. Antin waits for me at the end of the runner. As I reach Antin, he takes my hand.

"Wow," he says, inaudible to the crowd, "you look beautiful."

"Thank you," I mouth back to him.

Once each girl arrives and stands next to her mate, the ceremony begins. An elder Planner steps forward.

"A gift has been bestowed upon you. As the Planners of the community, you must care deeply for the responsibility to maintain the balance. All must be fair and equal. Keep prosperity, and eliminate what is forbidden. In front of us all, you now take the vow to love, honor, and work every day of your lives here on out to protect us, plan what is right, and forever love your community. If you accept, then say, 'I do.'"

In unison, we all say, "I do."

"Congratulations, new Planners. We welcome you."

The crowd cheers, and the seven couples walk together down the aisle, hand in hand, to the grand ballroom.

As we enter the ballroom, I stand in awe. The enchanted room resembles a winter wonderland. Real icicles decorate fir trees. Grand tables covered in food wrap around each tree. Smaller tables circle around a dance floor as a band plays. Planners attend the meal, and our year mates work as waiters and waitresses so they can enjoy the Wedding Day and congratulate us. The rest of the community eats in the main dining room. Occasionally, leftover food is delivered from the wedding in courses, or sometimes the leftovers are served the following day for lunch.

"Congratulations." Charm practically slams into me with her tray of sugar-covered fruit. "You look so beautiful. I can't believe you are finally married! How do you feel?"

"Great, Charm, thanks. How are you? We never get to see each other anymore."

"I know. I work a lot, but we can still try to get together when my shifts are done."

"Sure. I'd love that. How is marriage for you?"

"Fine," Charm replies slowly. "It's coming along slowly. We have a lot of adjustments to make. Well, we just need to sort of get used to each other."

"What? We were all besties!"

"I know, I know. Don't worry. With Antin, you won't have any of the problems I've got with Paine. Antin is the dreamiest! How did you get so lucky?"

I immediately think about Sky. I haven't seen him since this morning. I couldn't find him as I walked down the aisle, and I haven't seen him since I entered the ballroom. I try to erase him from my thoughts and concentrate on Antin.

"Not sure. I guess it worked out that way for me."

"Anyway, Merry, I gotta go circulate with the fruit. So nice seeing you."

"Bye," I say.

Most of the night, I rest by Antin's side and diplomatically greet Planners who welcome and congratulate me. Antin relishes in all of the attention. He grabs my hand from time to time and squeezes it warmly or kisses me gently on the cheek. I finally relax and give in to my new marital bliss.

Suddenly, I spot him by the cake. Sky sets out fresh slices of white cake covered in ivory frosting. Again, I resolve to remove him from my mind. Antin is my husband. He deserves all of my attention and respect. Sky should not exist in my new life. Anyway, he made his choice perfectly clear with his perfect match.

Antin chats with an elder Planner. I grab his hand.

"Let's dance."

"Gladly," he says. "Excuse me, please," he tells the elder.

As we twirl across the dance floor, I imagine I'm a fairy-tale princess. This is the best night of my life.

Skyler-18

Grabbing Marabelle and kissing her gives me the greatest pleasure in life. Chills run up and down my spine every time we touch. My nerves recharge with passionate electricity. I've never been so happy, ever. For some reason, watching the Planners marry reminds me of my own Wedding Day. I experienced my personal triumph in winning Marabelle as my wife. I think I might have even shed a tear during tonight's ceremony. Now, here in the kitchen, Marabelle walks in as I cut the enormous wedding cake into palatable squares. We embrace and kiss intimately but momentarily. Public displays of affection are still forbidden, so I steal moments with her lips when I can.

As I divide the cake into hundreds of pieces, I pull two slices to the side.

"We can take these pieces for later. I want to celebrate our own nuptials."

"Is that allowed?"

"Don't worry, Marabelle. We won't get into trouble. I promise. I'll set them aside and take them home for us to eat later."

"Are you sure?"

"Yes. Dance with me."

I pull Marabelle close and glide in a box step. She trips a bit and steps on my toes. Then I kiss her forehead.

"Tonight, we can celebrate ourselves and make a toast to our own marriage," I tell her.

Marabelle smiles and leaves to bus tables.

I relax and bask in my happiness. This must be how a newborn experiences life. Everything looks so bright and fresh.

The white cake glitters with crunchy sprinkles. I wrap a couple pieces in a napkin for later tonight. The Planners rejoice now, but my celebration takes place at home with my own bride.

I take a full tray of cake and push open the door, high on life. I consider getting us some vin since I have a key. Marabelle gets tipsy easily, but that might make our evening even more interesting. But alas, I decide on a sober night together. I'll surprise her with some vin later.

Planners gorge themselves on food and drink. My belly growls with hunger. Working tonight means I skipped my dinner. Marabelle might be equally hungry. I decide to wait for our shift to end to eat together. Being smaller, she doesn't eat as much as I do. I glance at my tightly cinched belt. My pants are getting looser and looser as I work longer and harder. Over this past month, Antin's pants have tightened. I see it in his fat belly. Less activity and more food work against his waistline. I sure hope Merry enjoys his flabby stomach tonight. She'll surely get a nice surprise seeing this man sans clothing in a few hours.

Merry sees me as I set out the dessert. She yearns to talk to me. I ignore her and clear my mind. I put Marabelle first now. Close by, I smell a hint of ginger and lemon. Marabelle must be nearby. She has mixed a nice spicy oil and applied it this morning. She also applied a bit of lip gloss that has since been kissed and licked off her face. That strawberry stuff drives me crazy and barely lasts once she applies it to her lips.

Poor Cecile sulks in a corner as Sasha works a nearby crowd. She lingers in her denial. Paine collects dishes, and Charm fills glasses with fresh ice water.

We are all here tonight, all 113 of us year mates. We have become Planners, Workers, and maids. Some of us celebrate; the rest of us work the party. I don't mind. I have what I want. The rest doesn't matter.

As the event winds down, the newlyweds feel the pressure to perform tonight, as consummation is definitely expected. I grow excited to eat my cake and feed Marabelle hers. She searches the crowd for me. Butterflies swarm my stomach. I hold out my hand as my best mate grabs my fingers. I kiss her cheek, and we head home. Fatigued, we both know our next day's work starts earlier than necessary, but we both look forward to that sweet sensation of fondant melting on our tongues. I'm like a little kid again, free to enjoy something sugary like Marabelle's company and a slice of gâteau.

My hands cover Marabelle's eyes. We walk in unison, my body touching hers from behind. The moon lights a path for me. I love it when the moon glows so bright that it outshines the sun. I breathe easier at night.

"Where are you taking me?" Marabelle giggles.

"It's a surprise. You'll see."

"How much longer till we get there?"

"Not too much farther."

"Well, it's taking a real long time."

"Patience, my love."

We stop at the water's edge. The lake appears black during the night.

"Ta-da!"

I remove my hands from Marabelle's eyes to reveal a small, wooden rowboat and a couple of oars.

"It's a boat. I made it for you," I say.

"You did? All by yourself?"

"For us, yes. It was nothing, really. I gathered the planks from time to time.

Working at the factory has its perks. It floats and everything."

"What are we going to do with it?"

"What do you mean, silly? We are going to row in it."

"Yes, but where are we going to go?"

"Now that is the real surprise. Get in."

We carefully board the boat. It wobbles, so I hold it steady for Marabelle.

"Don't worry," I assure her. "It won't capsize, I promise."

Under the moon, I row us farther and farther from land. No speakers sound off as we disappear into the night. I already tested that theory. I figure they don't worry about anyone leaving by boat because no one owns a vessel big enough to see if there is land on the other side.

We drift into the deep, too far to swim back to the mainland. A layer of fog surrounds our boat. Finally, we reach a tree-covered sandbar.

"Voila, Madame. We are here!"

Marabelle's eyes widen.

"Wow, what is this place?"

"It's called Apple Island—our enchanted spot for two, totally forbidden, totally for us."

I jump into the water and tow us to the beach.

"Look," I tell Marabelle, "I made us a picnic."

I lead her to a blanket. On it, I had organized two sandwiches, some grapes, a couple gold-wrapped chocolates, and two cups of vin.

Marabelle claps her hands and throws her arms around my neck and hugs me. We skip to the blanket and dig in, feeding each other the grapes and chocolates. After her cup of vin, Marabelle giggles even more and slurs her words.

"Thisssss is the nicest thing anyone has even done for me." She cries real tears.

"That's not all. I thought we could dance together tonight as well."

"Okay, but there is no music," Marabelle says but gets up anyway.

"No problem. I can take care of that."

I clap my hands together and command the birds to start singing.

"Amazing!" Marabelle cries as we dance like crazy together. Then we fall laughing onto the blanket. I roll over and look Marabelle in the eyes.

"I love you. This is the best day I've ever had too."

"Let's promise to come back here again sometime."

We hold each other and let the breeze blow around us, snuggling and kissing. When we return, I hide my small boat under some vines near a large tree on the beach. Typically, no one goes near the twisted bramble. The community rowing shed has a supply of boats and canoes, so who would even want my makeshift craft? So I don't worry about it being used by others.

Sleepily, we walk home to our slab. Sure it is small—we have so little—but I wouldn't want it any other way.

After a while, I forget what started this bickering between us.

"Why can't you just do it without asking so many questions, Marabelle?"

"Why do you always just expect people to do what you say without explanation? Is it because no one has ever questioned you? I am not that person! I don't just mindlessly do something without questioning it first!" Marabelle challenges.

"Fine!"

"Good! Is this what you really want? Then fine! I'll go along. But you need to recognize I clearly have a major problem with your authority!" Marabelle quotes her fingers around the word "authority."

"Great. I win? You don't have to do what I want just because I put up a stink! And what 'authority'? I'm not anyone's 'authority'!" I mimic her gesture using the same air quotations.

"Well, it certainly seems that you are used to getting whatever you want out of people, so you win."

"What authority, Marabelle? I'm not your authority. We are the same."

"Really, we are the same? Think, Sky, just think for a moment."

"What do you mean? Is it because you came from a *W* and I'm now an *S*? If so, I don't think that is so many steps closer to being a Planner."

"No, that's not what I mean. Never mind."

"Why are you making this so difficult? I don't even remember why we are fighting! But we are. We are fighting. I can't remember what started it, but here we are, our first fight. I love it!"

I pick Marabelle up under her arms and swing her in the air in a circle like a little kid.

"We're fighting! I'm so happy!" I scream. "You can fight with me anytime you like. You win. Do what you like. Don't listen to me."

I slow down, and we topple to the ground. I roll onto her, hugging her.

"It's so charming how you don't give in so easily. *I love this girl!*" I shout.

Then I cover her face in kisses and grab her face to tell her, "Don't ever leave me. Don't ever change. I like you for you." I turn this incident into a goopy love moment.

I didn't realize how much passion and emotion Marabelle would spark in me.

Merry-18

The sound of two people yelling echoes over a grassy hill and reaches the walkway where Sasha and I stand. At first I don't recognize the voices, but they sound angry. Then it hits me. Sky and Marabelle are fighting with each other somewhere close by.

"Let's take a peek and go listen," Sasha suggests.

"All right," I say, a bit hesitant. Part of me wants to relish in their disagreement, and part of me wants to forget Sky and put my mind at ease.

"What do you think it's about?"

"I'm not sure, but they both seem really mad."

"Good. That will make you grateful that you're not on the receiving end of that conversation. You and Antin seem to get along well."

"We do, but I don't think we are immune. We might occasionally disagree about something."

"Well, I'm stuck with Cecile. That's fine since I just have him running around like a cow with his head cut off doing stuff for me."

"Chicken."

"What?"

"It's chicken. The expression is 'Running around like a chicken with its head cut off.'"

"Whatever. Let's listen some more."

The fight continues and gets louder and louder. They really go at it.

Then Sasha says, "You know what they say: passionate breakup makes a passionate makeup."

"That does not make me feel any better, Sasha."

From the hills, we hear, "I love this girl!"

"See?" says Sasha as she turns to me to prove her point.

"Great, thanks, Sasha. What a pal. Let's get out of here." Now I will be moody the rest of the afternoon because of her.

Skyer-18

As Marabelle sleeps, I replay the day's events. I try to analyze what Marabelle said. She commented that we are not the same. I need to think about it. I turn her words around and around in my mind. I don't get what she means. I told her I want to be the same. She said we can't. I insisted that we were the same and we always would be. She refuted that we really weren't the same and never could be. I demonstrated that we were both Workers and not Planners, but I was fine with it as long as she was as well. So Marabelle patted my hand and reassured me it was okay. She knows what she is, and she's fine with it.

I'm so confused. Why aren't we the same? Why can't we be the same? Marabelle urged me to forget about it for now, especially since I seem so happy with the status quo. Afterward, Marabelle spent the evening trying to soothe me with her odd magic which, until now, worked. I've seemed to snap out of it. I yearn to wake her and get another dose of her sorcery.

I don't have the heart to disturb her. So I am stuck here thinking to myself and unwinding our argument from this afternoon. I still struggle to recall what started it or what it was I wanted her to do. I wrapped us up into the fact that she refused. So I guess she was right—people don't really refuse me, just her. Does that make sense? Could that even be right? Does everyone do what I say?

Staring at Marabelle, I bend down to smell her pretty hair, and a chill runs up my spine. My mind whirls with crazy thoughts I've never encountered before. I suddenly want a baby with her. But this is not a normal thought. I feel this intense and immediate urge that I can't stop or control. Having children without permission is not only forbidden, it is impossible. My hands shake. I'm nauseous and dizzy. I want to vomit.

"Marabelle, help me."

I sit up. She hugs me as her eyes flutter.

"What's the matter?"

As she grabs on to me, it stops. My sickness dissolves. Her touch cures me again.

"Nothing, sorry. Go back to sleep. I must have had a nightmare." I breathe in some air as my chest shakes.

"You sure?"

"Yeah."

She pats my back and falls back to sleep. I begin to think Marabelle and I have some sort of strong connection dating back from when we were little. I try to make a note in the back of my mind to talk about it later.

Cecile-18

Where exactly do I fit in around here? I ask myself that question daily as I run errands for Sasha's unending quest for perfection, although, to be honest, I'm not sure what she is perfecting. I think she sends me away to get rid of me. The Planners don't mind because they aren't exactly sure where to place me either. I am without purpose. I lack direction.

After picking up pastries from the kitchen, I stroll around the lobby of the main dining area. In the late afternoon, it appears empty. The lobby leads to a large set of stairs that takes you outside. Inside the lobby sits an old piano, slightly out of tune yet still functional. I sweep the dust off the bench and sit down. I plunk away at the keys and play a simple tune.

Marabelle walks nearby, scrubbing the floor with a mop. She wears a badly ripped shirt and very worn pants. Seeing that tugs at my heart. I feel horrible looking at her clothes. For some reason, I blame myself. I yearn to befriend her because I've always liked her company.

"Hey, Marabelle," I call. "Look what I can do."

She turns and smiles, puts down her mop, and comes over to visit me.

"I've had some time to pick this up," I tell her as I softly tickle the keys.

"Can you play a song?"

"Sure." I bang out a common nursery rhyme. As I play, Marabelle starts to sing. We both look at each other and laugh. I join her and help finish the song. So that our session doesn't end, I quickly turn out another song, and we continue harmonizing our words.

"I didn't know you could play so well, Cecile."

"I didn't know you had such a beautiful voice, Marabelle."

Three, four tunes go by, and I am at ease in Marabelle's presence. I pound harder and harder on the ivory as our voices get louder and more enthusiastic. Out of the blue, I grab Marabelle's hands and swing her arms, dancing and twirling with her as we pant in a fit of laughter.

"This is too much fun," I say, out of breath.

"We can hang out and sing again."

"Really?"

"Sure. Why not? Singing isn't forbidden, is it?"

"No."

"Okay, great. See ya." Marabelle pats me awkwardly on the shoulder, gets her mop, and resumes her chore.

Our encounter ends on a high note so to speak, I think, chortling to myself.

"Bye." I wave, pick up my box of pastries, and jog down the steps back to my home.

"Cecile." A voice comes out of nowhere.

"Huh?" I almost slam into someone.

I look up. It's a younger kid, Asher.

"Asher, sorry, you scared me. I guess I was so deep in thought that I wasn't paying attention. You see, I was playing that piano in the—"

"Cecile, stop talking. Listen to me. There are a lot of dangerous people on this compound. You need to really be careful."

"Okay, sure. Thanks for the warning."

"Cecile, really, I'm serious. Please listen to me. I'm not making this up, and I'm not exaggerating either. Danger exists here, and it's only going to get worse. You need to watch yourself. Unfortunately, in your situation, it's going to be really hard, but just … um … be safe. Don't trust anyone."

"Okay, er … can you be more specific?"

"No, not really, but I would stay away from Marabelle."

"Why? We are year mates. We're friends."

"She's married, and so are you. Relationships outside of marriage are forbidden."

"I know that! We aren't having a relationship. Besides, her husband is my best friend."

"Still?"

"Asher, why are we talking about this? I thought Marabelle was your friend!"

"She is. I'm trying to protect her too."

"Then go talk to her about it. I don't need protecting. You are still a little kid. Maybe you need protecting."

"Do I look like I do?" he asks.

I study Asher for a moment. He is no longer a little kid. He's a teenage boy, almost taller than I and still growing.

"No."

"I'll talk to Marabelle, then. She's on your side, but you need to stay away. Give your own wife some attention instead."

"Ah, wait. Never mind! Please don't. Don't talk to Marabelle about me. I won't bother her, but I can't stand her thinking badly about me. I would rather not lose another friend over a few songs."

"Fine," Asher responds and walks away.

My hands tingle where Marabelle and I touched, not in a bad way, but in a fizzy, sort of ticklish way—perhaps a souvenir from a girl I waited so long to touch. Last time we danced was when Sky fell ill. It was long overdue for us to have this chance again. As for Asher, what a whack job. I have no idea what he is talking about. I sadly retreat home for more nagging and complaining from my wife.

Antin-18

From a distance, they carry baskets of fruit from the orchard. I recognize Marabelle from behind. Her ripped work shorts reveal her curvy assets. Her walk mesmerizes me. She jokes with the person accompanying her. It's not Sky. Although he is tall, he has lighter brown hair than Sky and is pretty lean and not as muscular.

The two Workers laugh, chat, and tease each other.

"Stop," I hear Marabelle say, laughing and punching the male Worker in the arm.

The male continues to taunt her playfully.

"Marabelle," I decide to call.

All at once, the two Workers stop, and their bodies stiffen. They both turn and reveal polite smiles. I immediately recognize the other Worker's face. It's One, a younger kid who is not so young anymore.

I walk over to where they have stopped frozen in their tracks, waiting to hear what I want from them.

"Hi, Marabelle. How are you?"

"Hi. Fine."

"You look really good today."

"Thank you," Marabelle responds as she nervously peers over at One.

"I have a favor to ask you."

"Okay," she says.

One puts an overprotective hand to block her a bit for some odd reason. She mouths to him that it's okay.

"It's okay, One. You worry too much. I'm not going to hurt her. Marabelle and I are old friends. Isn't that right? I put in a request to have some rooms in my home painted. Obviously, Marabelle, your color-mixing talent makes you my top choice to aid my decisions. So I was wondering if you could come over my home tonight after dinner and look over some color swatches."

As we chat, a cold rush of air gusts through the warm summer day. The tall trees around us sway, and the leaves rustle like noisy maracas filled with dried-out beans.

The two Workers' eyes meet.

Marabelle answers hesitantly, "Okay. I'll come by and help you."

A blast of air whips past us, blowing Marabelle's hair in disarray, knocking several pieces of fruit out of their baskets onto the ground, forcing the two to put down their loads. They scatter around trying to pick up the fruit, chasing a few pieces around before they can retrieve all of the oranges.

I disregard the odd weather and watch them scramble.

"Great. See you later." I pick up an orange for later and take my leave.

The blue sky turns dark, and raindrops pelt my dress shirt. I hurry back to prepare for tonight.

Cecile-18

The wind whips around me. I struggle to hold on to my umbrella. I can't remember a summer rainstorm ever being like this. Sasha was well aware of the weather condition when she sent me out to get some ice cream from the market tonight. She emphasized it really could not wait until tomorrow. How could I argue with her? Knowing Sasha, she'll take one bite and either find fault in the flavor or insist she is not hungry anymore. Then she'll complain how difficult I am and what a burden it is to be married to me. I guess I'd rather hang out in the rain with my clothes soaked through than listen to Sasha whine at home.

Out of nowhere, something rushes against me, smashes into my body, and knocks me to the ground. The cold rain numbs my skin. I ache and tingle simultaneously. My head spins. I feel two hands pat my shoulders. I hear a voice and slowly open my eyes which blur in the rain.

"Cecile, are you all right?"

It's Marabelle. We rest on the ground together, her legs covered in grass and mud. Beside us lies a tree branch that resembles more of a log or a tree trunk than a stick.

"Yeah, I'm fine. What happened?"

"You were walking and not paying attention. You almost got hit, so I pushed you out of the way."

"Hit by what?"

She points at the dead wood.

"The wind must have picked it up. It almost knocked you in the head. You could have been really hurt."

"You saved me," I say weakly.

My bones ache from our collision, but I imagine a tree trunk to the head would have been much worse.

"What are you doing out on a night like this, walking around in the rain?"

"I could ask you the same question."

"Go home, Cecile. Go home to your wife, light a fire, stay in for the evening."

With that, Marabelle gets up and leaves.

"Wait," I call for her, but it is too late. She's already walked away, and my voice is inaudible in the wind.

Antin-18

With my parlor straightened up a bit, I set out the paint samples and some desserts. I glance in the mirror to fix my tie and make sure my hair is not out of place.

I jump as I hear a knock at the door and run to get Marabelle. As I open the door, I see Marabelle is soaked to the bone. Her work clothes stick to her body like a bathing suit fresh from the pool. Even in her wet condition, she smells sensual from vanilla-and-orange perfume.

"You look lovely, Marabelle," I stammer.

She gives me an odd look.

"I'll get you a fresh, clean towel to dry off with," I offer.

I run to a linen closet and retrieve a thick, white towel. I bet she's never seen a cloth this lush before.

She pats herself down a bit, wraps the towel around her body, and tucks it in under an arm.

"Please sit."

I lead her to a leather couch. Silently, Marabelle sits and waits for me to say something.

"Chocolate pastry, Marabelle?"

I hold up a tray of goodies under her nose to entice her. Her mouth drops open slightly, but she still remains silent.

"It's okay. You can take one. I got them for you. I know how much you enjoy sweet treats. It's not all business here. Relax a bit."

Reluctantly, Marabelle finally decides to take a minicake covered in chocolate ganache and takes a bite.

"Thanks," she says, breaking her silence.

I put the tray down and watch her eat.

"Enjoy," I say and smile.

The rain pelts harder and harder against the window outside. Marabelle shifts in her seat nervously.

"Did you have some paint samples you wanted me to look at? What are some ideas you have for your room?" Marabelle asks. Crumbs fly everywhere. She reaches for a napkin and tries desperately to contain her little mess. She wipes away at her fingers and sweeps the cake bits into her hand. Her cheeks redden a bit. It makes her entire face glow. Wow, she's beautiful.

"Later. We have time. Let's catch up together. It seems like we haven't had a chance to talk in such a long time." I inch a little closer to her. I try to put her at ease so she isn't embarrassed by her sugarcoated clutter.

"Um, okay, what do you want to talk about?"

The pace of the rain increases and turns to hail clinking against the glass. The wind howls and whistles. The windows shake furiously.

"You," I reply. "I want to talk about you, Marabelle."

As I start my conversation with her, a large chunk of ice smashes through a nearby window, shattering glass all over the floor.

"Oh my," Marabelle stammers, and she leaps off the couch. Grabbing a sheet of paper towel from under the samovar, she rushes to the floor and starts to sweep up the glass.

"No!" I shout. "You don't need to do that, Marabelle. I'll call a maid."

"Ouch." She stops.

Blood trickles down her finger. She sticks it in her mouth to suck off the blood. That's when I hear banging on the front door. It's more like thrashing, like someone's trying to kick it down.

"Let me in!" screams an angry voice.

I run to the door and open it a crack, revealing a very angry Sky.

"Where is she?" he roars. "Where is Marabelle? What business do you have calling her to your home late at night?"

His hair drips wet. He hulks over me in a beastly manner.

"What a temper you still have, Sky. It's strictly business, as you said, I assure you. I simply need help painting a few rooms in my house and seek your wife's assistance. She is known, after all, for her eye for color. Is she not?"

He pushes the door open wide and shoves me out of his way, running toward his wife.

"Marabelle." He grabs her by her arms, inspecting her hand and holding it to his chest. "Are you okay?"

She mumbles something to him.

In a typical manner, Merry wanders into the middle of the scene. Her eyes widen as she sees Sky standing in our parlor.

"Sky," she says in a delighted voice. "What are you doing here?"

Sky's eyes darken as he ignores her. Now I see. His true feelings for Merry become apparent—disdain. He turns away from me.

"You stay away from my wife. She is forbidden to come here after any approved working hours. You have no right to call her to your home."

Sky pulls Marabelle by the arm and takes her back out into the storm, slamming the door as they retreat into the night.

"What happened here?" Merry questions, looking at the broken glass with a small pool of blood.

"Nothing, dear. Don't worry about it. I'll call someone to clean it up. Don't touch the glass. I would rather you not cut yourself as well."

"Why was Sky here? Why was Marabelle here tonight? What's this food for? You didn't tell me we were having company."

"Company? Don't be silly, Merry. They are not company. Why would we ever socialize with a lowly Worker couple?"

"But what's the food for? You would have had to order that in advance."

"That food? That was for Marabelle. I've hired her to do some painting for us. You can't let a Worker go hungry, can you? She skipped dinner to be here, darling. How can you expect a woman to work and not eat? You don't want a Worker to faint in your home! Come, my love. Let's go to bed and talk about what color walls you would like tomorrow."

"Sure, Antin. I guess. But when did you decide to paint the walls? I thought we just had them redone before we moved in."

"We did, sweetie, but they didn't do a good job. We'll talk about this later."

I usher her into our bedroom, thinking about Marabelle.

Skyler-18

This has to be the happiest, most enjoyable summer of my life. Work often lasts several hours past most people's on the compound, but I don't mind. Marabelle and I skip dinner at the main dining hall and meet at the water's edge under the moon at least once a week. I try to pack ample food for us to have a picnic on our private island. For Marabelle, I take crusty-bread sandwiches, pickles, olives, salad, and dessert. I don't care what I eat as long as she's at my side. After our meal, we spend the evening laughing and dancing. This is the best way for Marabelle to get to know the real me, free from other people, negative exchanges, or other forms of influence that would otherwise turn her off me.

In my mind, I constantly plan the "what's next." It's only been a few months since we married, and you can't fit a lifetime of experience into a few evenings, but I'll surely try. Perhaps Marabelle might like a free day to walk around the zoo or the museum. They haven't scheduled a movie in a while. She might enjoy sitting near me in the theatre eating treats. Or we could find a butterfly garden together and have some laughs trying to chase them and having them land on us. My head swirls with ideas.

Antin-18

Sky, the person he is to this community, the position he holds on the compound or lack thereof, he, Sky, cannot and will not tell me what to do or prevent me from using his wife's services ever, ever again. I hold the real power here. I'm the man being groomed to become one of the top, leading Planners. Sky sits at the bottom of the alphabet as far as importance and influence. He cannot best me at anything ever again either. I will, someday, force him to recognize my authority over his. I am going to show him that I can take what I want when I want it, and he won't be able to stop me.

Sitting on my couch sipping some iced tea, I pretend to read as I watch. What a nice sight. Marabelle entertains me with her painting abilities from behind.

"Is the color to your liking, sir?"

"'Sir'? Why do you call me 'sir'?"

"It's part of the rules, sir."

"Rules? What rules?"

"In the professional painter's handbook. The part of the manual in which Workers deal with Planners, it said—"

"Marabelle." I laugh. "Cut it out. We are old friends and year mates. You can call me Antin. Stop being so formal. You crack me up."

"Okay, sir."

"Stop, funny girl!" I say, waving my hand at her to cease her silly behavior.

As Marabelle continues to work, I continue to study her from behind. Her T-shirt creeps up, revealing her soft belly. It's sort of round and soft like a peach. Merry's stomach is tight and lean. Marabelle's legs curve nicely as well, whereas Merry's legs are thin and bony. Marabelle turns to ask me something else, to showcase her large eyes and her batting eyelashes and her lush lips forming words from two red petals. She reminds me of this old animated cartoon we get to watch at the movies from time to time. I forget her name, but she is a curvy thing in a red dress that sings and dances with tiny animals and possesses springy dark curls much like Marabelle's. I love that movie. I realize Marabelle is the exact opposite of Merry. I'm taken back to my preschool days learning the difference between short and tall and dark and light. I relish in the memory of seeing little Marabelle sit in her seat at school, looking so lost and lovely.

"Excuse me, please. Did you hear what I said?"

Marabelle's voice snaps me back to reality.

"What?"

"Do you have some sort of sponge I could use? You know, the kind you get in the

lake? It's sort of beige. It's a natural sponge. Perhaps Merry has one that I could borrow? I'd bring you a fresh one next time. It seems that mine has gone missing."

"Sure," I answer as nicely as possible. "I'll go look for you. Be right back, Marabelle."

"Okay," Marabelle says in her dreamy voice and turns back around to paint some more.

I get up and stretch, flexing my muscles. I give a little groan, hoping she'll take note of my newly toned arms. Yet Marabelle stares at her wall, oblivious to what's around her, as usual.

I take the steps and head toward my bedroom. I have a slight clue about what Marabelle wants, but I'm not too sure where Merry keeps all of her stuff. I open her wardrobe and riffle around, tossing items here and there. I find many uninteresting things like lipstick and nail polish and frilly nighties. I whip it all to the floor carelessly. I take my arms and wade through her junk like I am swimming through a sea of garbage, pushing a path through her waste. My hand reaches to the back of the cupboard, and my fingers touch something rather foreign yet interesting. I stretch my hand further and pull out this treasure. I discover a small wooden box. Do I dare open it? Of course, now that we are married, Merry shall keep no secrets from me.

As the box opens, it lets out a small creak from its rusted hinges. At first, I'm a bit disappointed with its contents. The box contains dried flowers and broken toys, plus a stack of old papers, some brown with age. I pick up one of the sheets and unfold it. Magically I uncover old love notes from Sky to Merry. Delighted by my find, I laugh out loud.

"Fantastic!"

Once I start to read them, I can't stop myself. One by one, each note unfolds a story about their relationship from childhood till quite recently, before we all married. As I read the words, my mind starts to think these notes are pieces of a puzzle. They lead to a mystery Merry could not quite solve. I rack my brain, trying to remember how Merry got some of these notes in class.

"Of course!"

I try to keep my voice down. None of these notes actually have Merry's name on them. In fact they all start with an *M*. Not only does Merry start with an *M*, but so does Marabelle. Growing up, Sky would go out of his way to fight with Marabelle, and then mysteriously, Merry would end up with a note in her hand, delivered to her by Marabelle. And! And the note would always be wide open, which meant Marabelle had read the letter first.

"Aha!"

I seize the box, jumping up and down with excitement. I kiss it. Then carefully I collect the items and put the contents back into the box gently and return it to its right place. I clean up the mess from the floor and return it to the wardrobe, shutting it. Now Merry's treasures appear undetected. I would hate for her to find out I rummaged through her secrets. She may scare easily and try to remove her pieces of evidence. Yet she trusts me so blindly that she'll never guess I went snooping in the first place. I realize I have gone absent too long a time, and I retreat downstairs. Marabelle still works on the walls.

"Sorry, I couldn't find one."

"That's okay. I'll run and get one when I take my lunch break. I'll just eat on the run and head over to the supply warehouse."

"That sounds so unfair. Why don't you take some extra time to eat and then head down to the supply shop? I would hate for you to think me cruel for not allowing you a proper lunch hour."

"No, that's fine. I don't take that long to eat, anyway. Plus, it's a nice walk. I would hate to waste a perfectly sunny day like today in the dining hall."

"Well, let me go with you, then."

"That's okay. I'll be back real quick. If you'd like, I can pick you up something at the main dining hall as well. That way, you can keep working on whatever it is you are working on."

I check my watch.

"Shoot. I must meet Merry for a Planner brunch. Just let yourself back in, Marabelle. I completely trust you."

She smiles, puts her brush down, covers the remaining paint, and leaves on her mission. I straighten out my shirt and tie and head over to the Planner event. It slipped my mind as I kept Marabelle company, but now I remember it's my turn to give the speech on our Planning future, my vision of the compound, and where we must go to have a plentiful future.

Skyler-18

My first full-time harvest as a Worker wears me out by the end of the day. Sweat drips down my back, soaking my clothes. I have trouble taking in enough water to sustain productivity. Many of the older Workers take fierce verbal jabs at me and then pat me on the back.

"You'll get used to it," they say.

"Good old Sky."

"What a trooper for such a young man. He never gives up."

"Best Worker we got out here. He's like clockwork."

I spend my long hours thinking about Marabelle. I visualize taking my finger and tracing it down her nose and across her lips.

"Whatcha smiling at, boy? Get back to work."

Holiday approaches, so I concentrate on how Marabelle and I can celebrate together. After the harvest, the community feasts on a succulent dinner all together in the main dining hall. Planners and Workers sit together in harmony and balance and give thanks for whatever plentiful crop we pulled in for the year.

This year seems especially abundant. I've never worked this hard in my life.

I worry a bit about the seating arrangements. Families new and old tend to eat together as one. I'm sure Marabelle will want to dine with her parents. She misses them occasionally. I, on the other hand, dread spending a meal with mine. No doubt they miss me, but I'm done with them. I don't see a need to perpetuate our relationship. I'd rather sever ties once and for all. I can't tell them that. I'm not so malicious that I want to hurt their feelings. Still, we never had a close bond from the beginning, so it doesn't mean much to me now. I can tell they are anxious to get to know Marabelle. They have dropped several hints whenever our paths cross, which I make sure is not too often. As far as Marabelle's concerned, she has no opinion either way about meeting them.

As the wind tames the day's heat, I look forward to my row with my bride. I shower as fast as I can to rinse off my offensive stink from the day. I grab fresh clothes and hastily stuff food into a basket. I end up with bread, cheese, pretzels, olives, and grapes. I toss in a bottle of orange drink and a couple of cups and head toward the lake to seek out Marabelle.

As I arrive, the night sky darkens, and the stars shine brightly on the pathway. Soft footsteps approach, and I see Marabelle squinting her way over to me. I pull her close and kiss her, taking in her breath and smelling her wet hair. She showered before she came here as well. I put down my basket and look for my boat.

"Where's the boat?" Marabelle asks, squeezing her eyes even tighter, trying to see if she is missing it.

"I don't know. I put it right here underneath the brush."

I bend down, sweeping my hand along the shrubs and bushes, swirling around the sand underneath.

"What could have happened? You don't think someone took it, do you?"

"I'll keep searching. You stay here."

I roam around the vicinity, searching under every tree. Perhaps someone found it and moved it accidentally.

"Oh no!" I hear Marabelle cry.

"What?" I ask.

"I think I found it in pieces."

I stand over her shoulder and find a pile of splintered wood. My tiny boat was smashed into pieces quite violently—like someone took an ax or a sledgehammer to it. Whoever did it must have been very angry. The vessel is unrecognizable.

"Who could have done this?" Marabelle questions.

"I think I know who."

"Who? Who would be so mean?"

"I bet it was Antin."

"Really? You think? He's been a lot nicer now that he's married."

"Who else would it be?"

Some faces flash into my mind, but I hold my thoughts.

"Maybe the person who did it didn't even know the boat belonged to us."

"It doesn't matter, Marabelle. Forget it. I'll make us a new one. It's easy. You'll see. It will be even better than before."

I put the idea to investigate behind me. I'd rather not waste resources getting even when my free time should be spent with my love.

"Don't bother. It'll be winter soon enough, and we won't be able to use the boat anyway. The lake will freeze over. We can skate together instead."

"You're right. Let's just take our meal home and eat it together, snuggled in a blanket on the couch, and fall asleep. I am so tired that I feel like an old dog passed out under a porch. My body aches so much. Even my bones hurt."

Marabelle rubs my back and takes my hand. I'm glad we are in sync during nights like this. I realize she's also fatigued and wants to return home. Marabelle spends her days on food prep for Holiday when she's not assigned to other mundane Planner chores. We both deserve a day off to rest. In this respect, a broken oar presents itself as time off from physical activity, a blessing for us in disguise from a bad deed.

Merry-18

Holiday brings new functions I never thought existed. Planner ladies receive invites to all kinds of activities like card-game brunches and deep-cleansing facials. Who knew? Certainly not I. As a Worker child, it didn't occur to me that others on this compound existed so differently in lavished luxury. Workers serve as staff at most of these events. So either I wasn't told or telling was forbidden. Either way, I know now. Then for some reason, I wonder if Marabelle knows or will attend as a Worker. A bit of anxiety creeps up and enters my already-overwhelmed mind. What happens if I do see her? Do I ignore her? Do I talk to her? Do I even address her at all, or should I pretend like she doesn't even exist? Last time I saw her, she was in my own home, painting our walls. I felt my space a bit invaded, but I dare not mention it to Antin. I would rather not anger him over the color of our living room.

When I enter the event hall, I scan the room. Thank goodness Marabelle is nowhere in sight. Now I can rest easy. As I relax at my card-game brunch, I realize the majority of the Workers are busy harvesting the fields. Once they finish, they either prepare or store the food. I was that person once. I didn't question my place here at the time. I didn't know any different. Now that I do, should I feel bad about it? It is fair and equal here, but would Charm agree if she saw me sitting here sipping tea and eating cucumber sandwiches? And how about Marabelle? Does she care, or is she just glad to be married ... to Sky?

"Hello! Your turn." Sasha sounds annoyed as she waves her hand frantically in front of my eyes to get my attention.

"Sorry." I play my hand, poorly.

"Oh," Sasha scolds. She gets so impatient at times, and I'm stuck with her.

Less than six months have passed since I became a Planner bride. People treat me like I belong, but I don't. I'm uncomfortable here. I miss my parents. And despite Sasha's best efforts, I miss the rest of my friends. I even miss the people who weren't my friends. Plus, I'm kind of bored. I don't know what we are planning here, but they don't include me in those meetings. Antin does some "Planner work," but the rest of the time he spends leisurely doing nothing—like, and for instance, changing the color of our walls again and yet again.

"Sasha, do you think I should try to befriend Marabelle now that we are done with school?"

"Aw, this again?" Sasha asks, frustrated.

"Well, I was thinking, Sky thinks she is okay, and she did a good job painting our parlor. Perhaps she's not so bad after all."

"Merry, is this another attempt to get back into Sky's good graces?"

"No," I say meekly.

"Get over it, Merry! You don't get it, you just don't. Let me tell you something. Marabelle's not who you think she is. She appears all cute, and shy, and sweet, and innocent. Well, she's not at all that way. Don't underestimate this person. She's very clever and supercontrolling. You don't want to get caught in her web. She's a shrewish vixen. Eventually, Sky's bound to figure this out as well. My advice: stay away from her, and even farther away from Sky. He's not that great either. He's already deceived you. Want to make a bet that he'll do it again? If I were you, I would enjoy the good life. Stay content. Forget them. You got that? Let them deal with each other. Keep your distance. I'm speaking to you as a friend. I want what's best for you."

She stares me in the eyes. Then she takes my hand and holds it tight.

"Merry, listen carefully. I implore you to heed my advice! Take very good care of Antin, and make him very, very, very happy! He's your husband, and you want to keep it that way. Got that?"

"Yes, Sasha, I got it." I chuckle. "Don't be so serious. I was merely thinking out loud. Gee. I do take care of Antin. I adore him. I've never met a man more generous than he." I pull my hand away and set it in my lap. I use my other hand to massage away the pain. Sasha is stronger than I'd thought.

183

I shrug off Sasha's silly notions. I barely see any Workers unless they are serving my needs. Rarely does that involve Marabelle, and it never involves Sky. I've only seen him when he seeks out Marabelle. Even then, he doesn't mutter a word to me.

Sasha pulls me out of the fog as she snaps her finger at a Worker with a tea kettle. She wordlessly motions for the girl to refill her cup. Then she displays two fingers to indicate cubes of sugar and swirls her finger in a circular motion for the Worker to mix it all with a spoon. The poor Worker leaves without a thanks, a nod, or any kind of acknowledgment. I feel sick to my stomach.

"Pardon me, Sasha. I'm going to head home. I suddenly feel ill and need to rest. Thanks for playing with me. I'll see you later."

As I get up, Sasha grabs my hand and pulls me close.

"Just remember what I told you. Be a smart girl, and keep out of trouble."

"Okay," I say, pulling my arm out of her grasp. I leave and don't look back.

Skyler-18

The best part of Holiday this year is watching Marabelle cook for the feast. She enjoys peeling apples. She takes the knife and skins it in one swift move, leaving a curly skin. She loves making it fall to the ground. She slices the fruit so paper thin that the pieces are translucent, and then she makes beautiful dishes with the tiny bits. She cooks an apple crisp with a crunchy cinnamon-oatmeal topping. I ask her to put one aside just for us. She bakes sticky buns filled with apples and gooey brown-sugar topping. I pop a whole one in my mouth as it cools. She chops apples into a crispy salad topped with nuts and grapes. I spoon heaps into my mouth before she can take the bowl away. She simmers the fruit into a sauce and covers baked chicken with it. I pull off a bone and nibble it on sight. I relish the benefits of dishwashing duty and my current ability to feel safe talking to Marabelle at work.

"Stop eating so much." She slaps my hand. "There won't be anything left for everyone else, and you won't have room for dinner."

"That's where you're wrong. I always have room for dinner."

Marabelle boils sweet potatoes and mashes them for a soufflé. She arranges pickles and olives into bowls for each table. She pinches meats and potatoes into pastry crust for appetizers. She rolls chocolate dough into a circle to bake babka cakes. She heats coffee and steams milk for after dinner. I have orders to gather bottles of vin for our Holiday toast. I swing the key around my neck with childish glee that we get to prepare this meal together.

The other Workers bustling around us seem annoyed by my antics and encourage me to get back to the dishes so we have enough for the table settings. I respond by sticking my tongue out when their backs are turned. I also remind them I was not granted any time to rest in between my work in the field and my work now. So, a person running on such little sleep should technically be dead. This temporarily bothers Marabelle. Since she almost died when she was little, she suffers from great anxiety, which I must patch up with comforting her so she can finish making tonight's meal.

I hold my hands up at these annoying people as if to say, "See what you made me do? Upset my little Marabelle." I grab a cup and fill it with two sugars, half milk, and half coffee and deliver it to Marabelle. I steal a sprinkle cookie and a slice of cake for her before getting back to my dishes.

After long hours of food prep, we still stay to set up the tables and furnish them with decorations, utensils, plates, glasses, and starters. As we finally finish the last touches, we have less than an hour to wash up and dress in fresh clothing. This barely affords us time to look nice for the occasion.

I dread the actual dinner. My pleasure came from working alongside Marabelle and eating as she cooked. I wish we had our own kitchen at home. But we only have a hot plate and a small fridge, a tiny table, and a couch. If we had a full kitchen, we would never have to eat meals in the main dining hall again.

Like community tradition, some head Planner guy gives a speech about bountiful abundance and balance. Blah, blah. As always, I tune him out. We sit at a table for six. My parents attempt to chat pleasantly with Marabelle's parents. I have no idea if they are friends, and I don't care. I hold Marabelle's hand under the table and sulk in silence. I truly have little to contribute, which upsets my parents and creates an awkward scene for Marabelle. This setup was not my idea. I hoped for an intimate table for two. I shovel food into my mouth, quietly trying to catch a taste of it. It tasted better this morning when it was fresh. Marabelle makes such delicious food. I could have told the guests at the table this fact, but I decide to wait until we are alone tonight to share. I also make a mental list of several other topics I'd like to share later, including how much I hated sitting with our families.

The meal lasts several hours. We are required to stay for the "festivities." The main dining hall comes alive with the din of loud voices competing to share stories. I yearn to leave the stupid cacophony behind. My heavy eyes flutter with exhaustion. My ears buzz with words not detected by a normal person. I scan the room. It's Merry. She squirms in her chair at the other end of the room, hoping to catch my attention. I ignore her, but with my fatigue, I'm having a hard time blocking her thoughts. I consider calling the birds to pluck out her eyes so I can relax, but I suspect Marabelle may disapprove of this drastic measure. I turn my back on her and put my head down on the table.

Marabelle apologizes for my poor behavior and explains that I worked a twenty-hour shift. The parents look down at me empathetically. Someone pats my head. They move on to discuss their long work schedules. Finally, some head Planner man and his wife thank the crowd and dismiss us. A few people linger to chat. I practically run home to bed, dragging Marabelle behind me. I flop down on the couch, forgetting my items of discussion, and pass out. Only six hours until the next work day for me.

I welcome the cold, the darkness, the snow, the ice. I feel more at home. I look forward to long nights, gazing up at the moon and the stars. All along, I planned nighttime rendezvous on the frozen lake with Marabelle. Since my boat was destroyed, we lost our last chances to row to Apple Island. Now I pack a blanket and a basket for picnics on the ice. We walk or skate together, out of view of the compound. We relax and make snow angels, dance, and eat, laugh, and share each other's company.

After Holiday ended, many of the outdoor chores stopped for the season. I mostly work indoors at the factory or in the kitchen. Marabelle usually cooks or cleans. A request for her services by a Planner pops up on occasion. I also go on occasional vin runs so Planners may cook their hot glogg. Mostly, I live for outdoor evening meetings on the ice. Marabelle is adorable in her little hat and gloves as we walk hand in hand cautiously on the ice. I rarely worry about falling through. Although I do check the solidity and thickness, I am confident I'm safe out here.

I'm so grateful to finally skate with Marabelle. She's quite clumsy still, so I guard her. I also try to tie her laces so they won't lock together on her. When she falls, she laughs it off and tries again. She's such a good sport about it.

I relish the wind blowing around me, whipping snowflakes in my face. The trees sway as the wind whistles around the branches, making them dance. Blackbirds caw out my name, waving their wings as they fly over my head. My life has become peaceful and exactly how I wanted it—happy. When I'm with Marabelle, I forget everything around me. I drown out all unnecessary noises and distractions. I'm oblivious to anyone not Marabelle.

As I lie on a blanket, I close my eyes and have her feed me. I mixed a thermos of coffee to her liking and packed her cakes and cookies to go along. I take my gloves off and inspect my hands.

"Do you think my hands would turn blue if I stayed out here long enough?"

"Not sure. Let's not find out."

"I don't think they would. I barely feel the cold. I bet I don't even need a coat or a hat."

"Please keep them on for now."

I laugh at Marabelle's overprotectiveness.

"Do you think there are fish underneath the ice?" I continue.

"You know there are. People go ice fishing."

"But some big ones. Some kind of mysterious ones."

I'm sort of trying to chip away at my old enigma.

"The real mystery is to wonder how they survive in such cold temperatures. Do they feel trapped living under this solid ice?" Marabelle pounds her hand on the frozen ground.

"Do you think they can hear you do that?"

"Knock, knock."

"Who's there?"

"I'm."

"I'm who?"

"I'm so hungry. Give me my supper."

Okay, it was a bad joke, but we both laugh and eat at the same time. I want to tell her that I never had any real friends before we married, but she might not believe me. She might think all of those kids growing up were my friends. But they weren't. She's my first and only. This makes me a bit sad. It means Marabelle had more friends than I as a kid, and I waited eighteen years before I got one. My face reddens as I think about how much having a true friend means to me. I deserve this! I have earned this company through hard work and dedication. I'd rather die than let anyone come between us or take her away. I love Marabelle more than I love myself.

Cecile-18

Last night, I spotted Marabelle and Sky playing on the ice. It looked like they were enjoying themselves. I almost wanted to join them. Instead, I found myself returning home, trying to appease my miserable wife. Today, I skipped my Planner meeting. They'll get on fine without me. I find it hard to pay attention, which leads me to getting lost and leaving early at break time. So I decided to just avoid it altogether.

Instead, I put on my hat and gloves and head out toward the ice. I imagine it must be frozen over, because even though Sky's super lean, he is definitely taller than I am and more muscular, so he must weigh more as well. I'm a lot shorter and closer to Marabelle's height than he is. The two of them together would probably add up to more than my own poundage. Surely, a small skate around the perimeter wouldn't hurt.

As I reach the edge, I put my foot down gently and press. Seems solid enough. I cautiously walk onto the frozen lake with both feet and slide my way forward. Feeling more secure, I skid around faster and faster, leaving the edge of the beach farther behind. I lose myself, spinning and twirling around the slippery surface. I should have brought my skates.

Light snow starts to fall, decorating my hat with white flakes. I gaze up at the sun, allowing the snow drops to gather on my lashes. The rays warm my face and heat up my frosty cheeks. I should play hooky from work more often. I realize no one knows where I am, and I prefer it that way. With more and more time alone, I question who really cares about me. My parents often left me alone to go to events, and things aren't exactly working out with Sasha. Maybe I wasn't meant to cohabitate with the Planners after all, if that indeed is a word ... *cohabitate.*

I take a small step backward to get a running start and rush toward the center of the lake. Underneath my gliding feet, I feel a crackle. The brittle ice crumbles beneath my body, and I instantaneously drop through. I plunge down into the icy water fast—too fast to try to grip the edges and break my fall.

My lungs fill up with frigid water. My hand struggles to pound the solid ice over my head. A strong current pulls my heavy body lower.

My ears register a strange noise. Something above me glides over the ice. Whatever it is, it's very fast and impossibly light. Just as my breath gives out, bare hands grab my shoulders and pull me out of the water. Whatever it is pushes my limp body onto a snowbank, safe from the thin ice of the lake. Something hurdles over me and presses down on my stomach, forcing out the lake water. I cough up some more and let it dribble out of the side of my mouth. I struggle to breathe and gasp for air. A hand wipes my eyes and strokes my mouth, ridding it of the leftover spit. When I am finally able to look up, I see Marabelle. She doesn't have a coat, or a hat, or gloves, or even socks. She's in her work gear, a thin T-shirt, work pants, and flimsy plastic slip-on shoes for mopping up floors. I try to choke out some words.

"Shhhhh," she says, stroking my forehead.

"You saved me," I croak.

"I heard someone scream and saw you fall through the ice. What were you doing out there? They have not declared the ice solid! You know better!"

"How was it possible for you to hear me? You must have been so far away."

"Nonsense. I wasn't that far, and sound travels, silly."

"But I saw you on the ice last night."

"Don't be ridiculous, Cecile. Nighttime is colder that day. The sun has been out melting the ice, making it unsafe for people to play on it."

"Marabelle," I say, taking her hands in mine. "You saved me, again. What would I do without you looking after me? You didn't even have a chance to put on a coat. Aren't you cold?"

"I'm fine, but you need to get inside."

She stands up and pulls me up and holds me steady as my legs wobble beneath me.

"What about you?"

"I need to get back to work, but you need to remove those wet clothes and warm up, or your body will go into shock. Please, hurry home."

Marabelle drags me out of the brush and back on the pathway toward my house. Her wet T-shirt clings to her small body, and her shoes slosh as she walks on the crunchy snow. She pats my back.

"You're all right now. Please be more careful."

"I ... don't know what to say. Um ... thank you."

"Sure. No problem. See you later."

As I head back home, defeated, I watch her go back toward the main dining hall. It hits me in an instant. The main dining hall is pretty far from the lake. Even if the sound traveled over the hill for her to hear me, how did she get to me in time to pull me out of the water?

Skyler-18

As Birthday approaches, I rack my brain with ideas to impress Marabelle. I bet she's never received a special gift on that day, so I want to make our celebration amazing. I have so few resources that I will probably need to make her a gift. I certainly can't afford to give up my stipend to buy something.

I hint around at my plans, but Marabelle has been acting strange lately. She can't seem to get enough sleep. She's always tired and wants to nap instead of eat. When she does manage to eat, she gets sick and throws up.

"Love, I think you need to see the doctor."

"No, I'm fine. I guess the food didn't agree with me. Don't worry."

"It's not normal to be so sleepy either."

"They have us working twelve-hour shifts to get ready for Birthday. I'm just worn out from it. We never had to work this hard when we were at school. I'm not used to it yet. Plus, I caught a cold or something. You don't have to worry so much about me."

"But I do worry about you. You're all I have in this world. Look, I'll cover your shift, and you rest."

"That's ridiculous. You'll get sick too if you work that much. I'll take a short nap, and then I'll feel better. You'll see."

She revives herself a bit but not enough to stop my worrying. As she rests, I feel her head. Thankfully, she's not feverish, so perhaps she's just run-down with a cold. The change in weather often affects people's health around here.

A tad relieved, I refocus my attention to planning our day. April 1 also marks our first year as a couple. Racking my brain with ideas, I consider a day at the zoo, making her a necklace, cooking a feast, building a new boat. Wow! I'm going to be busy—busy working and getting my plans together.

Merry-18

Taking Sasha's advice proves more worrisome than I expected. All this time, I'd assumed Antin was infatuated with me. He treated me sweetly and spoiled me with gifts and affection for a while. Recently, he seems to have lost interest in me. I'm puzzled. Why the sudden change of heart? Now I'm drastically working to win him back. We've barely been married a year. We are forbidden to share notes on relationships, so I can't even tell if this is normal. I'm guessing no, it's not. I see Sky all of the time chasing Marabelle and laughing during his free time. Still, I wonder about him. On the other hand, I need to start to refocus my energies and concentrate on Antin. This is all my fault! Granted, I received some forbidden advice from Sasha, she suggests that I need to concoct a plan to put into immediate action. I kind of agree, so I guess I will.

I hear people plan for Birthday. So I decide to create a special anniversary night for the two of us. Perhaps I can recruit some people to make me look beautiful. I consider Marabelle since she's a pro at makeup, and then I realize that's probably not a good idea. I need to keep Marabelle off limits for now. Sasha would possibly help with my nails, and Charm may be able to help do my face. I could scrounge up some stipend merely for a new gown and hair accessories without Antin noticing. Now all I need is the perfect gift. It has to be amazing, something nobody else in the community has, something totally unique that will set me apart and bring us close again. I've got to get something that will force Antin to fall back in love with me again and stay that way forever. Thank goodness something incredible comes to mind, and I'm quite sure I'm the only who has it!

Birthday, April 1

Skyler-19

Sugar and spice and everything delicious sums up my day with Marabelle. We were granted the day off together, so I needed to prepare my special plans. I woke up my sleeping beautiful with a cup of her favorite coffee in bed. Marabelle enjoys half steamed milk, half coffee with sugar. I also prepared a plate of toast with chocolate spread and a roll with whipped butter. I could tell she enjoyed it because she squealed in delight and hugged me. I guess she's never had breakfast in bed before. I know I haven't. Then we took a walk around the zoo. I took the leftover crust from breakfast to feed the animals.

After the zoo, I led Marabelle to the vineyard where I had hidden a basket for lunch. I told her to open the basket and get me a drink. As she opened it, a small black felt bag perched on the top of our meal. Marabelle waved her hand in front of her face as tears fell from her eyes. Funny how touched she was, and she didn't even open the package.

I told her to go ahead and open her gift. As her tears streamed even quicker down her face, Marabelle dug her hand into the bag and pulled out my present. She stretched out some thin fishing wire strung with five round pearls I found from the shells that washed up on the beach. Marabelle cried how much she loved it and threw her arms around me, knocking me to the ground and covering my face with kisses. Then she cried because all she made for me was a card.

I spent some time rubbing her back and consoling her. I reminded her that I had to make up for all of my rotten behavior and looked forward to her card. Marabelle's mood quickly rebounded, and we relaxed and ate. We stared at the clouds and chatted about what we saw. She saw a giraffe. I said I saw a baby, and she blushed. I lamented how I wanted a family with her so badly because I loved her. She reminded me that having a child without permission was not only forbidden but impossible. Then it was my turn to cry out of frustration of being told what to do all of the time, which ultimately led to more holding and kissing.

Later, I put the necklace around Marabelle's neck, and she vowed to never take it off. I explained when she wore her gift around her neck it became an unbroken circle that represented my unending love for her and would never be broken. I corrected myself; it could never be broken. I assured her she was mine for eternity. I explained that we balanced each other and that one could not exist without the other. If one of us existed without the other, the world would be chaos. But together, we created perfect harmony. Her light would balance my dark and vice versa. Marabelle told me I was being poetic and kind of romantic.

We decided to show up to the main dining hall for dinner because they were serving chicken schnitzel and rice with pickles and slaw. That sounded better than toast since we ran out of food.

This year, the community used some of its resources to make fireworks to celebrate Birthday. Everyone gathered on a hill with blankets to watch. Even most of the Planners appeared for this event. Watching the lights with Marabelle in my arms was amazing. I'd seen fireworks before but never really appreciated their magic until now. Seeing them from this new perspective made my experience tonight awesomeness. Why can't every day be Birthday? Why can't I spend more lazy days in Marabelle's company?

The smell of burnt fire powder stung my nostrils. Suddenly, a chill ran down my spine. A bad sensation passed through me.

I turned my head and searched the crowd for signs of danger. I couldn't see anything suspicious, and the sick moment passed. I decided to shrug it off. Why spoil a nice night, probing for information?

I gently gripped Marabelle's little fingers and led her home to snuggle tight. Marabelle often suffers from insomnia, so I waited a long time for her to fall asleep. I can't say for sure that I didn't actually start to doze before her, but it's now the middle of the night, and I have awoken to process my day of the first year of our life together.

"I love you, Marabelle."

Merry-19

As hysterical as I am right now, I urge myself to get a grip and think about what happened today. I furiously wipe my tears from my face and examine my blotchy skin in the mirror. I've confined myself to the bathroom. It has become my refuge for the moment. I turn the faucet and splash cold water on my face. My hands shake uncontrollably. I still can't understand what went wrong. I intended this night to be amazing and unforgettable. Well, it certainly ended with an unforgettable memory, but why?

When I was a child, everyone clamored around me. I had an unending list of friends. All of the girls wanted to hang out with me. I thought most of them wanted to be me as well. I caught the attention of every male year mate. Sky spent his days flirting endlessly with me like I was the only person that mattered on the compound. Antin chased me as if I were the most desirable creature on the planet.

As soon as I married, life changed. At first, I thought it was for the better. Being a Planner brought wonderful privileges I never knew existed. Antin treated me like a celestial gift. I assumed I deserved the good life because I was the most desired around. Now I realize I was wrong.

It all started the morning of our first anniversary. For most of the community, May 1 marks an ordinary day. All Workers marry on Birthday, so they have nothing to celebrate. Planners, on the other hand, celebrate their weddings a month later, allowing Workers to help create opulent soirees or private engagements. I opted for a smaller, more intimate celebration for two with Antin. I gathered the most romantic ingredients I could for an evening to remember. I purchased a white silk slip, fit for an evening gown. I collected candles to create a mood in the bedroom. I ordered sugar-covered strawberries and an assortment of cheeses from the kitchen. I had a silver-and-gold ganache cake baked specially for Antin with his name spelled out using silver pearl sprinkles. Last, but surely not least, I secured and wrapped the ultimate present.

Obviously, I ignored all of the warming signs. Antin greeted me after his work day with a lukewarm embrace. He's grown less and less interested in me over the last few months to a point where I'm not sure he even wants to be married anymore. He doesn't look at me. He hasn't touched me in a long time.

As he entered our home, I tried adjusting my slip, pulling it down lower, trying to make my outfit more revealing. He smiled politely and walked away. I coaxed him upstairs. I feel so silly now remembering how he sighed like he was already bored with my frivolous ploy. I pushed him toward the bed and tried to feed him some berries. He choked down a couple and then declined the rest of our treats, claiming he already ate. I almost lost it at that moment, but I sucked up my emotions and continued my quest to win back Antin.

I took my fingers and placed them over Antin's eyes and removed the gift from its hiding place.

"Baby, I have a surprise for you!" I teased him.

"That wasn't necessary. Why did you do that? I've told you not to go out of your way for me."

"I know, but this gift is special. I wanted us to share something amazing that no one else on this compound has."

"Are you trying to tempt me? You know how I love being the only one to possess the most special things."

"Well, sweetie, this will definitely make the others quite jealous."

"What is it?"

"Just open it already."

Antin removed the silver wrapping from the small box and opened the lid.

"Ta-da!" I announced.

As he looked into the box, his face grew red with rage.

"What is this?" he yelled.

I stared at the bright red orb and sniffed out some tears.

"You know what it is," I answered quietly.

"Yes, I recognize it. How did you get it?"

"I thought you would be happy."

"Happy? Happy? Are you kidding? It is forbidden! You could get us both killed! What kind of gift it this?" He sneered in my face.

"I don't know! I wanted you to have something no one else had. It was a mistake."

I could feel the snot flow out of my nostrils into my mouth.

"How could you do this to us, Merry? The forbidden fruit is forbidden for a reason. Who gave this to you? How did you get it?"

"It's just that I love you so much," I cried. "And you don't seem to notice me anymore. I wanted something to bring us closer." My eyes stung with mascara mixed with tears.

"I don't get you, Merry. I give you everything, and this is how you treat me. You thank my generosity with a death wish?"

"No, Antin, I love you."

"Where did this come from? Did you pick it yourself? You couldn't have picked it yourself."

"I don't know."

"Just tell me! Tell me!"

"Fine. Sky gave it to me."

"Sky? Is Sky your secret lover?"

"What? No! Why would you think that?"

"I don't know, Merry, you tell me. Do you still have feelings for him? Do the two of you have secret rendezvous together when I am not around?"

"Please, Antin, stop. I love you! Only you! I don't even see Sky. You know that."

"No, Merry, I don't know that. He gave you this." Antin shook the fruit in my face.

"Please believe me. I didn't mean to insult you. I saved it for us."

"I want to believe you, Merry. I really do. But you have now put us in an awkward position. We possess the forbidden fruit in our house. Now I need to come up with a plan to get rid of it."

Antin got up off the bed and grabbed the box.

"Where are you going?"

"Where do you think I'm going? I need to rid us of this fruit before we're found out and someone punishes us both."

Antin stormed out of our bedroom and slammed the door, cracking the frame. I ran to the bathroom, seeking shelter to try to calm down and comfort myself.

I rock back and forth on the floor, gritting my teeth. I want to wake from this nightmare. I pinch my cheeks to stop the emotional pain I have caused this evening. I shake with fear and dread facing Antin. Who knows what he'll do to me. Perhaps I will fall to his feet and beg for forgiveness. I will confess that it's all my fault. I will swear on whatever he wants that I love him.

I collapse onto the rug in another crying fit.

"Please help me get through this night. I'm not a bad person. I just want someone to love me."

Skyler-19

As I lie in bed, a sudden darkness disturbs my slumber. Chills run up and down my spine. Someone has been watching us sleep, the same someone who often creeps by our window. It has been happening for quite a while.

One eye opens and darts around the room. I cover Marabelle protectively as she sleeps curled in a ball. She takes shallow breaths. I rub her back.

It pounds loudly on my door.

It screams, "Wake up!"

Marabelle grabs the covers and cowers under them. She's a bit shaky.

"Shhh, don't worry. Go back to bed," I reassure her.

I climb off the cot and stumble to the door. Standing before me is Antin.

"Get your key. I need some vin."

Antin-19

As I pass Sky and Marabelle's window, I peek inside. Little Marabelle sleeps at the edge of the cot, wrapped in a thin blanket, curled in a ball. I strain my eyes to see what she is wearing. An eye opens immediately and scans the room. It belongs to Sky. He sneers. He's already angry with my arrival. He displays his overprotective nature and covers Marabelle with a duvet and shields her with his wiry, muscular body. This charade raises my blood pressure as I feel the boil inside my stomach. My hands shake with rage over Sky's stupid games.

Even my breath shakes as I pound on the door to summon Sky.

"Wake up!" I shout. I'm now out of breath as if I just ran a mile.

Sky opens the door and towers over me, trying to make himself look even bigger. He puffs out his chest like a vulgar peacock. He wears those worn-out shorts. I doubt he even owns a pair of pajamas.

He turns back to Marabelle, who hides under the covers.

"Shhh, don't worry. Go back to bed," he says to her, waving his hand.

I can't stand his patronizing ways.

"Get your key. I need some vin!" I command him.

Sky stands in the doorway for a moment silent, staring me in the eye.

"Well? What are you waiting for?" I mutter impatiently.

He walks back to his wardrobe and searches for his lanyard. He hangs it around his neck and pulls some pants over his shorts, puts on an old T-shirt, and slips on a pair of battered shoes, forgetting his socks in a sleepy haze. He puts out his hand, indicating that I lead the way and closes the door to his slab behind him.

We walk in unison in the darkness to the main dining hall and make our way to the cellar door.

"I've changed my mind," I finally say.

"What?"

"I've changed my mind."

"About what? About wanting some vin?"

"No ... about Marabelle. I've changed my mind about Marabelle."

"You can't change your mind about that. Bidding is way over. What's done is done. All marriages are final."

"Oh, really, Sky? You don't seem to understand the power I have around here. As always, you underestimate my abilities."

He stands silent, just looking at me.

"You don't have to answer me, Sky. But I have something you might be interested in seeing."

From my pocket, I pull out the shining orb and reveal it to him.

"What's that?"

"You know what it is, Sky. In fact, I bet you know how I got it."

He says nothing. He stands very still, listening to my words very carefully.

"You don't think I catch on to your games? You are very clever," I continue. "This is not the forbidden fruit, is it?"

I take the perfect orb and smash it on the ground. It splats all over the tile, juice running red like blood. After it spatters, several tiny black snakes crawl out of the pulverized meat of the fruit. I jump back a bit, shocked. Then the remaining flesh blackens and turns to ash.

Sky smiles and looks the other way.

"That's funny to you? Huh? Well, here's the kicker, Sky. I know who the forbidden fruit really is. It's Marabelle."

Sky's mouth curls to a frown.

"Answer me!" I yell.

"Yes," he says quietly.

"I see what you did, playing those games to protect her all of those years. Pretending to offer her to me and then snatching her away."

"I didn't offer her to you."

"Yeah, right, sure it wasn't you. Who would send her to me, then?"

"Are you nuts? Why would I send her to you?"

"You're such a massive liar! Well, it doesn't matter anyway. I changed my mind. I decided I want her now after all."

"You can't do that, Antin. We already bid on our brides. You won Merry."

"Watch me," I respond, stepping so close to him that he darts back nervously, lowering his eyes.

Nervously playing with his fingers, he summons up the courage to tell me, "Well, that's not going to happen."

"Are you sure, Sky? Now I am truly feeling a little celebratory. *Get me my vin!*"

Skyler-19

Antin's crazy behavior confuses me. His brain swirls with half-formulated ideas and pictures about me and Marabelle and Merry. He's truly gone off the deep end. How can this man feel so threatened by me? I have so little in this world. I live as a Worker in the smallest possible domicile, with the tiniest pension, with a woman previously bound for maid-dom. He possesses an enormous house, little responsibility, and the most beautiful woman on the compound. How much more could he want? What is it about me that drives him to jealousy, enough to take the only thing in my life that matters? Marabelle.

I give that daft dolt his vin and send him back to his luxurious home. He leaves me only so that I may worry about Marabelle. Of course, I need to protect her against angry predators like Antin. I must stand and guard the only thing worth living for in this empty life of mine.

Fatigued, I rub my eyes. If I hurry back, I can get a couple more hours of sleep before I must return to this kitchen for work. I ponder whether or not I should discuss what happened tonight because I don't want to alarm Marabelle. I gather I've started crying because a tear trickles down my lips, and I taste the salt in my mouth. What if Antin really can take her away from me? Then what? What he said is true: I have such little power in this world. Who is going to save me?

Merry-19

My heart beats rapidly in anticipation as I spot another note hidden away from everyone but me. The day has finally come. Sky loves me after all. I knew he did. What a relief! It has all been an act after all. We discussed having some sort of secret plan when we were young, but I had given up hope. I guess Sky was working behind the scenes at reuniting the two of us after all. I'm ashamed of myself that I gave in so often to Antin and sacrificed so much of myself to him. I let him carry me away with promises of status and luxury. It worked too, but now I must try hard to ground myself. I've come to the resolve that Sky and I were meant to be.

It started a couple of days ago. As I retrieved my laundry bag, I noticed a note sticking out of a dress. I took it inside and sat on the couch to sort my clean clothes while casually opening the note. At first, I thought a piece of clothing got ruined in the wash and that it was a written apology. But then I realized it was so much more important than that. As I read it to myself, tears poured out of my eyes, first out of guilt and then out of relief. I tucked the note into my shirt and ran upstairs to read it again. I cautiously looked around to make sure Antin was totally out of sight and then read it out loud.

> M,
>
> Time is running out for us. We were meant to be together, but it is forbidden. Our union was written in the stars, and as I gaze deeply into your eyes, you will know my love it true. I only hope you can love me back one day.
>
> S

As I read the note, I jumped up and down in delight, excited that he wanted me back.

"He loves me, he still loves me," I squealed. "Oh no. He doesn't think I love him back anymore!"

I panicked and pulled apart my wardrobe to get to my box and shoved my note deep inside.

"It seems like he left me a riddle that I need to sort out soon. Time is running out because we are both already married, and there is no way we can be together. But our union was written in the stars, so he will contact me sometime during the night. He will gaze at me, indicating the time is near and that he wants me to reassure him of my affections some how. I'm so brilliant," I gloat.

I jumped up and down, proud I could read between Sky's lines. I knew Sky was clever. He often works at the laundry, so that seemed like the perfect way to communicate with me. After getting my first note, I struggled to search the compound to find him. When I finally did, it was awkward at best. I spotted him at the dishwashing line. I could tell he was not in a good mood. As I approached him, he scowled at me.

"Sky, I think we need to talk," I began.

"Not right now, Merry. In front of all these people? It's not the best time, um ... it's lunch rush. I'm kind of busy right now."

"Okay. When then? When can we meet to talk?"

"Really?" He looked at me, kind of annoyed.

"Oh, I'll find you later, then."

"Fine."

"Bye."

Well, that exchanged backfired, but I realize doing it in front of the entire community could have gotten us in a lot of trouble and caused us to be punished severely. Sky is bright, so I understand I have to be a lot smarter than this and wait for his next clue.

Finally, it comes. I turn his note around and around in my fingers, too scared or excited to see what it says. It has been about two weeks since our weird exchange, and I was getting seriously impatient. I slowly unfold my note and skim the contents. I hug it to my chest and then reread it, more slowly this time.

M,

I'm so sorry! Please forgive me for what I have done to you. I didn't mean it. I get so jealous sometimes. I just can't stand the thought of you being with anyone else. It hurts me to see you sad. I hate to admit it, but when you cry, I cry too. I know it is hard, but please don't tell anyone how I feel about you. Remember my promise to you.

I love you.

PS

Meet me tonight in front of the forbidden tree so we can finally be together at last!

I kiss the note a thousand times and fold it back up, concealing it in my shirt again. My mind swirls around. I swoon with dizziness. I have so much to do to prepare for tonight. I can hardly wait! Sky has a plan to escape, and it's with me after all!

Skyler-19

As I return from a long day of work, I can already sense that something is wrong. My slab door is cracked open a little. I peek through the entry and see blackness. The room is dark. My heart beats rapidly; it pulses in my throat. My breath stifles. I can't seem to gulp. My hands shake. I want to pass out. I think I am going into shock.

"Marabelle?" I speak quietly into the abyss of my front door.

I push open the door. It creaks. My throat goes dry, and I pant.

"Marabelle, are you in there?"

My vision blurs. I'm too dizzy. My heart thumps in my chest. I shuffle my feet farther into the slab. My mouth gapes open. Someone tore apart my possessions. My

place has been ransacked. I slap my hands over my forehead and panic.

"Marabelle?" I say louder.

I run to the bedroom and overturn the cot. I look under every blanket, too nervous to realize it's useless. I continue my futile efforts searching my small room. My foot smashes something on the floor. I hear a big crunch. Tears stream out of my eyes. I pick up Marabelle's broken glasses. I almost faint.

"Marabelle!" I scream.

I punch the wall. I don't know what to do. I run out of my slab, heading for nowhere. I can't get a sense of where she is. I can't feel Marabelle. I hate this. She's one of the few people I can't listen for, and it's killing me.

"Marabelle!" I yell so loud that windows vibrate as I rush past the main dining hall.

"Help!" I scream.

Who out there can really help me? Who really cares what happens to me? I have no one to turn to in this situation. I am at the bottom of the rung in this community.

"Marabelle!" My voice grows hoarse with every call. Every moment I don't locate her I waste going in useless circles. I breathlessly blow air out of my mouth and suck air back in my nose. My lungs fail to give me enough oxygen to function.

"Marabelle, please!" My body propels me to the edge of the compound. I guess where my feet are taking me. I was left with no clues. I reach a dead end. I see a figure in the fog. The night plays nasty tricks on me. It's a female, but not Marabelle. I rush to the edge of the orchard to warn the woman who awaits me in the darkness. I push the hair out of my face. I need to get to Marabelle before it is too late. Someone has taken her, and she can't see without her glasses. I know she must be scared. She must be saved. I vow to be her hero. I suck in air through my teeth to catch my breath. I slow down to a walk and try to calm my body. I press my hand to my heart to slow the beating and blink back tears. Marabelle needs my strength. Time is running out, and I must reach her before she truly faces danger.

I see a face and struggle to speak. Before I can get a word out, she says something to me first.

Merry-19

Clutching the notes to my heart, I wait in the darkness. As the fog gently rolls in, I worry that Sky won't show. Time seems to pass slowly as I anticipate his arrival. What will I say? How will I react?

A figure appears in the night just as I almost give up and return home.

"Sky, you made it."
"Merry? Is that you?"
"I knew you would come for me."
"Merry. Stop. It's a trap!"
"What? What do you mean?"

"We've been set up! We need to leave now. We have to get out of here before it's too late."

"Oh, Sky, I'm so happy. Where do you want to go?"

"Go? Merry, we need to get back to our homes before it is too late! We've got to go now!"

"But, Sky, why would we go home? Why did you ask me to meet you here if you just wanted to go home?"

"Merry, I didn't invite you here. Please, run as fast as you can."

Sky grabs the letters to look over.

"Merry? Are you daft?! These are old letters! And look, this isn't even my handwriting."

He points to the spot where it says to meet him.

"It's not even in the same color ink," he growls.

I'm so confused. I freeze in my spot, unable to move or speak.

Suddenly a siren goes off, and lights flash above us.

"Merry-19 and Skyler-19, you are in violation of community rules. You are under arrest for conspiracy to run away and commit adultery. Adultery is strictly forbidden. Please remain still as we collect you."

A group of Planners surrounds us quickly and point laser taser sticks at us. I smell a charge, and static jumps from one stick to another like strands of blue lightning.

One of the men announces, "Merry-19 and Skyler-19, please come with me."

Seven strong men watch as our wrists are zip tied, and then they drag us back up the hill. I sob uncontrollably. Sky quietly follows along.

Skyler-19

My feet pull me into the darkness, and I know why they lead me down this path. She was dragged out of our home and pulled this way. I pick up her scent. The fragrance of citrus and vanilla lingers in the air. She was pushed past the forbidden tree and then carried away by someone. She's no longer here.

Marabelle was forced to walk as a sick clue from a puzzle I was meant to solve. Whoever did this knew I would come running. I was led to this dead end. To my horror, I find Merry waiting for me. Marabelle's disappearance remains a mystery.

"I knew you would come for me."

"Merry. Stop. It's a trap!"

I try to warn her. I urge her to leave. An element of danger surrounds us. I fear it's too late to flee the scene. It's become obvious someone wants to rid the compound of the two of us, and poor Merry doesn't get it. Plus, my main concern right now is to retrieve Marabelle.

"Go? Merry, we need to get back to our homes before it is too late! We've got to go, now! Merry, I didn't invite you here. Please, run as fast as you can."

I reiterate the need to leave immediately. Merry stands, confused, crying, flashing me old letters I wrote her long ago, unable to recognize how aged they appear. Someone found her stash and added a couple of lines in a different handwriting. Merry, too blind to see the difference, wanted these letters to come from me. I didn't think she would still want to be with me so badly after she got the taste of a better life, but I guess I was wrong. Instead, she patiently waited for me to plan our escape together, and here it is, a botched situation. All this time, I meant to escape with Marabelle, and it backfired. I had forgotten my main purpose and spent the past year relishing in my own happiness, and now instead of finding Marabelle, I am facing Merry. I work out some options in my head when a siren goes off, and announcements blast from the loudspeaker.

"Merry-19 and Skyler-19, you are in violation of community rules. You are under arrest for conspiracy to run away and commit adultery. Adultery is strictly forbidden. Pleases remain still as we collect you."

Before I can react, a group of Planners with taser sticks surround us. I curse under my breath and bite my lip until is bleeds. At this point, I have little choice but to obey and follow them. I realize this may be my last chance to locate Marabelle, so I need to concentrate my thoughts and come up with a new idea to free us.

"Merry-19 and Skyler-19, please come with me," a big Planner guard commands.

Then they zip tie our wrists together like handcuffs. Merry sobs uncontrollably while I just go along. As my hands fall to my waist I realize I could easily break the plastic that binds my hands, but why play any of my cards in advance? I decide to wait and see the outcome of this ridiculous game.

Merry-19

Sky and I are led to an outdoor amphitheater where summer concerts and lecture series are often held. Most of the compound has been roused out of bed and take up most of the seats surrounding the platform in the middle. Several old Planners sit at a table on the platform, awaiting our arrival. The Planner guards shove Sky and me into the middle of the stage so that we can face the audience of angry, sleepy eyes. In the corner of the platform rests Antin. He's holding the wrists of a confused Marabelle. She squints, and tears roll down her cheeks. Someone has dressed her in maid white. The flowing dress shows off her small waist and curvy figure. Antin gives us a triumphant smile as we arrive.

"Boo!" The crowd jeers us as we arrive, and we are pelted with small stones and wadded-up garbage. Snot runs down my nose as I cry harder. I've never seen anything like this before. Crimes never happen in this community. Sky stands still, stoic, and silent. But even his composure lasts only a moment as he tries to make unsuccessful eye contact with Marabelle. She can't see him without her glasses. I have no idea how she lost them, but it looks like she is trying to listen to what's happening around her. Her head tilts toward the noise. She wrinkles her nose in concentration.

"Marabelle!" Sky screams. "It wasn't me! I didn't do anything. Please believe me!" Tears now pour out of his eyes. "Marabelle, listen to me. I'm going to fix this," Sky pleads in her direction.

"Silence," calls the elder Planner.

"Skyler-19 and Merry-19, I have been provided ample evidence of your plans together to escape this community to commit adultery. Both such behaviors are strictly forbidden and punishable by death."

Upon hearing these claims, my head spins, and my legs give out beneath me.

Before I can faint, Sky grabs on to me and keeps me stable. Even during this nightmare, he stands behind me and protects me.

"Skyler-19, I hold here evidence of your ultimate plans to commit this crime. Are these your letters written by your hand?" The elder Planner holds up a handful of letters taken from my box I buried in my wardrobe.

"Yes, but those weren't meant for Merry," he pleads. "They were for Marabelle, my wife! I wrote them to Marabelle."

Then Sky turns his head and shouts, "Marabelle, believe me those letters were for you. You know that's true. This whole thing is a lie. I love you."

"Silence," calls the elder.

Confused, Marabelle cries in the corner, still in Antin's grip. She turns her head toward Sky's voice but doesn't appear to see him well.

"So, Skyler-19, you admit that you wrote these letters."

"Yes."

"These letters were not in Marabelle's possession. They were in Merry's possession. Is this correct?"

"Yes, but sir, they are old! I wrote some of them when I was a kid. Is it forbidden to write?"

"Merry-19, is it true you recently received these notes?"

"Yes," I say weakly.

"Is it true the two of you planned to meet and conspired to run away as a couple?"

"Um," my voice quivers, "I thought so."

Sky turns to me and says, "Merry, please don't do this. You know those were old notes. I've made it very clear now they

211

weren't for you! Why do you think I had Marabelle always pass them? Please, think! Tell them!"

"Silence! I have made my decision. Skyler-19 and Merry-19, I condemn the two of you to death for violating community rules. Please submit and come with me."

I let out a scream, "Nooooo!!!!!!" Then I collapse.

Sky yells, "Forget this!"

He breaks his hands free from the ties, yanks on my arm, lifts me to my feet, rips off my bindings, and pulls me off the stage.

"Run!" he yells, and off we go as the crowd gazes, stunned by the entire display.

As we leap off the stage, the elder summons his guards.

"After them," he calls as Sky and I run toward the mountain.

Part 4

Skyler-19

Desperate to get away from this ridiculous compound, I run to the mountain, pulling Merry behind me. I'm stuck with her for now, but I plan on trying to find other people out there to release her for her personal safety. I don't intend to keep Merry around. I need a way to get back and rescue Marabelle.

Merry cries continuously out of fear and confusion. She slows me down.

"Aye! Pick up the pace, Merry! Is this as fast as you can go?"

"I can't keep up, Sky. I need to stop and catch my breath. I can't go any farther," she pants.

"We can't stop now, Merry. They'll catch up to us and take us back. We are as good as dead if that happens."

This sends Merry into another round of panic and tears.

I stop. Merry tries to catch her breath. Her whole body shakes with terror and exhaustion.

"Come here," I tell her. She approaches, and I put out my arms.

"Hop in my arms, and then put your legs around my waist. Hold on really tight. I'll carry you out of here."

We can see the guards approach from a distance.

"There they are!" they call.

"Hurry, Merry!" I scream.

Merry runs and jumps into my arms and straddles my waist. I pick up her arms and place them firmly around my neck. Then I run like I've never run before, racing toward the orchard. My legs speed faster and faster into the maze of citrus trees. The guards can't keep up with my pace. They stop. In the distance, I see a couple throw their hands up in the air, giving up. As we get closer to the mountain, another alarm sounds off.

"Skyler-19 and Merry-19, you are in direct violation of trying to leave the compound. Turn around and return immediately."

This time, I ignore the alarm. I can see the mountain ahead. My heart beats fast in my chest, and I dive past the last tree while holding Merry in my arms. A sudden jolt rushes through our bodies. I feel it enter my head, travel down my chest, and exit my feet. My heart skips a beat, but I'm okay. I've survived our escape thus far. Merry, on the other hand, does not fair the surge as well. I stop at the foot of the mountain and lay her body down on the ground. I grab my two hands and pump them on her chest several times. I lift her mouth and cover it with mine and blow into it. Merry shakes back to consciousness, gasping for air.

"What was that?" she asks.

"I'm not sure. Maybe some kind of electric fence. But that doesn't matter. We need to start climbing now."

"Climb? Climb what?"

"The mountain, Merry. Let's go."

"I can't climb now, Sky. I'm too tired," Merry cries.

I pick her up again, this time putting her on my back. I have her put her legs around my stomach and her arms around my neck. With Merry secure, I start to climb up the rocky mountain. I've never done this before. I try to secure my feet into the small crevices so I can lift our bodies farther up into the air. I cut my hands on several jagged edges as I go up, stopping to wipe off the blood on my pants so my hands don't get too slippery. I don't want us to fall to our deaths after all of this. As I go higher into the air, it gets harder to breathe. I finally reach a small opening. It's a cave big enough for two, with a small, flat area at the entrance to look down below at our former home while I build a fire.

Merry-19

This whole event has left me in a confused daze. I sit on the cold mountain ledge, shaking. I rock back and forth a bit. I want to vomit. I try hard to hold back the tears, but they keep flowing freely from my eyes. What just happened? How did Sky and I end up here, high in the mountains? I remember heading toward the edge of the compound, and I see where I am now, but how I got here seems a little fuzzy. I'm still quite jittery from something.

"Sky," I wail, "I thought you wanted to run away together. You wrote those letters to me."

"Sorry, Merry," he says as calmly as possible. "I did not intend those letters for you. Sorry. I take full responsibility for that. It's all my fault, but that was the only way I could safely correspond with Marabelle without drawing any attention to how I felt about her."

"No, it's not true," I cry. "It can't be."

How could he love such a person? He hated her! What's so good about her, anyway?

"I'm sorry, Merry. It's true. Also, I'm going to have to ask you to clear your mind. I can't really concentrate when I hear you think so much, especially if you are thinking bad thoughts about Marabelle."

"What? How ... could you know that?" Sky is starting to scare me.

"Uh, sorry. I have another confession to make. Here's the thing ... I can read your thoughts. I can hear everything you are, um, thinking. Sorry!"

It can't be true.

"Merry, it is true, so please keep your mind as blank as possible. You don't want to make me angrier than I already am. I'm desperately trying to keep my composure, but it's really hard. I don't want to end up throwing you off the side of the mountain."

I cry even harder. Sky's gone mad!

"I'm not mad. Just shut up for a bit."

Obviously, shutting off my brain is easier said than done. Thoughts swirl around my head. Images of myself with Sky, Sky and Marabelle, and our days at school keep resurfacing. Look at her, look at me. Why does he like her?

"For goodness' sake, Merry, shut up! How many times were you mean to her?"

"What?"

Again, Sky catches me off guard. I can't wrap my head around the fact that he seems to hear me.

"Marabelle! How many times did you mistreat her? How many times did you call her names? How many times did you accuse her of things that didn't exist?"

"You weren't exactly pleasant to her either."

"Obviously, I know that. I can never make amends for what I've done, but why did you do it? Was it because I did? Did it seem acceptable to you to be mean to someone just because I was? Did I make it okay for you to be mean to another human being? Why didn't you stand up for her? Was it because you wanted me for yourself, or was it because you are a lousy person?"

"Stop, Sky, just please stop! Why are you doing this to me? What have I ever done to you besides be loyal? I'm sorry! I'm sorry I wasn't nicer. I trusted you. I thought I knew you."

"Well, you thought wrong."

Sky picks up a fistful of pebbles and throws them fiercely off the ledge. I sit holding my arms around myself, trying to keep warm. My eyes feel puffy, and my nose runs. My tears stop, but I'm terrified and sobbing on the inside.

Sky stands up and gathers bits of branches and dried grass. He arranges them in a pile in front of the cave. He finds a couple rocks and hits them together.

"Do you know what you are doing?" I ask.

He doesn't answer. He just gives me a dirty look and clicks the rocks together again. As he does that, something very curious happens. Sparks fly from his hands, linger on his fingers for a moment, and then land on the pile. The small fire ignites, and the pile becomes consumed with a small but steady flame. I blink a couple times, unsure of what I just saw. I think to myself, was it simply the rocks or did something strange just happen?

I rub my hands over the flames to try to get warm, but as the night grows later, the temperature seems to drop. Sky grimaces and mumbles under his breath and then removes his shirt. He hands it to me.

"Here. I'm not cold. You can use it instead."

I slowly reach out my hand, unsure of how to take this gesture. I wrap the shirt around my shoulders. It's oddly warm, almost hot like the towels they give you before a swanky Planner dinner. Sky doesn't even shiver. I stare at him for a moment. He's even more handsome than when we finished school. The boy I knew is gone, and here before me stands a man. He is still extremely lean from lack of calories, but he has grown even wider and more muscular. His chest has more hair than when he was younger, and his chin is even stronger than I remember. He must hear my thoughts again because he rolls his eyes and lets out a huge sigh. He seems very annoyed with me for the moment.

Sky stands up and walks to the edge. He takes his hands to wipe at his eyes, all the while sniffling a bit. He chokes out a groan. Sky is crying. He closes his eyes and yells louder than I've ever heard a person yell.

"Marabelle!"

Then he looks at me again with rage as he says, "Look what you made me do! This is all your fault!"

He hits the side of the mountain hard enough for me to hear a creak. Rocks start to fall around us and rush off the cliff.

"Stop it!" I yell. "What are you doing?"

I've never been so frightened in my life. The tides have turned, and I think Sky is going to kill me.

Antin-19

"Please let me go," Marabelle cries, squinting up at me as she pats her hands around the floor in a sweeping motion.

"Get up, Marabelle." I pull her up and put my hands on her face.

"I never realized how beautiful you are."

"Antin, please. I can't see. Where are my glasses? I need to get back to my home."

"You don't seem to understand, Marabelle, that's not your home anymore. You don't live there anymore. You will have a new home now, with the other maids."

"Please," she pleads, "just let me go."

"Marabelle," I say really slowly, "you are mine now."

"No, please don't," she whispers. A large tear slides down her chin.

"I could have you, you know, right now. I've watched you so many times."

"Excuse me? What do you mean?"

"And from what I've seen, you have completely changed my mind. I do want to be beneath you."

"Antin, stop, please. You don't know what you are saying," she still pleads and cries.

"Sure, I could take you now, use you for my love needs. You are a maid now, and, well, I'm a bachelor looking for love. But instead, you are going to be my new bride."

"Huh?"

"That's right! You'll be bid out again, and I am eligible for a new wife. You'll see; you will grow to love me as much as I love you. I know you will. And we'll have a child together soon after. I'm sure our year will get the letter to consummate and populate."

With this Marabelle, vomits all over the floor. Spit and mucus drip from her nose.

"What's your problem?" I yell. "Clean this stuff up!" I throw a towel at her. "I'll find you some glasses soon, when I remember."

I watch Marabelle fall to the floor to try to mop up her barf. She squints from the tears and her lack of sight. Even now she looks beautiful. Why did I even turn her down to begin with?

The compound is still abuzz with what just happened. Several Planners offer me their condolences for my marriage breaking up. They pity me for being fooled by Sky and Merry's

219

adultery. A couple of maids scurry over to Marabelle to help her clean and take her to her new quarters. She must live with them now.

As I head back to my home to rest, a loud noise echoes through the hills. It almost sounds like a human voice. Then the ground shakes suddenly, and bits of gravel pop around like corn on a fire. It's pretty odd. As I reach my door, a little kid named Asher approaches me.

"You shouldn't have done this, Antin!"

"I don't know what you are talking about."

"You need to stop this immediately."

"Hey, I'm the victim here," I insist.

The ground shakes again but even harder this time. I hear glass windows around us shatter to the ground.

"And now it begins," answers Asher as he leaves.

Merry-19

Never in my life have I been so threatened. Sky walks around angrily and then breaks down and falls to the ground. His cries are so intense that the ledge shakes. He mumbles Marabelle's name and cries out for her. He shakes his head and curls up into a ball. I've never seen him act out so emotionally in my life. The normally calm, cool Sky sobs like a newborn unable to self-soothe.

"I had a plan." He talks not to me but to no one in particular. "Why did I stray? Why didn't I pursue it to the end and take Marabelle away from here? Maybe I was too happy, too preoccupied with having fun for once in my life. I'm so, so sorry, Marabelle. I'll save you. I'll find a way."

He gets up from the ground and pounds the side of the mountain again.

"Stop, please, Sky. Take a rest," I plead.

He turns and looks me in the eye.

"Don't worry. I'll find some other people out there and drop you off before I go."

"Sky, no, please don't leave me!"

"Why? You would rather go back to the compound and face death? I doubt they want you back."

"Well, maybe we can explain it was all a mistake. Perhaps we'll be forgiven. We didn't actually do anything wrong."

"I understand that, and look how well that turned out the first time. They won't believe us, and they don't care. That's why I should find a way to protect you and then go get Marabelle. The longer we wait, the more dangerous it becomes for her."

"She'll be fine," I offer weakly.

"Fine? Really? Antin has her. Who knows what he's going to do to her. Wait. Actually, I know what he wants to do with her. I need to get there now!"

Sky rushes to the ledge. I quickly hold him back from diving over the edge.

"Wait. We need a plan."

"You're right. I'll call the birds."

"What birds, Sky?"

"Oh, I forgot to mention I can speak to certain animals too."

"Really?"

This predicament gets weirder and weirder as time goes on. I guess Sky was right. I have no idea who he really is!

Skyler-19

My poor decisions have caught up with me. I failed to look deeply into Antin's thoughts. As always, I guess I felt ignoring them would make us better off, but I was wrong. He left too many clues: the broken up boat, the snooping at my window, the slight but steady harassment he focused on Marabelle that ultimately led to spending private time alone with her. I blinded myself with the love and joy of living in the moment. I failed myself miserably, and I failed Marabelle even more.

I summon some birds to travel to the compound and spy for me. I need them to check up on Marabelle and see what Antin is up to. I also assign some birds the task to seek out more human life. I got this far away from the community, so maybe they will be able to stretch out their distance as well.

Merry rests before me, crumbled on the ground. She shakes with fear and from the cold temperature. She's causing me a bit of a distraction. I need to find a way to get rid of her. Her ignorance did not allow her to see Antin's plan either, but our current reality slowly sinks into her brain. Although I'm having a super difficult time tuning out her thoughts, I keep trying to concentrate on my rescue. Merry chats incessantly in her mind ... she loves me ... she hates me ... she wants to touch my chest to see what it feels like. How could I fall in love with ugly Marabelle? Why did Antin betray her for a dummy maid? It goes on and on and on.

I ponder my issue for a moment. Perhaps I can't tune her out because I am trying to reach the others left down below. If I give up that pursuit, I can redirect my attention to a solid plan. Yet my emotions interfere with my concentration as well. My eyes swell with tears again. My hands shake as I try to wipe my face. I mumble Marabelle's name because I hate myself for what happened, and I need her here to comfort me. Since we married over a year ago, I haven't lived a day without her. I can't cope with my loss. So many years I wasted by waiting to be near her, and in less than two years, I am alone again.

I lurch my body over the ledge and peer down below. If I jumped, would it hurt, or would it stop the pain? If I died, would she move on? My heart beats in my throat. I cry some more. Then I slap my face. I recover temporarily, but the pain creeps back into my body. I start to pace, moaning quietly. I'm really scaring Merry now. From the distance, the sun rises. A new day brings new challenges. The birds have yet to reappear.

Cecile-19

This whole thing is so messed up! I have no idea what Antin thinks he's doing! But, seriously, I've got to do something. No matter what's happened in the past, Sky and Marabelle are like my best friends, and I need to help them. I know them, and what Antin says they've done is not true. They are good people who love each other. It totally broke my heart to see Marabelle up there crying and Sky being accused of adultery. He would never harm Marabelle or leave her for another woman. I've seen them together day and night. They never leave each other's sides if they can help it. Those plans to leave with Merry are a lie! Flat-out falsifications!

Sitting in the stands tortured me. I witnessed Marabelle, bawling and confused, snot pouring out of her nose. I'm almost ashamed of myself for not intervening, if that's even the right word. How can I live with myself? I watched, as did the entire community, as Antin persecuted Sky and Merry. I should have stepped up and protected my friends. I suppose at the time I was either too much of a coward or it didn't occur to me to speak up until now. I'm not sure which one. But now that I've thought about it, I'm not going to stand idle. I'm going to face Antin and let him know he made a huge mistake.

As the morning sun rises, Sasha covers her face and rolls away from me. That's kind of normal for her. Yet today, she acts differently. As she faces away from me, I see a panicked expression. Last night's events affected her as well. Even after a year, we barely communicate, so I'm unsure how to broach the subject. Should we discuss what happened or not?

"Sasha," I start.

"Leave me alone, Cecile."

"Don't you think we should—"

"No!"

"You don't even know what I am going to say."

"I think I do, and I don't want to talk about it with you."

"Why?"

"I just don't! End of discussion!"

"But, um, please? I sort of need a friend right now. My mind is so confused,

and—"

"Cecile?"

"What?"

"I'm not your friend."

"Oh."

With that last word, Sasha gets out of bed and walks away from me. Funny, when I was young, Sky would be the person I could turn to after an exchange like that. He always said the right things to make me feel better. Marabelle, on the other hand, was the person I wanted to confide in. I tried a couple of times when we were in school. Then over the past year, it got easier to approach her. We even developed a small rapport, whereas my relationship with Sky deteriorated for some reason. Now I miss him.

The light out of my window glows fuchsia. I roll off the bed and head to the kitchen in search of the coffee press. I cut open a bag of milk to steam and place the rest in a jug. I deposit it back in the fridge. I pop several slices of bread into the toaster and grab the butter and jam. As I prepare my breakfast, the room slowly heats up like an oven. At first, I think it's because of the toast. Then I realize the warmth is coming from outside. Now the temperature is rising rapidly. I run to the front door and yank it open. The light burns my eyes so intensely that I pull the door shut as fast as humanly possible. Then I lift up the edge of the window shade slowly. I cower down and shade my eyes to protect them from the bright rays. The sun lights the outdoors with a bright red tinge. It's as if I were looking at the world through a bright red balloon at Birthday. What is happening?

A cup behind me drops and shatters. I turn and see Sasha starting at the sky.

"What's happening out there?" I ask.

"This is not good," she responds. "We need to go tell somebody about this immediately."

"Who can we tell, and what are they going to do about this? It's not as if somebody can control the weather."

"I'm not so sure about that."

"Really? Someone here can control the weather?"

"He isn't here, here! But he is nearby. Go get Asher. He'll be the one to talk to Antin."

"Asher, why Asher? He's a younger kid. What does he have to do with Antin or the weather?"

"Just hurry, Cecile. You won't want to be around if things get worse, which is exactly what will happen if you don't get Asher!" she shouts in my face.

"Okay, okay, all right, Sasha. I just wish you would be a little nicer to me."

"Now's not the time for niceties!"

I crack the door open slowly and then realize I'd better get some sunglasses. The bright blaze is unbearable for more than a few seconds. I rush to my room and find a pair of black shades on a dresser. I think they belong to Sasha, but I guess I don't have time to care. I slip them on and venture outside again. It's pretty warm, but not as hot as you would think, looking at the color—at least not yet. As I walk, my feet burn from the heat rising off the pavement. It normally doesn't reach this kind of temperature here till later in the summer and often not until late afternoon. With every painful step I take, I feel like I'm already sacrificing myself for a cause. What the cause is exactly I'm unsure of yet.

My feet burn so badly that I scurry quickly to Asher's house. As I move along the path, eyes appear from beneath window shades, curious and afraid. Air-conditioning units run at full blast. Most families hide indoors. Confusion fills the compound. I'm part of that confusion. I'm not even sure what I need to talk to Asher about.

Since Asher is a little kid, he still lives with his parents. I don't remember how many years younger he is, maybe like four. The weird way they have our names with our years has always confused me. I can barely remember my own age. Why should I know someone else's? Well, obviously Asher is an *A*, so he comes from a long line of privileged Planners. But unlike other people in his position, Asher is rather pleasant and often happy. He has a nice rapport with Marabelle since she would take care of the younger kids when we were at school. Maybe Sasha wants to gather support for Marabelle among her true friends (although Sasha herself never truly cared for Marabelle).

I inch closer to my destination. Desperate eyes plead with mine to find out why we are cursed with this weather. I sweat. Water pours from my hairline. I think part of the sweat comes from my anxious nerves. My tongue sticks to the inside of my mouth. I hope Asher can give me something to drink. I'm so faint that I think I'm going to die out here.

Antin-19

Last night, I got the best night of sleep in my entire life. I finally rid the compound of that pesky Sky. True, he did not die, but still, he is gone forever! I also managed to get rid of Merry—a bonus. She proved to be quite lame. She only cared about herself and what she could drain from other's pockets. Sky and Merry deserve each other.

Yes, I sort of falsified the documents to aid in my removal of these sinful creatures, but Sky really did write those notes to Merry. I couldn't care less that they were allegedly for Marabelle. Sky used them to keep me away from Marabelle. So in that way, he deceived me into going after Merry. For that, he deserves to be punished. Marabelle should belong to me. Sweet, kind, shy, beautiful Marabelle needs a man like me. In my point of view, I'm saving her from a life of misery with Sky. She'll be happier with me, she'll see. I hate Sky for keeping such an angel from me. I gladly sacrificed my wife to get what I really want—happiness. Yes, Marabelle will make me happy. I watched her charm Sky for over a year. He never smiled so much until now. Once he married Marabelle, he beamed day and night. I must say, that should have been me. I should go after my father next for not insisting that I bid on Marabelle.

Right now, Marabelle sleeps safely in the maids' quarters. Those old biddies will watch over her for me. They have been given strict orders to keep her away from other men who could use her for their love needs. I've claimed her as my own to marry next Bidding Day. She must remain pure and untouched until then.

My toes stretch out to the edges, and my arms reach across either side of my king-size bed. I really enjoy having the entire bed to myself. As I hop out of bed, I run to Merry's possessions on the dresser. I pick up the garbage can and sweep my arm across the surface and push her stuff into the can, glass and metal crunching and clanking as it hits the bottom. I laugh out loud. I didn't realize how much fun it would be to erase Merry from my life. I run to the closet and rip her clothes off the hangers, scattering them all over the floor. I could set fire to them in the fireplace, or I could barbecue them in a fire pit. I have so many ideas that I'm getting excited. Maybe I should save a few nice items for Marabelle, although they probably wouldn't fit. Marabelle is shorter than Merry, and also more ... not fatter, but more womanly, I guess. I find a pair of silver scissors and hack at the pile. I'll buy Marabelle all new clothes, whatever she likes. No more old, worn-out work clothes for her. She won't need to wear another holey outfit again.

The room is in total disarray. Fabric is scattered everywhere. Bits of feathers fly in the air from a formal gown Merry used to own. I need to summon a maid to clean up. I consider requesting Marabelle, but that would just be cruel. On the other hand, she and I would be able to spent time together this morning in the aftermath of this tragedy. I could use this opportunity to comfort the woman whose husband just cheated on her.

I laugh to myself all the way downstairs. I am so clever, thanks for noticing. I'll probably have this place wrapped around my finger within the next year! I plan on taking over eventually as top Planner of the community. I imagine I'll be the youngest man in history to pull off that feat. But I've accomplished so much already. I have positioned myself to head all affairs (ha-ha) concerning the compound. Plus, I've established my ability to punish and excommunicate undesirables. The Makers have granted me just about everything I've ever wanted, and I'll take care of the rest.

Buried so deep in my thoughts, I almost don't hear the pounding on my front door. I leisurely walk over and open it.

"Antin-19, the community has expressed some serious concerns that require your immediate attention," an elderly Planner pants at me, completely out of breath.

"What could possibly be so wrong that I don't get to enjoy my breakfast first?" I respond casually.

"Antin, have you not seen the sky yet?"

"No, what's wrong?"

I swing my door open wider, revealing a fluorescent pink backdrop.

"So the sun rises with this color from time to time," I say upon inspection.

"Please, Antin, let me in. My feet are burning, and we need to talk," he says with desperation.

"Later," I answer and slam the door in his face.

That serves him right to come bother me at this hour. He can suffer and wander back from where he came. I saunter to the kitchen to get some coffee and toast. I want to enjoy this victorious morning, not ruin it with "pressing affairs" that can obviously wait.

Merry-19

My existence has become a living nightmare. I'm here as a witness to Sky's emotional meltdown. Chunks of rock fall onto us as he hits and rocks the mountain. I fear for my safety. He spends his time murmuring to himself and crying for Marabelle. Since I've learned a few frightening facts about him, I try to guard my thoughts, which proves nearly impossible, and Sky yells at me for thinking anything! I'm scared that Sky is going to randomly drop me off with foreign strangers—if they even exist out there. Somehow, he has willed birds to do chores for him, including spying on the compound. He told me he talks to them, but I don't even hear him say anything. The birds don't seem to speak back either. Several have flown back and forth from the trees to this ledge, but I've yet to hear them communicate beyond the occasional normal chirp.

I wrap Sky's shirt tightly around my arms. I can't seem to get warm. There is no indication that the frigid temperature affects Sky. He doesn't shiver, and I don't see goose bumps anywhere. He doesn't seem to care that we have no food or drink either. I feel quite faint and extremely light-headed.

"Sky," I whimper, "I don't feel so good. We haven't eaten in a very long time."

"Oh," he responds, as if it hadn't occurred to him.

"Please help me. I don't want to die here."

"Sorry. I'll look for something. Stay put."

Sky takes off and leaves me alone. A chill runs down my spine. I've never been left alone in the wilderness like this to fend for myself. None of us have, really. Even Workers have always been provided for on the compound. We lived in a world of abundance and balance. No one taught us how to search for food or water. I cry a little as Sky walks out of sight.

"Please come back soon," I call after him, sick to my stomach that he may never return.

I pray Sky's instinct will take over. He's not the person I once believed him to be. He's changed into a fantastic creature capable of mysterious things.

Alone, I run through the worst-case scenarios. If Sky never returns, I could try to get down the mountain myself. I could make my way to the orchard and find something to eat. Then I could beg the Planners for forgiveness and opt for a lesser punishment. I could become a maid and serve out the rest of my days husband-free. I'll do just about anything to live there again, even become a love slave if I have to. I fear death more than anything else.

A flock of blackbirds circles over my head. They make me nervous. I grab the shirt around my shoulders even tighter and try to warm my hands by the fire. Then I ease onto the ground and close my eyes. I drift into a sleeplike state half filled with reality and half plagued by nightmares.

Cecile-19

My walk to Asher's house lasted past an eternity. My pants stick to my legs, wet from the sweat that poured off my body. My tongue hangs out the side of my mouth as I tap the door with the back of my hand.

The knob turns slowly, and two blue eyes stare at me. They belong to Asher. He pulls the door open. We stare at each other for a moment. Asher is a nice-looking person. His light blond hair sticks to his forehead. Even the air conditioner cannot defeat the heat. And although he is younger than I, he is already taller. I look up at him, trying to decide what to say.

"Asher, I, uh, am here, uh, at the request of, uh, my wife, uh, Sasha. She seems to think, uh, you might know what to do. So, well, uh, you see, um, I took the trip over here to ask you if there was a way to try to help, and um ... well ... could you please give me something to drink? I'm feeling faint."

"Sure," Asher says, dragging me into his house by my arm and shutting the door. He leads me to a couch to sit down and rest.

He fetches me a glass of orange drink, which I down in two seconds flat, and then I let out a loud sigh of relief. He pours me another glass, which I sip a bit more slowly.

"Go on, Cecile," Asher says with a calm smile after I've quenched my thirst.

"Wow! I can't believe how calm you are, Asher. I'm freaking out! Anyway, I guess Sasha felt since you were friends with Marabelle, you could help."

"Are you sure it's because we're friends?"

"No, I just assumed that's what she meant. I know Marabelle spent a lot of time taking care of the younger kids, and I've seen you wave at each other."

"She did. We have. But that's not why Sasha wants my help. Anyway, I think it's too late."

"Whatcha mean?"

"Well, the scales have already been tipped. It's over. I don't think we can ever get back to where we were."

"Oh, okay. No, I don't get it."

"Fine, let's start from the beginning of your life."

"Okay." I have no idea where he is going with this.

"Cecile?"

"What?"

"Please pay attention."

"Okay."

"Here on the compound, our goals are simple: we strive for balance. Life here means all is fair, all is equal. Now while I don't truly buy into that concept, I do work for the preservation of balance. Balance brings us abundance, and abundance keeps us all safe and happy. We have beautiful gardens of fresh food and animals of every species, and people who work hard to maintain the status quo. I'm sure you have heard about the hard times of our past, but since your birth year, the compound has experienced its longest reign of prosperity."

"This sounds so familiar."

"Did you pay attention at school?"

"Uh, yeah."

"Anyway, someone here made the biggest mistake and tipped the scale off kilter."

"Who?"

"Cecile, for real? Antin, obviously!"

"Oh, how did he do that?"

"By getting rid of Sky and taking Marabelle!"

"Sure. So how do we fix it?"

"I don't think we do. I'm sorry. It's too late."

"No, I don't accept that! It can't be too late. It's never too late to do something. Marabelle's my friend. She would help me if I were in danger. So it's my turn to try to help her. What do we need to do?"

"I guess we need to go get Sky back."

"Fine. How do we do that?"

"Convince Antin to stop his crazy rage and have him summon Sky. But, Cecile, even if we do this, I'm not sure it will help. The damage seems irreversible."

"Oh. Explain."

"Sky the man may possibly forgive and forget, but the, um, the force inside of him may not. In fact, for him, humans are selfish beings that don't want or deserve balance. And, Cecile, without balance, there is only chaos."

As Asher tries to explain himself, the lights start to flicker. A sharp buzzing sound alarms me. I jump. Then a loud explosion shakes Asher's house, and the lightbulbs break around us. Then the air stops.

"What happened?" I whisper.

A burnt smell enters my nose.

"The generators died. It's too hot, and the compound couldn't handle the intense heat. Our electricity is gone, and so is our cold air."

"Do you think they can fix it?"

"Doubtful, Cecile."

"Really?" Asher is scaring me.

"Really, Cecile. Again, sorry."

I press my lips together. I don't want Asher to see me cry in the dark.

"Don't give up, Cecile. You are being very brave. Marabelle won't forget this gesture. You are a good friend to her."

"How do you seem to know so much? You're a little kid."

Asher laughs at my statement—perhaps enjoying the irony of it, if that's indeed the correct term for it.

"You are right, Cecile. I am a little kid still. It's too bad too. I kind of looked forward to my turn dancing and bidding. Oh well. Anyway, I still need your help. Let's try to find a few people who can aid us in our chore. First, we need to locate One. He'll assist. Then we need to get to Antin and perhaps help secure Marabelle. One can watch over her the best. Our goal is to stop Antin from taking over and convince him to not only bring back Sky but beg for Sky's forgiveness. This might

Cecile-19

The wave pushes back to the lake, full of fury, dragging our forbidden tree deep into the darkness by its roots. It is sucked down in a rapid spiral like a vortex of a tornado. The branches filled with red fruit spin and vanish into thin air. As the tree disappears, my eyes play tricks on me. Several hands appear out of the water and wrap their fingers around the branches as the tree is pulled into the darkness. I blink, and these strange apparitions are gone.

People around me run in mass panic toward the edge of the compound, making their way through the orchard. As the light from the sun disappears, many smack into tree branches or fall to the ground. Several of the fallen get pummeled by the frightened stampede. I hang back a bit, frozen in my tracks.

Antin remains on the ground, coughing water out of his lungs. Asher stands over him like he's waiting for Antin to stand up. Asher wears an angry face like he's about to punch Antin.

"You moron," Asher spits. "I gave you the chance to bid on Marabelle, and like an idiot, you rejected it. 'Oh, she's too opinionated. She won't submit,'" Asher says mockingly. "So fine, she went back to where she belongs. No harm done until you got the brilliant idea that you wanted her back. I'm not sure how that happened. Maybe you snuck around their window. Maybe you didn't like your replacement bride. Whatever it was, you knocked us all off balance, and now we all pay for your greedy mistake."

"I still don't know what you are talking about, Asher," Antin says, sneering back. "How is it that you're the Messenger and barely anybody knows about it? How is it that you are the only one who knows about this so-called Light Maker and the rest of us are in the dark about it?"

"I was born a Messenger, just as you were born a pompous ass. I said before that I'm the only one of my kind here. Only a few know. It's safer that way. I deliver the messages to those who need them. I don't grant wishes, I don't cure the sick, I don't save the dying, and I don't communicate with the Maker. I was born knowing what to say and when. I did not tell anyone I was the Messenger because I am not able to make a difference in your everyday lives. It is only and always up to you to make good choices to keep the balance. This is your home. I'm just here to watch over you as a guardian and, more importantly, to offer you Marabelle, who you didn't even want until, I guess, now. Then I had to get you to apologize for taking what was forbidden, which you didn't do. So now I will watch over you to see how your life on this compound ends."

Antin stands frozen, looking at Asher, speechless. I stand close by, unable to dissect the meaning behind Asher's message. Since the tree was pulled up, the water has started to retreat. We are no longer in danger of being flooded. A few other people stand by Asher and Antin as well. One and Marabelle remain close by, just listening and observing this exchange. None of the people huddled in this small circle seem fazed by what Asher just revealed. In fact, I seem to be the only one surprised by what just occurred.

One finally breaks the silence. His eyes blaze red with rage.

"Get up!" he yells at Antin. "You are coming with us to the edge of the mountain. It's time to face him. Your judgment day has finally come."

Skyler-19

I make my way down the jagged rocks, Merry in tow, weeping. As I carry her, I see a crowd gathered at the bottom of the mountain. They all share the same scared look in their eyes. I search for Marabelle. I don't see her. This causes my heart to drop. A bird flies overhead, and I plea to it.

"Find Marabelle, please!"

It whisks away. I lick my lips. They feel very dry. I haven't had anything to eat or drink in a very long time. I climb down shirtless since my shirt has been wrapped around Merry during this entire ordeal. I stop for a moment to wonder why the reverse the damage that has been done. Finally, we need to placate Sky, give him Marabelle, and return balance to the community at once."

"I'll do anything it takes to get back to normal."

"Good. But be prepared for hardship, because I don't think Antin will go down without a fight. We may need to bid adieu to normal."

Skyler-19

By the time I make it back to the ledge, Merry is nearly passed out. Now I feel bad, in fact worse than ever. I kneel down close to her body and try to rouse her.

"Merry, I'm back. I brought some food for you."

Well, at least I brought what I could find. It barely passes for food. My escape didn't come with a preplanned way to survive. It also never included Merry.

"Ahhhhh." Merry can hardly respond.

"Merry." I pull her into my arms and pat her cheek gently. "Open your mouth."

She pries it open slightly. I take some leaves that I've gathered and squeeze the condensation left on them into her mouth. Droplets dribble on her face, and I wipe them off with my hand. Then I give her a couple unripened olives for her to chew. This seems to do the trick, as she slowly comes back around. She tries to sit up a bit, so I hold her against my chest.

"Merry, I just want to take this time to apologize to you. When I went off in search of food, I had some time to think. I guess I'm not really that good of a person after all. So I need to say sorry. I really haven't been good to anyone, especially to you and Marabelle. I sort of regret it. So there it is."

Merry takes a few minutes to respond.

"That's okay. I forgive you. I suppose I'm not such a good person either. But I guess you and I are the same. We do what we need to in order to survive. You wanted Marabelle. I get that now. So you did what you felt was necessary to protect her, even if it meant hurting her. I never really knew what I wanted, so I played all my hands, hoping something might turn out. I think it's not our faults, really. We were so restricted that some other instincts inside of us took over."

"I suppose. But I tried to always be up front with you, in a way. And now I need to be honest again. No matter what happens, my goal is to get to Marabelle. I'll keep you safe for now, but you can't stay with us, no matter what!"

"I understand. I get it, Sky. We won't be together, ever."

"No, not even in the same company, Merry. One of us must go. Once we get back to the compound, things will never be the same."

"Maybe that's not such a bad thing."

"I have a bad feeling it won't be a good thing either."

A large blackbird swoops in from the sky as Merry and I talk. It caws at me. I wave it away with my hand but it pecks my fingers.

"What?" I ask it.

"I'm back from the farthest point, as you requested. I bring word about others."

My stomach flips in anticipation. I may finally find new people.

"What did it say? Tell me!"

"The bird from afar says there are no others."

This news devastates me. Vomit rises in my throat. The bird can tell I'm disappointed.

"Wait," it says. "There's more. This bird told me to say that you, Sky, you will create a world with new people."

"Hold on. That doesn't make sense. I've never said anything like that."

"Really." The bird persists. "It said you told it you will make sure people populate the world. That's why you can't find any yet."

"No," I say, "I don't believe that for one minute. I haven't talked to any creature about populating the world. I've only asked the whereabouts of others."

"It said you wouldn't remember but to believe me that it was you who said this," the blackbird insists.

"What's going on?" Merry pipes in on my conversation. I almost forget she can't hear it.

"The bird said there are no others out there because I haven't put them there yet."

"Ridiculous. What does that even mean?"

"How do I know? I've always felt like we can't be the only ones here. I've searched for years to find more people, but I've never had any success."

"Could we be the only ones? Is that why we have been kept so protected?"

"I suppose. I need to think about this for a bit."

My head swirls with too much information. I seem to lose my ability to concentrate again. I still need to pull together a plan.

Finally, I add, "Let's wait for the next bird to bring us news about the compound. Then we'll decide our next move."

Merry agrees glumly. I hand her more olives to munch while we wait. She winces from their sour taste, but they help satiate her for a while.

As for myself, even in her presence, I still feel alone.

Antin-19

Mass panic only makes me more invincible. As the power goes down, shrieks erupt all over the community. Fear will not create chaos. I'll simply take command.

As I finally leave my house, the sky has turned a darker maroon color. The heat slowly dissipates as some wind in the air cools down the temperature. I seek out some elder Workers and assign them power grid duty. As soon as we get the electricity working again, I will be able to restore confidence.

After about an hour, a Worker approaches me.

"Antin-19, sir, we do not seem to be able to restore power to the compound. The heat blew the fuses, and the grid is fried."

"So try again."

"You don't seem to understand. None of us feel we will ever be able to restore the power."

"Impossible. You've only been trying for an hour. Go back and do it again."

"Yes, sir."

Incompetent fools. I'd restore it myself if I had the time. We've faced bad weather before. How bad can it be?

I head to the main dining hall. The wind blows harder, and the windows rattle as I enter. I wish I knew where Sky put his key. I could use a bottle of vin at a time like this. I bet it's still around his neck, wherever he disappeared to. The place is practically empty, so I help myself to an extra helping of schnitzel and rice. The wind sings an eerie tune outside. Gusts of air slam against the building. The noise emits a low hum. The branches shake on the trees outside. It reminds me of a broken pearl necklace with beads being spilled onto the ground. The wood frame creaks out a long squeak. The last few residents scatter while I eat. As time ekes by slowly, I gather my thoughts. I'm getting a bit uneasy about the deteriorating conditions around us after all. As I munch, I can simply hear two things—the wind and my own chewing. The power is still out, and I'm now all alone. This is creeping me out. As I look around me and everyone has gone, the wind bangs the windows against the foundation. My heart pumps loudly in my ears. A hand reaches out from the abyss and touches me on the shoulder. I jump.

"Ahhhh!"

I turn around and face Asher.

"Asher, it's just you. You scared me!"

"We need to talk."

I let out a huge sigh of relief. I'm not sure who I was suspecting—perhaps some creature from the darkness.

"I know, this weather is crazy, right?! Let me finish my lunch, and then we'll chat."

"No. Now. It's important."

"Can't it wait, Asher?"

"You? A little ... You are the Messenger?"
"Yes."
"For how long?"
"My whole life."
"Are there others?"
"No, not exactly, not like me. Not now."
"Liar. I don't believe you. You mean to tell me in this entire place there is only one Messenger?"
"Yes. For this entire community, I am the only Messenger for the Light Maker. And until now, I was only needed once, as I stated, about two years ago."
"Is the Light Maker here?"
"No, not in human form."
"There are two Makers, then?"
"Yes, sort of."
"You talk in riddles, Asher."
"This is neither a riddle nor an explanation."
"Okay, if you represent the 'Light Maker,' then who is the Messenger for the 'other' one?"
"One is."
"And who is the 'Other Maker'?"
"Guess," he snarls.

At that moment, a wave comes out of nowhere and engulfs the crowd. Screams bubble out of the water. As the wave pulls back, it rips the forbidden tree out of the ground by its roots and carries it back into the black of water at the base of the lake.

Many of us collapse to the ground and gasp for air.

"We need to make our way to the mountain," someone from the crowd suggests.

I lie close to the ground, catching my breath. Asher stands over me, unfazed by what just occurred. I think he's waiting for me to react to his madness.

security issue. He can't come back. If he does, he needs to face his death sentence."

"You need to fix that!" One yells as Asher pushes him out of the way.

"Look, Antin, you need to stop what's going on around here. Please, go get Sky and apologize. Okay? Just bring him back. It's our only hope of saving the compound," Asher says with a straight face.

"You are just as crazy as One," I answer.

"Please, Antin," Asher says, raising his voice. "I know it's going to be hard to believe me right now, but I'm telling the truth. We are all in danger if this weather doesn't stop. All of our lives are at stake here. You need to end this! Go get Sky, and give him back Marabelle."

Suddenly Marabelle yells, "I don't want to die!" She runs toward the rushing water.

"Stop her," Asher commands.

One takes off after her and grabs her before she can get too far.

"Get off of me, One!" she screams and struggles as he pulls her back to safety.

"What is going on here, Asher? You can't tell me what to do," I challenge him, still wondering about Marabelle's motivation for running toward the water.

"Yes, I can."

"Might I remind you I am above you in station? Only a Messenger or Maker can tell me what to do!"

"Well, you're in luck," Asher screams, "because I am the Messenger!"

The fleeing crowd gasps and stops to listen. People slowly creep closer to hear our conversation.

"Liar," I challenge him.

"That's right, Antin, I'm the Messenger. You can ask your father. I'm the one who told him to invite Marabelle to your bidding visitation."

I look around and spot my dad. He lowers his eyes to confirm that Asher speaks the truth.

Just as we reach the door, the building starts creaking and swaying to a point that several beams crack and break like kindling. Chunks of drywall fall on our heads and cover us in chalky white dust. Asher arrives at the door just in time to pull us out safely as the entire building collapses at our heels.

"Asher, thank y—" I start to say, but One interrupts me.

"What are you doing here, Asher? You're not a part of this."

"I'm as much of a part of this as you are, One!"

"Don't fight," Marabelle pants, breaking the tension between the two of them.

"I thought you were friends," I say.

"We're not," One answers.

"We are not enemies," Asher adds.

"It doesn't matter," Marabelle comments.

I break down in tears. The three of them stand calmly beside the rubble of what used to be the maids' quarters. But for me, the pressure is too much. I don't understand what is going on, and I don't see how we will be able to fix the places we call home. I look beyond the skeleton of the quarters. The water rushes toward us, engulfing the old hill where we used to relax during our old school days.

"Marabelle?" My voice shakes in a new panic.

"I'm sorry, Cecile," she apologizes.

"Why are you sorry, Marabelle?"

"We don't have time for this," Asher urges. "We need to get to higher ground."

The two younger boys push me to get my feet moving. As we begin our quest for safety, I notice hundreds of other community members working at escaping our deteriorating compound. Men, women, and children on foot make their way to drier ground. The four of us join the pack and blend in as we walk toward the orchards. Many around us cry, but the four of us go in silence.

As we approach the fruit trees, Antin jumps out in front of Marabelle and snatches her hand.

"And where do you think you are going?" he asks her.

The wind blows around our eyes, swirling leaves and dust into our faces. I cough and duck again. My eyes tear up as I wipe at them. Out of nowhere, the ground rumbles and brings us both down this time. I hear a crack. From a distance, I see a slab collapse onto the ground. Screams and cries follow.

"I'm so confused," I confess, wanting to give up our pursuit.

"Look!" screams One. "We're almost there." He points to a building so shabbily built that it practically sways like a child's swing in the wind.

I summon some energy and get back up. We finally reach the maids' quarters. One swings open the door. A blast of wind catches it and blows it so hard that it shatters against the wall. We push ourselves in and call for Marabelle. One rushes from room to room, calling her name.

"Here," she says as she emerges from the dark hallway.

Marabelle hugs the wall and feels her way to our voices. She shuffles her feet so she doesn't trip and holds on to the doorknobs to get to us. She's wearing a different pair of glasses that don't fit. Someone probably lent them to her, but I can tell they are practically useless.

Marabelle's hands shake, and her face appears pale and blotchy. She bends over, vomits a little on the floor, and then spends a few moments spitting and dry heaving.

"Marabelle, are you okay?" I ask.

"She's fine," One snaps at me.

"I'm fine, Cecile, thanks for asking." She gives One the best dirty look she can muster without being able to see straight. "I just need a drink of water or something. This rocking back and forth in here is making me a little dizzy. Plus, I can't really see out of these glasses. I lost mine, so some maid gave me this pair. So now I have a bit of headache."

"Oh, um..." I stammer.

"But don't worry, Cecile. I'll be all right."

She reaches out to me, but One grabs her hand to help lead the way. The building shakes again. One makes sure to steady Marabelle. I hold on to the wall and angle my feet so I don't fall again.

"Come on, guys. Let's go," One says, trying to get us out of here.

Antin-19

The bad weather could not have come at a better time. This will be my chance to take position to lead the compound. I know I've always been quite convincing. Merry fell for it. Marabelle, well, I need to work on her a little more. But the rest of the population didn't even question my word against Sky's.

Obviously, many buildings have been destroyed. But the wind will die down, and the water is bound to recede. We have the manpower and the tools. It will take a strong leader like myself to put things right. It could take a while, but we have nothing but time here.

As most people around me panic, I walk leisurely. Citizens everywhere stampede like a wild herd toward the orchards. I stay back a bit. I would hate to get hurt over nothing.

In the midst of this mess, I see Marabelle. She's surrounded by Asher, One, and Cecile of all people. The boys rush toward the trees, huddled around Marabelle. It seems awfully suspicious, like they are taking her away. I quicken my pace to retrieve her for myself. I weave behind some trees so they don't see me and pounce in front of them.

"And where do you think you are going?" I ask her.

I try to pull Marabelle toward me, but One takes his arm and knocks her hand away from me.

"Don't touch her, jerk! This is your fault, and you need to fix this right now!" One screams loudly in my face. He inches close enough to feel his hot breath.

"This has nothing to do with you, One. You'll get your turn in a few years. This girl is mine."

"She belongs to Sky, and you know it. So go get him back now."

"You're crazy. Sky betrayed his wife and the community. He is a traitor and an insane criminal. Luckily for you, he's been banished. He can no longer threaten our high standards of living on this compound or poison the minds of the other Workers. It's a

Skyler-19

Out of nowhere, a flock of birds rushes toward us in formation, nearly missing us before they turn upward.

I turn to Merry.

"They are distressed about something," I say.

This really worries me. Something is happening below to make the birds react this way. Upon hearing this, Merry reacts rather nervously. Tears stream down her cheeks again. I want to join her. My heart pounds in my chest. I keep on telling myself that I need to be strong for Marabelle.

"I don't understand this, Sky," Merry bellows. "How is it you can talk to birds? Did you ever once ask yourself this question?" Then she runs for the ledge. "I need to get out of here."

I catch her in my arms and hold her tight while she cries.

"Hush now. Let me ask them."

I summon them back and several swoop down from a high-up branch.

"You were supposed to bring me news," I say. "What's going on down there? What's wrong?"

"It's all falling apart down there."

"What is?"

"That place you used to live."

"What do you mean?" I demand.

"That place where you were. The buildings are collapsing, and the water is following the people."

"*Enough!*" I shout at them.

"You are right. We need to get out of here!" I yell and pull Merry back toward the ledge.

"What? What, Sky? What did they say?" Merry's voice shrieks with panic.

"They said the compound is demolished. I've got to save Marabelle before it's too late."

"How are we going to get back there?"

"We climb down."

ground, causing several small explosions. Sparks fly in our direction. I shield my face.

"What will it take for you to believe?" he calls in my ear.

"A whole lot more than this!" I yell back. "This is a bad storm, Asher. We've had storms before. It's that simple. Why are you acting so crazy? Get over it."

"Then be prepared for more," he answers.

Then he gets up with a bit of a struggle, shielding his eyes from the particles swimming in the air from dust and leaves, and heads toward the maids' quarters.

"Where are you going?" I yell.

But he refuses to answer. As he walks, the wind pushes him over, and he falls to the ground a couple of times before he walks out of sight.

I squint and look across the field. Suddenly, I see the water from the lake rising to dangerous levels and creeping toward the beach. Now I'm concerned.

Cecile-19

One and I run toward the maids' quarters. The wind pushes our bodies back so hard that we fight back at it with each step. The force of the air knocks us down, but we resist and slowly make our way toward our destination. One is able to move easier than I and must double back every few inches to help catch me up to him.

"What's happening?" I yell at him.

"Just keep moving, Cecile, or we'll never reach her."

I turn and see water from the lake rushing toward us, and I panic. I turn back to get out of the way, but One yells, "Don't stop, Cecile! Hurry, or you'll get caught in the tide!" He shoves me out of the way in the nick of time. The tail end of the wave catches my foot and trips me up as it retreats back to the lake. I fall into a puddle of soggy grass. One pulls me back up.

"It's not safe here, Cecile. Keep walking," he urges me to move.

"I don't think so, Antin. Don't you see what is going on around us?"

"Yeah, the power is out. So? What's new with that? It's not like we've never had an outage before. Is that supposed to worry me? They've assured me they'll have it fixed soon."

"I really think you are in some kind of denial right now. We need you to get off your lazy posterior and go get Sky back!"

Asher's voice starts to rise as he gets more anxious by the minute.

"I have no idea what you are talking about, Asher!" I sneer. "Sky made his decision when he broke the rule. Adultery is forbidden, and he knew it. That didn't stop him from pursuing my wife. The punishment is death, and he eluded it. I think he's lucky to be alive."

"That's all a lie, and you know it, Antin."

"What do you know about it, Asher?" I challenge him.

"A lot more than you think. Now let's go! You need to find him and apologize. If you beg for forgiveness, maybe we'll have a chance at rebuilding what we've lost."

"You're nuts, do you know that? I'm not apologizing for anything. Let him rot out there in the wilderness. What evidence do you have that I'm lying? You're just a little kid. You have no power here, and you certainly don't have any power or influence over me. You'll regret even asking."

"No, you will. We all will! I won't even get a chance to grow up and find a mate like you did. You've ruined all of our futures here. Now I'm stuck in this crazy situation you created with your power-hungry selfishness, and there's very little that can be done."

"What madness are you ranting about, Asher? What situation?"

"Look."

He grabs my arm and takes me outside. We stand on the steps of the main dining hall. The wind whips our hair in our eyes and pushes us to the ground with such amazing force that we lose our balance. Something creaks ahead of us. The poles supporting the electrical wires come crashing to the elements haven't affected me at all. Very strange. I swallow hard and take a deep breath.

"What is wrong with me?" I say quietly.

I put Merry down on the solid ground at the bottom. She curls into a ball and collapses. The people at the bottom react with shocked groans and gasps as Merry looks at them, pleading for them to rescue her. They don't. They stay put, still and frightened.

Finally, someone from the crowd shouts up at me, "Help us, Sky!"

A murmur of shared agreement echoes around this call for help. I process this for a second.

"Help you? Help you? You want me to help you? Where were you when I was condemned to death for a crime I didn't even commit?" I ask.

I feel the anger working up in my body as I face the community that didn't care the last time I was surrounded by them.

Then I call, "Marabelle!" I can't stop screaming. "Marabelle, where are you? Come quick! Please! We need to get out of here!"

A man runs forward. It's my dad. His eyes plead with mine.

"Sky, please help us. We beg you. We're sorry."

"You're sorry?" I say. "Marabelle? Can you hear me? Bring me Marabelle now!" I shout.

"She's right here," a voice says from the crowd. Then I see One drag her toward me.

"Marabelle," I call excitedly.

She's wearing new glasses but still can't really see. Her eyes dart toward where my voice is coming from, but they go in the wrong direction since the sound bounces off the rock walls of the mountain.

"No, over here, by the mountain," I say again.

She squints as she tries to focus them toward me. Still her face looks blank, like she's in some kind of shock or she's unhappy to hear from me. I worry she's not pleased that I've come back for her.

"I love you," I call.

She opens her mouth to speak, but One interrupts her by saying something in her ear. So she stops.

"What is happening here?" I ask as I walk closer to the crowd. I climb on top of a pile of stones at the foot of the mountain so that I can see above the crowd.

"I will tell you, Maitre," answers One.

"What? What does that mean?" I ask. A chill goes down my spine.

Part 5

Dark Wings—An Introduction

*It's not so much a residence as a state of mind,
and yes, I have been there and back.*
—Marabelle

Skyler-19

"Marabelle," I call.

One finally pushes her toward me. She looks back a moment and proceeds to walk to me slowly until I scoop her up in my arms on top of the rock.

"Are you okay?" I whisper.

Marabelle nods her head.

"Are you hurt?" I ask.

She shakes her head, indicating no.

I push the hair out of her face and cover her cheeks with kisses and hug her tight. I don't really care what One is talking about or what these people really want. I hold Marabelle tight and don't want to let her go. I grab her face and look for some sort of sign of emotion or an explanation, but her eyes still appear blank. She does smile up at me, which reassures me a bit.

"Maitre," One says, bringing me back to the present.

"Huh?"

Marabelle narrows her eyes at One and then turns my head toward her lips.

"Sky, don't be nervous. I'm here to protect you," she says so faintly that sound barely escapes her mouth.

"No, I'm here to protect you," I mouth back.

"You can trust me," she answers back.

"Can I trust him?"

"For now," Marabelle says, barely audible.

"Maitre," One says again, loud enough for most of the compound to hear him this time.

"What? What, One? What are you saying? What are any of you saying? Here I am, before all of you! Your outcast, not your hero. I played your games. I followed all of your rules. I worked for you. I worked very, very, very hard for you. I took direction. I obeyed! All I wanted from you was one thing. That's it. Simple! One thing! I wanted Marabelle to be my wife. I even worked hard for that. I followed all of the rules again! It worked. The end. I was happy, ready to live out the rest of my life with her—until that day—the day you thought you could take her away! And for that," I scream, "all of you will be punished!"

With that statement, the sky cracks with thunder, and bolts of lightning hit several trees, which collapse around my audience, trapping them from reentering the compound. Screams and cries of terror erupt around me.

I take a deep breath. I don't even know where that came from. Did it come from me?

"Please, no, don't do this, Sky. Let us back in," someone begs.

My parents are shoved in front of me. I ignore them.

"No!" I shout. "You are all forbidden to come back here. You are all punished. I am casting you out to fend for yourselves. You are all forbidden from ever stepping foot back in here again. Out!" I roar, pointing my finger to the foot of the mountain. I'm showing them the way out of here, but I don't even understand why I'm doing this. It's like some odd inner instinct is taking over me.

Through the panicked cries and sobs, One mounts the rock and stands next to me.

"You heard our Maitre. He is the Dark Maker. You are now purged from the community. You must exit. You are now forbidden to reenter for eternity."

Another clap of thunder erupts above us.

"I ..." I turn to One and stammer.

One looks me in the eye, kneels down on one knee, lifts his arm to the sky, and turns his thumb down to the earth. It was the same thumbs-down he exchanged with Marabelle in the past.

"Marabelle," I stammer. " She ..."

"Yes, she is one of us. Oh, but don't worry. She's yours."

"But what are you?"

"We are yours. We are here to serve you. We are your Dark Angels, we are the Dark Wings."

"Are there more?"

"Yes, a few more. I will tell you who can stay. Plus Asher, of course. He is a Light Angel, but he does not serve you. Don't get me wrong. He is also here to protect you. We are not enemies. We work together to create balance, the Light and the Dark. It's them who throw it off, those selfish humans." One points to the crowd. Several people shrink back, afraid of what his finger might do. Nothing happens, but several people still duck out of the way, shaking their heads. Mostly frightened, few comprehend how to take this information. Several have hope that I will change my mind and that they will be able to return home.

My rage subsides a little until Antin marches up from and confronts me.

"You!" He sneers.

I feel something strange inside me bubble up and take over.

"Don't," Marabelle speaks up. She places her hand in front of me to hold me back.

"She's right," One adds. "He'll be banished soon anyway."

I shake my head in confusion.

"I'm sorry. I'm not getting this. What are you again?"

"We are here to serve you. We are the Dark Angels placed here by you for whatever reason you desire. We do not always know that reason. Some of us are born knowing who we are, and others are not. We do not tend to show up for any particular reason. We never show up to save humanity. It's usually something more self-serving on your behalf. Life often goes on around us. We are not out to harm anyone, just live in peace as fellow human beings—which is what we are right now. You, as you can guess, were not born knowing, which is why you are so confused. You must have had a reason, but it is usually not expressed to me or anyone else, for that matter."

"I don't believe you," I tell him.

"You don't believe me? Well, you don't have to. But ask yourself this, why would you be able to do all of the things you can do if you were an ordinary human? How is it you can talk to birds? Why can you hear their thoughts? Why can't you hear mine?"

"How do you know all of this?"

"It's my job, Maitre. I'm your number one."

"What can I do? What are my powers?"

"You can do anything. You are the Dark Maker. But all you see is who you are before us now, Sky. Sky is a man. He is just a grain of sand in the universe of what you really are. The Dark and the Light are all around us, trying to keep the balance of the universe."

"Do I control the seas?"

"Yes, I guess."

"Is there something in the water?" I need to find out what grabbed at Marabelle.

"Yes."

"What is it? What's in the water? Was something after Marabelle?"

"It's not human, if that's what you are thinking. But forget it. Leave it alone for now. It doesn't really matter because it obeys you as well. We'll explore that later. Now we need to decide who stays and who goes."

I feel hurt and betrayed, particularly by Marabelle. What did she know? Did she know at all? Why didn't she tell me? She looks at me meekly as I take in all of this information. Part of me wants her dead. I'm so angry that I could kill her with my bare hands, and part of me loves her so much that I'm ashamed of my thoughts.

I still want to take her and run away from this land. I want to forget all of this information and start anew, just the two of us. I sense Marabelle understands this, and she reaches for my hand. I take her fingers and squeeze gently. I feel this tiny spark of energy. It's like this momentary hit of recognition that zaps my brain, like I've seen her before, like we've know each other in the past, in a time that does not exist here and now. It's some kind of déjà vu. For a second, I remember Marabelle, and I remember who I am, and then it's gone. Sadly, I'm left just Sky, just a frustrated nineteen-year-old standing on a rock, facing a crowd of frightened people.

One waits patiently for a moment and then starts calling off names. He only summons a few before he gets to Sasha.

"And Sasha," he tells me.

"Oh, thank goodness," she squeals.

"And no," One adds, "you are no longer married to him." He points at Cecile.

"Finally." She sighs in relief. "I was drowning in that marriage. Good riddance." She shouts at Cecile and walks toward us.

At that moment, Cecile's eyes grow real wide, and he juts out of his corner and runs forward.

"No, Marabelle, please don't make me go." His eyes plead at her. "Please don't kick me out. I swear I'll be good. I don't need a wife. I'm fine," he stutters. "I'm your friend. Please save me. I'll do whatever you want. I can't go with them. Please!" he begs.

"Fine," I say against my better judgment. Marabelle lowers her eyes and looks down. I don't think she would betray me quite in the same way Merry did. She's built differently. Yet I bet her allegiance to me is more as a skeptical follower and not an eager one like One or Sasha. Marabelle strikes me as slightly rebellious and somewhat unwilling. Sadly, it is I who has this uncontrollable desire for her, strange flames that cannot be stopped or contained, almost as if I've followed her here to retrieve her for myself.

"Then it's settled," I finally say. "The rest of you must go now!" I point again toward the mountain and witness a shocked mass exodus.

I remain on the rock, but the others climb down. Blackbirds soar around my head, chirping in triumph. Those who remain with me watch as the others leave, taking little to nothing with them, just the clothes on their backs as I had to do when I was banished. A few Dark Wings exchange knowing glances, like Sasha and One. Where does this leave us now, I wonder. My heart pounds furiously in my chest.

Asher mounts a nearby rock, stands tall, and looks at the others who remain. A full moon rises over our heads and shines its light down on me as if I glow brilliantly under it.

Asher raises his hand toward the dark sky and then turns his thumb up toward the heavens.

The Dark Wings gather at my heels and drop to one knee. One pushes Marabelle down. She hesitates slightly and then goes down as well. They all lower their eyes and all in unison extend an arm down toward the earth and then point their thumbs down, opposite of Asher.

I stand to witness them in the light of the moon, trying to remember my identity as the Dark Maker.

The End of the Beginning